DRAWING
DEAD

DRAWING DEAD

Sandy —

Friend + Law-Living?

Neighbor

Best wishes always —

BENNETT SHELFER

UNLIMITED PUBLISHING LLC

First Edition

PAPERBACK ISBN-13:
978-1-58832-226-5

This fine book and many others are available at:
http://www.unlimitedpublishing.com

Acknowledgements

The author wishes to express his sincere gratitude to: Anina Morgan, the conscience of the characters, for the first and last read and the boundless encouragement in between; to authors Karen White and Karna Bodman, for their unselfish gift of time and advice on what it takes to become a writer; Dr. Doug Lyle, for his guidance on forensics, and his invaluable books, which are a service to all writers; Robert Macomber, Robert Norris, Don Reichardt, and Sara Williams for their invaluable insights and inspiration that only authors could give.

And personal thanks to dear friends Annabelle Hutson for her unabashed support and the use of her first name for 'Belle'; to Maj. Gen. (Ret.) Gordon Duquemin for his service to our country and for the use of his last name for 'Belle'; to former Secret Service Agent Rick Kerr for his tutoring on weapons; to Sue Nichols for her bountiful cheer and incomparable humor; to Dr. Jennie Block for her copious courage, character and charity; and to Nancy Rhodes for persuading me to write my stories in the first place.

And to my beautiful wife, Baxter, for everything. I chase rabbits, and she smiles.

Contents

"Nothing…"

"Nothing?"

"It's just I'm flying to Jacksonville today for a luncheon. It's okay. I'll balance it out with a reading from the tarot deck. I'm sure I'll be fine. Hey! It's time for you to go. Don't want you to miss your bus."

Jason grabbed his backpack and started for the door.

"Bye, sweetheart. I love you," she said. She kissed him and held him tightly.

"I love you too, Mom." And Jason was off to school.

Not a good day for a funeral.

The northwest wind was freshening, carrying a chilling mist to finish off the overnight deluge of the first cold front of the season. The forecasters called for clear skies by noon. Obviously that was not going to happen. The early winter weather systems had a way of stalling out by the time they reached north Florida, and it appeared this one would do the same. More drenching for the dirt roads and the farmland countryside near Tallahassee. They were called dirt roads, but they were mostly clay roads. Especially the hills. Red clay. Georgia's gift to its neighbor to the south. These wet clay hills made for treacherous driving, especially for the usual city car without four-wheel drive. And more difficult for a hearse. Even a brand-new 1979 Cadillac hearse.

Not a good day for a funeral.

The procession maneuvered the turn into Hillside Cemetery without anyone sliding into the ditch. The funeral director had a

Prologue

Jason Lancer ambled quietly into the kitchen.

"Good morning, sweetheart," Laurie said. Her voice was little more than a sleepy murmur. "Shuffle up and deal. Your eggs and bacon are almost ready."

Jason knew the game was on; three hands of Texas Hold 'em, with the short stack doing the dishes. He loathed doing the dishes almost as much as Laurie Lancer loved playing poker. Nonetheless, he felt obligated to do his part, even if it meant losing to her in poker. Which he did with regularity.

"You want to cut 'em?" Jason asked?

"You wouldn't cheat me, would you, Hon?" Laurie glanced at Jason as he ruffled-up the dog-eared deck of Bicycles.

"Of course not," he said. A hint of a smile betrayed his shyness.

Jason dealt the cards, and the fate of the dishes was decided in one hand. After the turn card hit the table, there were three spades along with the king of hearts showing. Jason went all in and Laurie immediately called. Of course, Jason was bluffing. He pretended he had a spade flush, and Laurie's pair of kings won the pot and a pass from the kitchen.

"How did you know?" Jason asked. He wolfed down the last bite of his eggs.

"I can read you like a book, cutie pie," Laurie said. She tried not to laugh and then laughed anyway. Jason shook his head, a little embarrassed, and began clearing the table and putting the dishes in the dishwasher.

"You should've checked your horoscope," Laurie said. She continued the morning routine by opening the newspaper to the astrology page.

"What does it say?" he asked. He looked away, not wanting to show he was really interested.

"Let's see." She glimpsed to see if Jason was watching her. "Libra. Libra. Here it is. It says, 'Today is not the day to deceive those you love. Play your cards close to your vest, and success can be yours.'"

"It does not." He almost shouted from the kitchen sink.

Laurie laughed as if she knew she had him going there for a moment. "Alright," she said. "It says, 'It is not too soon to make plans to achieve your ultimate goal. If you can dream it, you can do it. Be the one to define your destiny.'"

"Yeah, right."

"No, really."

"What about yours?" Jason asked. He knew he was about to hear it anyway, as he did every morning.

"Let's see, Pisces. Pisces. Uh oh!"

"What is it?"

"Oh, nothing. It says, 'Leave nothing to chance today. Keep both feet on the ground in mind, body, and spirit.'"

"So what's wrong with that?"

farmer, one of the nearby landowners, standing by with a tractor, in case it was needed.

Eleven-year-old Jason Lancer watched the pallbearers lift his mother's casket and carry it slowly to a small tent erected beside the soggy grave site. She had been everything to him; now she was gone.

Moisture ran down Jason's face, a mixture of cold rain and warm, salty tears. He cast a perpetual blank stare at the distant cornfield. It lay empty, shredded and spent from the recent fall harvest. That was exactly how Jason felt as he clutched the single rose he was carrying.

Jason tried not to listen as the minister talked softly to the stunned crowd. Whenever he peeked at the huddled mourners, he seemed to establish eye contact with each one. Then each nervously looked away and gazed at the casket, as if they knew there would be no comfort for Jason today.

The pattering drizzle on the tent muffled the already-faint refrains of "The Old Rugged Cross" sung accappella by a slight, middle-aged woman. Jason recognized the woman from the church choir, but he closed his mind to the events unfolding around him. His thoughts wandered back to three days ago and the frightened expression on his mother's face as she read her horoscope. *Leave nothing to chance today. Keep both feet on the ground in mind, body, and spirit.*

The preaching and singing ended.

"Jason, Jason," his Grandmother said. "Don't you want to put the rose on your mother's casket?"

"Yes, Ma'am," Jason whimpered. He stepped forward and gently laid the red rose on the mahogany casket. Then he stumbled into the pouring rain toward the waiting cars.

Not a good day for a funeral.

PART I

Chapter 1

Monday, September 10 (Moon in Gemini) A productive Monday awaits. Keep your focus on long term goals. Cancer and Aires may be involved, but these associations may produce more pain than gain.

September 10, 2001.

"What's this?" Sandra Thompson asked. Abdul al Din closed the door behind them to Room 201, the Honeymoon Suite, of the Mount Vernon Holiday Inn. She looked apprehensively at Ali al Din sitting naked on the huge four-poster bed. "You didn't say anything about there being two of you." She snarled, not taking her eyes off Ali as she turned for the door.

"No, wait." Abdul pleaded. "He's my brother."

"I don't care who the fuck he is. I'm not doing two of you for five bills."

"No, no, of course not," Abdul said. "We will make it very much worth your while."

Abdul was not worried about the money. They had been given twice the amount they needed to accomplish their mission and had plenty left over. And they sure weren't going to need it after tomorrow.

With a bounce to her step and an aura of satisfaction she hadn't experienced in a long while, Sandra walked past the front desk. As she exited the Holiday Inn, she nodded nervously to Muhammad, the bell captain, who appeared to recognize her from the Brown Derby. When she reached her car and opened her purse for the keys, she was shocked to find a wad of 100-dollar bills. Sandra was a thousand dollars richer. She would have had to tote drinks for almost two weeks to earn that amount. Still she felt guilty. Guilty because she had enjoyed a one-night stand with a man she didn't know, and guilty because he had given her money.

The very next night Muhammad came into the lounge and ordered a drink at a high-top table in Sandra's area. He assured Sandra her secret was safe with him and asked her to hear him out. Muhammad explained he would select only clean-cut, professional men who could pay top dollar. Because she was very attractive and very well-endowed, he told her he was confident she would command no less than 500 an hour. And for this screening service, and for smoothing things over with hotel security, should it become necessary, Muhammad would ask only ten percent.

At first Sandra was incensed, but after realizing her mother was requiring new medications and remembering the excitement of last evening, she decided to give it a try. Muhammad assured her in a year, two at the most, she would be in school to be a paralegal or maybe even a lawyer. Before Tiffany was old enough to remember anything, Sandra would be on her feet again and on her way to finding a husband for herself and a father for Tiffany. Then the happy-ever-aftering could begin. She could do this, Muhammad had said. She must be very careful, and she must always insist on using protection, but this could be her ticket to the future.

"I don't have a rubber," Ali said. He was unable to take his eyes off her breasts.

"Let me take care of this." Sandy adroitly retrieved a prophylactic from her jacket on the sofa. Ali let out a loud, guttural groan when Sandy, in one motion, removed the rubber from its packet and slipped it on him. The moans continued as Sandy pulled Ali's face between her breasts and hugged him lightly, swaying back and forth. After playfully pushing him back on the bed, she straddled him and began to slowly guide herself down onto him.

Without warning Ali withdrew from her slightly, instantly reached down and snatched off the prophylactic and thrust himself deeply into her.

"What the hell ..." was all Sandy could scream before Ali had his hand over her face, cramming the rubber into her mouth.

"I said no rubber, you infidel bitch." Ali began squeezing the breath out of her with his other arm behind her back.

Sandy fought fiercely but was no match for Ali. Abdul sprang like a cougar to cover her mouth, still stuffed with the prophylactic, with duct tape. He quickly tied her with rope facedown, spread-eagled, with her hands and feet each tied to a different bedpost.

Abdul and Ali took turns sleeping and raping Sandra Thompson throughout the evening. It was like a contest of manhood between them to see which one could be the last one screwing.

Sandy showed few signs of life during the night, except for an occasional gurgling sound. Abdul thought she might be choking on the rubber, but he could not risk taking the duct tape off her mouth for fear she would scream. Besides, she deserved whatever happened to her. *Infidel bitch!*

Chapter 2

Tuesday, September 11 (Moon in Gemini to Cancer 12:07 p.m.) The objects of your attention jump to the front burner. Keep yourself a safe distance from the flames. Go gently with Pisces.

September 11, 2001.

The orange glow on the horizon to the east was not yet strong enough to diminish the lights of the city and suburbs that lay below the stylish ranch bungalow on Overlook Lane on the western edge of Georgetown. The mirrored calm on the distant Potomac River was being disrupted by a scull with a crew team, rippling its way upstream toward the Key Bridge. The lights of the Iwo Jima Memorial and the Marriott Hotel were still shining brightly, with Arlington Cemetery stretching up the hill to the southwest. The predawn silence was serene, broken only by the competing echoes of howling dogs. They seemed to be barking not because they sensed an intruder, but because they were afraid the other dogs sensed an intruder they did not.

The inside of the house was also quiet except for the purring of the fans of the window units in the bedroom and kitchen. The exhaust fan ran overnight in an attempt to purge the cigar smoke from the house, only one of many remnants of the Monday-night football and poker party. Empty pizza boxes, beer bottles, and wineglasses were strewn throughout the family room and kitchen. The partygoers had merely gotten up and departed.

The phone rang in the bedroom. And rang. And rang again. Finally after it was knocked off the nightstand and retrieved by the cord, it was answered.

"Hello."

"Jay-man, my G-man. Did I wake you up, old buddy?"

"Hell no, I've been up all night waiting for your call. Perez, are you crazy? What time is it, anyway?" Jason recognized that distinctive Southern accent immediately.

It was incumbent upon FBI Special Agent Jason Lancer to register the obligatory complaints about the early call, but he knew his old friend from college, Tony Perez, would not be calling him if it were not important.

"It's Tuesday, man! Oh! I get it. Did you have your little game-game last night?" Tony asked, referring to the Monday-night football and poker party he knew Jason sometimes put together for his FBI buddies.

"Yes, thanks for asking, so you'd better make this fast, Tony. I think I'm about to wake up."

Jason Lancer and Tony Perez were both criminology majors at Florida State University in Tallahassee. Tony had graduated a year before Jason and turned down a job with the FBI. Other than within his family, it was a secret whatever happened to him, but Jason knew he had taken a job with the CIA. When Jason graduated at the top of his class the following year, he accepted a job as a codebreaker for the FBI, a job which had always appealed to him. After training and two years of doing classified work, he longed to see the outside of a cubicle and applied for a transfer to the field. He served three years each in the New York and Miami field offices before he was assigned to the growing Joint Terrorism Task Force (JTTF) attached to the Washington office.

"Easy, easy, now old pal," Tony said. "I'm not even supposed to talk to you, remember?"

"I know. In fact, I'm not even sure we're having this conversation. Maybe you have the wrong number, or maybe I'm dreaming, or both."

It was no secret none of the alphabet agencies had a propensity to share information with the others. Whether it was for pride, a turf battle, or departmental rivalry, the rule, which filtered down from the top was: operational information generated by an agency stayed with the agency.

When Jason and Tony were home in Tallahassee the previous Christmas, they had met at a party and renewed their old friendship. They eventually got around to hinting at what each did in his work and were amazed at the parallels of their efforts. They decided inasmuch as they worked for the same country with the same goals, they would discreetly help each other regardless of the informational firewalls in place. They never met face-to-face, but would occasionally talk on the phone, usually with Jason in Washington and Tony at Langley, Virginia. But usually the phone calls didn't come at this untimely an hour in the morning.

"So, Jay, I know the Broncos had the Giants all bagged up by halftime, so what kept you up so late? Was it the poker game, or did you have a little 'poke her' game afterward?"

"Tony ..."

"I knew it! Lancer, you slash hound. Who's the unlucky girl?"

Jason had had a bit of a reputation as a lady's man in college because he had dated many girls, but none for a very long time. Nonetheless, he secretly enjoyed the tag of being a Casanova. Jason certainly was not a womanizer. He had never liked clinging vines, and he didn't believe in leading women on or promising tomorrows for a romp in the hay, so he had never allowed himself to get too close to anyone. Until now.

Jason turned to stare at the empty pillow on the other side of the king-size bed, for the first time realizing she wasn't there. He turned to notice there was no light in the bathroom or the kitchen. Where was she? Where was this incredible sexual creature?

"Tony, tell me what you got. I gotta go. I'm serious now."

"Okay, here's the scoop. We got a hit on VORS a couple hours ago on someone you might be interested in, Jacob Lachman."

"Jacob Lachman, Lachman. Never heard of him."

"Well, that's the name he gave the operator for the international collect call, but the magic box named him Ali al Din."

Jason knew very little about VORS, the Voice Recognition System, or the magic box, as it was referred to by Tony. He knew it had the ability to monitor and record millions of voice transmissions around the world at the same time. Any voice segment recognized and identified through its voiceprint analysis capabilities as a previously designated person of interest would be highlighted on the mainframe computer and forwarded to the interested party.

"Ali, my old terrorist pal ... where have you and your brother been so long?" Jason mused as much to himself as to Tony over the phone.

The brothers had gone to ground after being in Florida for several months, hanging around commercial jet simulators. They were easy to monitor because they used cell phones. They may as well have had LoJack automobile theft locators strapped around their necks, because their exact location could always be pinpointed regardless of whether their phones were on or off.

"Who did he call?"

"He called his wife in Dharma."

"Did he tell us any secrets?"

"Not really. I'll get you the translated transcripts. He sounded very remorseful, the interpreter said, like he had something to apologize for. Maybe something he had done."

"Or maybe something he's about to do," Jason said. "I knew we should have picked them up in Palm Beach. Tell me he's still in Florida, and tell me he used a cell phone."

"No, and no."

"Damn. Did he mention his brother Abdul?"

"Not at all, but he was talking in a very hushed voice, as if he was afraid of someone hearing him, and also there was a strange echo to the sound of the recording."

"Do you think he was in a phone booth?"

"No, I think he was in the Holiday Inn in Mount Vernon."

"No kidding."

"We couldn't trace the call past the switchboard to get a room number, but I thought you would like to know where he is, thus the wake-up call."

"Thanks buddy. I owe you big-time."

Jason hung up the phone and once again glanced at the empty pillow next to him, which still retained the impression of her head. He pulled the pillow to his face and was aroused by her lingering scent, which was part natural and part Shalimar. The fragrance drove him crazy. The scent reminded him of the oleander blossoms his mother used to pick from the yard and use as centerpieces.

Jason knew he had embarked upon a very slippery slope. Special Agent Cassandra Reilly, or Cassie, as he had screamed her name in ecstasy only a few hours ago, was absolutely forbidden territory. Not only was she another FBI agent, but she was also his partner. How could he let this happen?

Or how could it not happen? Reilly and Lancer had been teamed together for over a year, both getting the assignment they desired on the JTTF. Jason could never forget the first time he laid eyes on her. He had been called into the office of the assistant director on the top floor of the Hoover Building.

"Come in, Jason." Alfredo Russo had beckoned with a pleasant smile, which immediately made Jason wonder what this was all about. Before he knocked on the open door, Jason had noticed a woman with long, black hair in a black pantsuit sitting at the desk with her back to the door. "I want you to meet your new partner."

Jason thought the Task Force's new policy to organize into teams of two would result in his being paired with one of the guys from his cell, not some new guy. Or new girl, which apparently was the case.

"How do you do? I'm Cassandra Reilly," she said. She rose from the chair and extended her hand to Jason.

"Jason Lancer." Jason was surprised at the firmness of her handshake. "It's so nice to meet you," he said. He noticed he was staring almost dead level into her deep, blue eyes.

"I look forward to working with you," she said. Her manner was polite, but the tone of her voice indicated she was strictly business and could take care of herself.

"Likewise," Jason said. He tried not to appear struck by her manner or her looks. Attractive. Extremely attractive. She looked like a tall, blue-eyed sister of a Jill Hennessy or maybe even a Catherine Zeta-Jones.

He wondered if she was a Scorpio: intense, emotional, and passionate, with a tendency to be secretive.

Assistant Director Russo looked at Jason and nodded towards Cassie. "She won the turkey shoot at Quantico, she speaks fluent Arabic, and she can dunk a basketball," he said. Jason knew he didn't have to justify why she was picked to be his partner.

"Wow!" Jason said. He knew the winner of the turkey shoot was the best all-around marksman in the training class at the FBI Academy. "Then it's all settled. She'll do all the talking and all the shooting, and I'll do the backup and paperwork."

Cassie Reilly had attended the University of Connecticut on a full-ride basketball scholarship. She was the starting point guard for the UCONN Lady Huskies who lost to Tennessee in the finals of the NCAA National Championship. She majored in communications and minored in Arabic languages. It was natural for her to speak Arabic because she spent many years in Riyadh when her father was the U.S. Ambassador to Saudi Arabia.

After graduation from college and a strategic phone call from her father to his friend, Al Russo, Cassie went to work for the FBI. Upon completion of the vigorous and extensive program at the Academy, she went back to Saudi Arabia as a LEGAT, a legal attaché who works overseas with officials from the host country to stop crime or acts of war before they can reach the shores of the United States. Two years later, with her mother battling cancer, she asked for and was granted a transfer to the JTTF in Washington to be near her parents. Tragically, after her mother died, her father seemed to withdraw from everything and everyone. Although he had a history of heart trouble, Cassie knew he was slowly dying from a broken heart.

Jason gently placed the pillow back on the other side of the bed and smoothed it out while trying to collect his thoughts. He knew he had to act quickly, but first things first. He opened his laptop computer, which was already booted to high-speed Internet, and hit the top selection of his favorites list. The screen shifted instantly to his daily horoscope.

Libra for September 11, 2001: Beware of changing winds. Attention will be on you today so this is a time to shine. Put personal matters aside. Aries and Scorpio may be involved.

What a bum horoscope, Jason thought; things are changing, so be careful. No kidding. How could this be relevant? Ali was a Cancer, so how could this have any real meaning? Wait! Abdul is an Aries, so he must be involved.

Jason knew what he had to do. He opened the top drawer of the kitchen cabinet and retrieved the tattered deck of tarot cards. He shuffled them three times and cut them once, then pulled a card and placed it on top of the deck. The Five of Swords brought a grimace to Jason's face because it raised more questions than it answered. It was the prophetic meaning of the card that was most troubling: destruction, degradation, and infamy.

Regardless of the vague horoscope and the poignant tarot card, Jason knew he had to act quickly. He grabbed his cell phone and hit the speed dial.

Chapter 3

Tuesday, September 11 (Moon in Gemini to Cancer 12:07 p.m.) Beware the dawning of clear skies, from whence dangers may appear. Ignoring threats will not make them less menacing. Today is not a day for the timid.

The black-and-white taxi from the Arlington Cab Co. raced through the traffic which turned north along the Potomac River. The blinding bursts of sunlight reflecting off the river and through the trees were distracting to the anxious driver while he pressured the accelerator. This was one of those chamber of commerce days with a definite taste of fall in the air. The huge hardwood trees of northern Virginia were still clinging to their leaves, though the caramel coloring had begun. This was a battle they would soon lose.

Abdul al Din and Ali al Din slouched in the backseat.

"Look," Ali whispered to his brother pointing to the operating permit of the driver enclosed in a plastic cover on the dash. "Siyavash Abrashamian."

"Shhh," Abdul said. His menacing look admonished Ali. "We are not to do anything to call attention to ourselves."

Still Abdul pondered what would be the reaction of Siyavash Abrashamian if he knew the historical significance of the fare he was carrying. Would he shout, "Praise be to Allah?" Would he turn them in to the nearest law enforcement officer? Probably neither. More than likely, judging from his neat grooming and new Dockers, he had migrated to the West and had become one of them. The truth was that, in appearance, the brothers and the cab driver looked very much the same, except the cabbie still had a mustache. Last week Abdul and Ali had splurged at a local men's clothing store for a new pair of pants and trendy silk shirts, along with belts and socks. Everything except shoes. After the painful process of shaving their beards, they went to a barbershop to complete the transformation. Indeed we have succeeded, Abdul thought when he glanced at Siyavash's image in the rearview mirror. The only difference in them now was that Abdul and Ali had a single mission in life: to kill infidels. Siyavash had weakened. He had succumbed to the decadent culture of the West, and now he was an infidel.

"Which airline?" Siyavash asked. They almost sideswiped a van which changed lanes while they were speeding past.

"Delta Airlines." Abdul said.

"The shuttle?"

"What you mean, the shuttle?"

"You know, the shuttle; the flight that leaves for New York every hour."

It made a difference because the regular Delta flights and the shuttle were in different terminals in the airport, and if they were taken to the wrong terminal, they might miss their flight. Abdul knew Siyavash was trying to do everything possible to keep him happy and get them to the airport by seven forty-five to earn the extra 20 he had been promised.

"No, not the shuttle, as you say. We are not going to New York today."

The tickets they had purchased with cash last week were for Los Angeles. Abdul could hardly contain his excitement as the gravity of the day superabounded his mind. This day culminated years of planning and training and sacrifice. For Abdul, his brother, and the others acting with him, this was the day they would reap the rewards of their commitment. They were holding tickets for Los Angeles, but this flight would take them to paradise.

Abdul glanced at Ali, wondering if he was as tired as he looked. Not to worry, he thought. There'll be an eternity of rest very soon. Before he slept again, Abdul would be with Allah and with his father and his father's father. Not to mention, of course, the 72 virgins. The thought of the 72 virgins brought a glimpse of a smile to his lips. His prayer was that the 72 were only half as good as the infidel slut he and Ali had ravished throughout last evening.

The two brothers had left the "Do Not Disturb" sign on the door to their room and exited through the side entrance to catch a taxi on the street. Having paid cash for the room, they knew they would already be in paradise by the time the housekeepers found the hooker.

Abdul glanced nervously at his watch as the taxi sped north on the expressway, relaxing somewhat when he saw a sign which read "Reagan National Airport" with an arrow pointing straight ahead. He noticed Ali was looking down at his shoes, grimacing.

"What's wrong?" Abdul asked.

"These shoes are killing me," Ali said. He whispered so the driver could not hear.

"You must do nothing to call attention to your shoes. They are absolutely essential to our mission. Do you understand?" Abdul was stern with his caution.

Ali continued to grimace.

Although he would never admit it, Abdul sympathized with his brother because his shoes were also cramping his feet. Maybe they should have paid more attention to detail and tried on the shoes ahead of time, or maybe even worn them for a few days to break them in.

The network had supplied them with the shoes for the mission based on the shoe sizes the brothers had supplied to them years ago. The shoes were ordinary business casual, leather shoes but with a specially designed heel held on by what appeared to be larger than average nails. The shoes on a person's feet are too low to be scanned by the average metal detector. Even if the shoes were scanned by a handheld metal-detecting wand, the alarm would only alert the inspector to the obvious presence of metal. The inspector would immediately conclude the nails in the heel had caused the alarm and would look no further. Indeed, he would not twist the heel, which would separate from the shoe, revealing the hidden compartment containing the blades to the weapons. The handles to the weapons were made of cheap plastic and could be concealed anywhere because they would set off no alarms. And if they were discovered, they were only harmless, nonthreatening pieces of plastic. When assembled with the razor-sharp blades, however, the result was a simple box cutter. Or a deadly throat cutter, depending on the person holding the handle.

At precisely 7:40 a.m., Siyavash brought the taxi screeching to the curb at the Delta terminal at Washington Reagan National Airport. He bounced out to open the door for Abdul and Ali, remembering they had no luggage in the trunk. He watched to make sure they didn't forget the small bag each carried with them.

Siyavash bowed slightly towards Abdul who handed him a 50-dollar bill and told him to keep the change. "God bless you,"

Siyavash said. To that remark, he received a quizzical glance from Abdul and Ali before they darted into the terminal.

Chapter 4

Tuesday, September 11 (Moon in Gemini to Cancer 12:07 p.m.)
The mixing of business and pleasure is a folly for the fool-
hearted. A slippery slope should only be attempted by the bold.
Be bold today.

"Hello."

Cassie awoke from a dead sleep and had checked the caller ID
to see it was the one call she always had to answer, her
partner's call.

"Good morning, good-looking." Jason was all pumped up about
the phone call from Tony Perez and ready to start barking
instructions, but the moment he heard her voice, he softened.
"I'm sorry to wake you; I was hoping you would still be here
beside me."

"No problem, I'm wide awake. I couldn't be there beside you
because I'm finishing up this sexual harassment report."

"Really, what does it say?" Jason asked. He suddenly had a
momentary twinge in his gut, fearing she might be serious.

"It says you would have been a perfect ten if you hadn't fallen
asleep so quickly afterward. I had to knock you down to an eight
point five for lack of cuddling and conversation."

"Whoa! You're tougher than a French skating judge. Are the Russians paying you off? I demand another try!"

"What you need is some rest, big boy. I don't want you to hurt yourself."

Jason loved the bantering with this intriguing woman, but he knew time was of the essence if they were to have a chance to pick up the al Din brothers for questioning.

"While I'm resting up, we have some work to do. I'll pick you up at Starbucks in thirty minutes. We're rolling."

"You're serious?"

"I'm afraid so. We got a tip telling us the brothers are in the Holiday Inn in Mount Vernon."

"What kind of tip?"

"A very reliable tip."

"Did Russo call you?

"No, he doesn't know yet."

Jason had vowed under no circumstances would he ever disclose his relationship with Tony Perez to anyone. He wasn't worried so much about himself, but he owed Tony the protection of his confidentiality. Still he could understand Cassie's curiosity.

Jason added, "Please get me the usual latte Grande. See you shortly."

Cassie had always been very reserved about her private life. Jason knew she lived in Crystal City, near Reagan National. When asked where, she would simply say, "Just a flat in Crystal City." Jason could tell she didn't want to divulge exactly where she was living, so he didn't pursue it. Whenever he picked her up, it was always at the Starbucks near the Crystal City Marriott.

The rising sun had broken free from the horizon and Jason pushed his new gray Crown Vic near 80 miles per hour southward toward Mount Vernon. Traffic out of town was still light, but the opposite inbound lanes on US 1 were filling with morning commuters on their way into Washington. With the blue bubble light flashing from the dash and no siren sounding, it was eerily quiet as Jason and Cassie sipped their coffee.

How does she do it? She actually looks well rested, Jason thought to himself, stealing a quick glance at Cassie buckled into the passenger seat. Her face always had a made up without makeup look. Even today, when he knew she had had very little sleep. Her eyes were clear and bright with no signs of redness or fatigue, except for a little more moisture than usual, probably from a massive dose of Visine. Whatever works, Jason thought, smiling to himself.

Cassie wore dark-gray slacks and a black soft leather jacket, draped midway on her thighs. Even with the jacket unbuttoned, it adequately concealed the Glock 19C 9mm which hung from a shoulder holster underneath her left arm. It was much lighter than Jason's SIG SAUER .357 magnum, but with the magazine it still held 18 rounds. He knew she also had the customary Derringer strapped to her ankle.

Cassie spoke to finally break the silence. "Did you call for backup?"

"No, I want to be sure of what we have before sounding any alarms," Jason said. His voice did not exactly convey confidence. But he was sure the heavens were aligning for him because of the horoscope he had read earlier: *Attention will be on you today, so this is a time to shine.*

More silence.

"Jay." Cassie was looking straight ahead and speaking very softly. "I'm sorry about last night."

"Sorry! Sorry for what? I thought you were incredible."

"Oh! You know what I mean . . . I'm not sorry it happened, but I showed poor judgement staying after the poker game. I should have left when all the guys left. You know how people talk."

"I'm not worried about it. If they talk, we'll deal with it. I'm crazy about you, Cassie, don't you know?"

"That's just it, Jay, you can't be crazy about me. We're professionals here, doing a job which can't be compromised by personal feelings."

"How about if we're professional during the day and crazy all night?"

"Jay, I'm serious," she said. She checked the rapidly approaching exit sign. "Slow down, here's our exit!"

"I know you're serious," He swerved onto the exit ramp to where the Holiday Inn was located. "We'll talk more when we're off duty. Now, let's go catch a bad guy."

Chapter 5

Tuesday, July 10 (Moon in Pisces) Respect your intuitions. If the cheese doesn't pass the sniff test don't eat it. Things are not always as they appear. Be not tormented by the rebuff of Scorpio.

July, 2001.

During the summer the Bureau had a call from a flight simulator instructor working for Florida Sim-Tech in Boca Raton on the southeast coast of Florida. The company owns two Boeing 767 simulators and rents them wet or dry, with or without flight instructors, to airlines, governments, or individuals for 767 training. The usual program is a series of eight or nine four hour simulator sessions in conjunction with an FAA approved ground school program, the result of which is a rating to fly the airplane.

The flight instructor, Paul Ledford, a Captain and Check Pilot for the former Pan American World Airways, became suspicious after his first instructional period with Abdul and Ali al Din. After seeing thirty years of sunrises and foreign cities from the cockpit of a Pan Am 747, Captain Ledford was seldom surprised at anything. But there was something about these two that didn't add up from the very beginning.

Abdul and Ali had approached Frank Graveler, the sales director for Florida Sim-Tech and said they were interested in booking a series of familiarization flights in the 767 simulator. They had represented themselves as citizens of Saudi Arabia, having gained entrance into the U.S. with student visas. They provided proper identification and documentation including Saudi passports, U.S. student visas, and Florida drivers' licenses to substantiate their legitimacy. The brothers said they were majoring in English at Florida Atlantic University in Boca Raton, but their long-term goals were to be commercial pilots. After graduation they planned to return to Riyadh to continue the flying lessons they began before they left for the states to attend college. They simply wanted to buy some simulator time with an instructor to be exposed to an overview of commercial airline flying so they would be ahead of the program when they resumed pilot training.

The brothers' story was indeed different, but feasible nonetheless. But Abdul said they would pay cash. This was extremely unusual inasmuch as the total bill for the ten simulator sessions they were requesting was forty thousand dollars. When Frank asked them how they could afford to pay so much money in cash they responded revealing their favorite uncle was a Saudi Prince who took good care of them. Their uncle insisted that they deal strictly in cash so they could not overspend, which he was sure would happen if they used credit cards.

Frank Graveler regarded this to be one of those deals that occasionally happens along. The story was altogether believable, especially in light of the middle-eastern oil opulence manifested by the walled-in monster mansions along the southeastern gold coast of Florida. Besides, Frank's job was to sell simulator time and make money. They wanted to buy time and had plenty of money, cash no less. Such a deal! So Frank gave them a receipt for the forty grand and assigned Captain Paul Ledford as their instructor.

On the first day of training it was apparent to Captain Ledford these two had no interest in the technical or academic aspects of flying the 767. They did not want to perform, or even see, any abnormal or emergency procedures such as engine fire or single engine landings. In fact, they did not want to practice landings at all, usually an item of major emphasis in all flight training programs. All they wanted to do was to fly the airplane in cruise and learn how to navigate from one city to another using the Flight Management System. They wanted to learn how to connect and disconnect the autopilot and how to operate the transponder, the radar encoding device which allows air traffic control to identify and track the flight.

This should have been good duty for Captain Ledford. He didn't have to teach, demand, or even expect any degree of proficiency from these students; all he had to do was show up and operate the simulator and collect his paycheck. Yet, he was feeling very apprehensive?

When Captain Ledford and the brothers returned from the ten minute coffee break halfway through the first simulator session, he thought it would be useful to demonstrate some of the visual capabilities of the state-of-the-art simulator. This full motion training device, a twenty million dollar computer in a self-contained capsule on hydraulic jacks, can simulate any phase of aircraft performance. Once the door is closed and the bridge raised, the capsule moves in response to any throttle or flight control movement by the pilot, who feels the movement in the seat of his pants, as if he were sitting in the airplane. And when the pilot looks out the window he sees a realistic computer generated image of whatever airport or city or weather conditions the instructor has programmed.

Captain Ledford positioned the simulator at two thousand feet over Kennedy Airport heading west at dusk with unlimited visibility. The entire New York City skyline could be seen ahead, including the Empire State Building and the Twin Towers of the World Trade Center. The brothers' eyes lit up when they saw the city ahead. They asked if they could fly between the buildings, pointing to the Twin Towers. Captain Ledford had no objections. After all, it was their nickel. But he was surprised at what happened next.

Abdul from the left seat, the Captain's position, flew the aircraft toward the buildings as if he would fly between them. Then at the last moment, he turned the aircraft and flew directly into the north tower. The brothers gave a gleeful fist pump to each other when they quickly emerged from the other side of the generated image of the building. They repeated the process with Ali flying from the Co-pilots' seat, once again turning at the last moment to fly into the south tower; more fist pumping and giddiness.

Captain Ledford was somewhat puzzled by the unusual actions of these two foreign students. Noticing his lack of enthusiasm, Abdul made a hushed remark to Ali in Arabic, after which their behavior was more reserved. This raised additional red flags for Captain Ledford. He did not feel his instructional talent and experience should be wasted on students who had no interest in the basic fundamentals of flying, regardless of the fact he was being paid for his time. But witnessing such bizarre behavior by these bearded foreigners made him feel uneasy, without being able to really understand why. The following morning Captain Ledford relayed his concerns to the Miami field office of the FBI.

The Special Agent who received the call in the Miami office forwarded the report to the JTTF agent attached to that office, who in turn forwarded it to the JTTF in Washington. From there it was given to Jason for investigation.

Jason immediately called Captain Ledford and was given the entire story firsthand. He thought the situation was a little suspicious, but even more, he could sense these guys made Captain Ledford, a seasoned veteran, feel uncomfortable.

"I'd like to meet these guys," Jason said to Captain Ledford. "Is there a way I could do that during one of your training periods without them knowing I'm with the FBI?"

"Sure, you could pose as an FAA inspector."

"What do you mean?"

"Well, the Federal Aviation Administration is responsible for making sure our training and our instructors meet the required standards. So occasionally an FAA inspector will drop by unannounced to observe us to ensure compliance. You could be that guy."

"I'm not so sure. I don't know much about flying."

"You don't have to know anything. Simply walk in and introduce yourself as the FAA, ask for our credentials and identification, and I'll take care of the rest."

"Perfect. Thanks, Captain Ledford. I'll see you tomorrow."

Jason flew to Palm Beach early the following morning and drove straight to Florida Sim-Tech to meet confidentially with Frank Graveler before the brothers arrived. Frank told him the entire story and admitted they were a little strange, but insisted he had asked for and was provided proper identification. In fact, he received three forms of identification, which he copied for his records.

Jason inspected the copies of the passports, visas, and driver's licenses and made additional copies for himself. He noted with interest that for a local contact, they listed the number of a cell phone. It was impressive how authentic the copies of the documents appeared. Maybe these guys were for real.

Frank listened while Jason told him he was posing as an FAA inspector to observe the brothers and cautioned him to keep his visit a secret. What he did not tell him was he was wired to record all conversations. Jason was not so much concerned by what was going to be said as he was for getting a voice sample for his buddy Tony to input into the VORS database.

They did a quick tour of the facility before returning to Frank's office to await the arrival of instructor and students. Captain Ledford arrived first, with Abdul and Ali following a few minutes later. Jason discreetly photographed them from Frank's office when they approached the building from the parking lot.

The brothers were sitting across a small table from Captain Ledford when Jason knocked on the door of briefing room number two. On the table was a small TV/VCR monitor with a stack of videotapes on top. Behind Captain Ledford was a whiteboard with an eraser and several different colored magic markers. The other walls of the room were almost completely covered with actual size photographs of the entire cockpit of a Boeing 767. Captain Ledford motioned for Jason to enter.

"Captain Ledford?" Jason asked.

"Yes."

"I'm John Lane, with the FAA," Jason said. He shook Captain Ledford's outstretched hand and glanced at the apprehensive expressions on the faces of the brothers.

"I'm Paul Ledford, and these are my students, Abdul al Din and Ali al Din."

"Hi, guys, nice to meet you." Jason smiled affably and shook each of the brother's hands. "Are you guys related?"

"We're brothers," Abdul said. He quickly added, "We didn't contract for the FAA."

"Oh, I'm not here for you," Jason said. "I'm here to observe Captain Ledford for his annual evaluation."

The brothers looked at each other with concern. If they knew the FAA was the government agency which ensured compliance for air carriers and pilots, they could not have expected to have to interact with someone from that agency.

"Not to worry, guys," Captain Ledford said. "He's only here to make sure I know how to operate the sim, right, Mr. Lane?" He nodded to Jason.

"Absolutely. And if you'll let me see your licenses for the record, I'll sit here like a bump on a log for the rest of the period."

Captain Ledford, familiar with the routine, reached into his wallet and pulled out his pilot's license for Jason to examine.

"We do not have a pilot's license yet," Abdul said.

"Doesn't matter," Jason said. "Any ID with your name on it will suffice."

The brothers each retrieved a Florida driver's license from their wallets and handed it to Jason.

"Thank you very much." He gave a cursory glance at the licenses and handed them right back to the brothers. Of course, he had copies of these same licenses in his briefcase. It occurred to

Jason that Ali had not really spoken at all, and he needed to gather his voice sample.

"Ali, where are you from originally?" Jason asked.

"Saudi Arabia," Ali said.

"Riyadh?"

"No, Dharma."

"Where's Dharma?"

"One hour drive west of Riyadh."

"Very nice. Welcome to our country and good luck to you," Jason said. He knew he had heard enough.

After a quick briefing, Captain Ledford and the group went into the simulator for the training session. Jason sat in the observer's seat behind Captain Ledford at the instructor panel, which consisted of only two touch-screen computer monitors with countless activation icons. He said not a word but was impressed at the realism of the aircraft simulator, especially the computer generated visual presentations. After about an hour and forty-five minutes of climbs, descents, and basic navigation drills, Captain Ledford brought the sim down so they could have a coffee break.

Jason accompanied the three of them to a small break room nearby. He purchased a Diet Coke from the machine and noticed Abdul had a Coke Classic and Ali had a Sprite. Captain Ledford drank coffee.

"Nice job," Jason said to Captain Ledford. They were finishing their beverages. "I think I've seen enough. I'm going to cut out on the second half of the period. You're a great instructor, which will be reflected in my report." He extended his hand to Captain Ledford.

"Thanks, it's nice to meet you," Captain Ledford said. They shook.

"Good luck guys; hope to see you again," Jason said. He shook hands with Abdul and then Ali.

"Thank you," Abdul said. Ali nodded. The brothers appeared relieved.

Jason tossed his Diet Coke can into the empty trash can, noticing it contained only a clean plastic liner. He left the break room quickly and ducked into an empty briefing room until Captain Ledford and his students were back in the sim.

When the boarding bridge was raised indicating the motion was on and they were totally isolated, Jason hurried back into the break room, which was now empty. From his briefcase he pulled out two evidence retrieval kits. After slipping on a pair of plastic gloves, Jason labeled one of the kits Abdul al Din and the other Ali al Din. With tweezers he carefully plucked the Coke Classic and Sprite cans form the trash can. With a DNA moisture recovery swab he thoroughly swiped the opening of the Coke can where Abdul had placed his lips slurping Coke only a few minutes before. He sealed the swab in a small container and placed it in Abdul's kit, along with the Coke Classic can. He repeated the procedure for Ali and the Sprite can. Confident he had what he needed, Jason dashed for the airport and flew back to Washington.

The following morning Jason discreetly forwarded the voice samples to Tony Perez at the CIA, then personally delivered the evidence kits to Quantico for DNA and fingerprint analysis.

Jason's further investigation revealed some interesting inconsistencies. The Saudi passports were valid but Immigration had no record of them having student visas. The Florida driver's licenses were authentic, having been issued on the legitimacy of the passports and visas.

Jason gave Assistant Director Russo a detailed account in his office on the top floor of the Hoover building. Russo acknowledged something was wrong with this picture and commended Jason for his prompt and thorough investigation. Jason pleaded with Russo to let him pick up the brothers for questioning to see if they would provide some answers. Russo refused, saying they needed more than an immigration infraction to detain them. In the meantime they would track them by their cell phones.

A week later the legal attaché in Riyadh reported that the story about them having a rich prince for an uncle was totally false. If they didn't have a prince for a rich uncle where were they getting all this money? By the time Russo decided to apprehend them, they had discarded their cell phones and disappeared.

Chapter 6

Tuesday, September 11 (Moon in Gemini to Cancer 12:07 p.m.) Stand strong. Just because you keep your guard up doesn't mean you can't be hit in the gut. Beware the wolf in sheep's clothes, especially if he's an Aires.

The brothers walked briskly to the flight status board near the Delta Airlines ticket counter.

"Perfect," Abdul said to his brother. He looked around to make sure no one was close enough to hear. "Flight 249 is at Gate 17 and is departing on time at 8:45. That should give us enough time to get through security and meet the others before we board the flight."

Ali nodded. He was very quiet this morning, so much so it was beginning to make Abdul nervous.

"Do you see them anywhere," asked Abdul?

"No," Ali said. Abdul could see he was not really looking.

"Me either, perhaps they are already at the gate. And don't forget, they are going to look as strange as we do." They would also be clean-shaven, wearing western clothes, and new, uncomfortable shoes. They would be very strange in appearance to each other, but very ordinary to the average minimum wage airport security guard.

As they walked towards the security checkpoint, Abdul studied his little brother, looking for signs of weakness and doubt. Surely at this critical stage of the mission, Ali wasn't having second thoughts. Abdul was never certain his brother would have made this commitment without his influence. He was very proud. Still he felt, but would never admit even to himself, a twinge of guilt.

Ali, after all, had a beautiful, very obedient, wife and young son. After today, Ali would be their hero forever. Abdul on the other hand was far too committed to the cause to become seriously involved with a woman. It always became complicated when that happened. Like last evening when Abdul was having his turn and his way with the infidel bitch, he heard Ali on the phone in the bathroom placing a collect call to his wife in Saudi Arabia. He was reaffirming his love for her and the hope Allah would always watch over them. Abdul had decided not to intervene, feeling certain, regardless of the security breach of the phone call, it would take the Americans forever to discover its significance.

Only a few people were ahead of them when they reached the entrance to the concourse and the security checkpoint. Abdul noticed the usual airport cop sitting behind a table off to the side reading a newspaper. When they approached the I.D. screener, the proper documents consisting of a boarding pass and driver's license were out and available.

Abdul didn't want to appear clumsy or show apprehension at this point. He looked down with disdain at the name on the Florida driver's license, Abraham Itzack. Why did they have to give him a Jewish name? It seemed like a slap in the face on this the greatest and last day of his life on earth to be answering to a Jewish name. Someone in the network, maybe even the Director himself, thought Jewish names would raise far less suspicion than Muslim names, especially when operating in

America. The network had supplied them with fake names and addresses and a genuine looking driver's license to validate their identity. The clean-shaven picture on the license, taken almost two years ago in Afghanistan soon after the training for the mission began, made Abdul look much younger. Abraham Itzach, residing in Palm Beach Gardens, Florida. *Not for long*.

"Good morning, sir!"

"Good morning." Abdul almost stuttered to the matronly bleached blond security guard, while she examined his boarding pass and driver's license.

"Thank you. Have a nice flight, Mr. Itzack." she said. Her smile showed teeth that appeared like they had never met a dentist.

Ali repeated the process behind him.

The guard returned Ali's license and boarding pass to him. "Thank you, Mr. Lachman," she said.

Within a few steps Ali placed his bag behind Abdul's bag on the conveyor belt which transported passenger carry-on luggage through the scanning device. Abdul removed his laptop computer and placed it in a separate plastic tray. The bags were small canvas bags, one blue and one green, the type you would take to an exercise facility to hold some shoes and workout clothes. They were very ordinary and very similar. Even the grips were similar. However, carefully wrapped and snapped in the grips of each bag were two plastic handles. They were made to fit the grip of a hand and the blade of a box cutter. *No boxes would be cut today*.

Abdul was not concerned about the bags because a week ago on the practice run of the mission the bags had sailed through the scanner without raising a single red flag. Besides, he knew the majority of airport scanning devices were designed to alert for substantial masses of metal, like guns or large knives. The only thing different about today was this was the real thing, not a drill. And today he had on a pair of very uncomfortable shoes.

Beeeeeep!

The magnetometer emitted a shrill beep when Abdul walked through it towards the waiting security guard. Abdul was somewhat surprised when the machine alerted on him and he opened his palms and raised his arms slightly in a quizzical gesture directed at the guard.

"It's probably the belt buckle. Step over here, sir," the guard said. He motioned for Abdul to step off to the side. "Let me check you out."

The guard was a large man, straining buttons at every seam. A small hairless head, the color of dark Lady Godiva chocolate, topped a chiseled body, supported by no discernable neck. Abdul rarely felt intimidated, but this was one of those times.

"Stand with your feet apart and your hands straight out," the guard instructed Abdul. The guard ran a metal detecting wand all along Abdul's body. A little chirping sound was heard when the wand passed the metal buckle of the belt. The wanding continued down Abdul's torso and down and up and around both his legs without further chirping. Abdul observed with great relief that the guard did not take the wand completely to the floor.

"Just as I thought, the belt buckle," the guard said. His remark reflected a tone of self-satisfaction. "Have a nice flight."

"Thank you," Abdul mumbled. Perspiration started to form on his slick upper lip.

Abdul watched behind him to see Ali come through the screening without incident. The leather belt he was wearing also had a leather buckle, which would set off no alarms. Abdul was thinking he should have picked out a similar belt. But it didn't matter now, because they were in the clear and on their way.

As they walked down the long concourse towards Gate 17, Abdul found it difficult to concentrate on the task at hand. With people and objects passing by him in slow motion, it was as if he were walking the longest mile. *Indeed his last mile.*

Chapter 7

Tuesday, January 22 (Moon in Taurus) Great orchestras have great conductors. Find your maestro and follow his direction to make music that will please your fathers.

Years earlier.

Abdul and Ali were born and grew up in Dharma, a small town west of Riyadh, the largest city and one of the two capitols of Saudi Arabia. Mecca is the other. Their mother had died while giving birth to Ali. The boys' father was the only shoemaker in town and had been very busy and preoccupied keeping everyone in shoes. While this kept food on the table, there wasn't much time for the boys. The father fulfilled his religious obligation, however, by ensuring that the boys attended Mosque every day for their spiritual and educational growth.

The Mullah at the local Mosque became a very important figure to the brothers during their teen-age years. They came to realize how fortunate they were to have such a learned Mullah who could give them the exact, correct interpretation of the Holy Quran. They were taught how Islam was the religion destined to dominate the earth. They were taught that Allah's will to advance the cause of Islam justified any action, and any deed accomplished on behalf of Islam had the eternal blessings of Allah. In fact, no matter how distasteful or heinous the deed appeared to the perpetrator, there was no worry of condemnation if it were done in the name of Islam. They learned repeatedly that all infidels, anyone who did not embrace the Mullah's teachings of Islam, must die.

The brothers also learned from the Mullah that women were sent by Allah to serve men in all ways. They were to make bread for them and come to their bed whenever the men wanted, even if they were making bread at the time. Any sexual act the man desired was considered a gift from Allah, and it was the woman's duty to perform it for him upon demand.

When Abdul was eighteen, he accompanied the Mullah to Riyadh to attend a seminar on the advanced teachings of Islam. When they arrived, he was surprised to see many men with guns surrounding the Mosque where the meetings were to take place. Although the guard at the door readily recognized the Mullah, they were both searched for weapons before they were allowed to enter. Inside the Mosque were several other Mullahs and many young men who appeared to be about the same age as Abdul. Soon a tall man with a long beard dressed in a white shepherd's robe entered. It was then Abdul first laid eyes on the Director.

Young and extremely impressionable, Abdul was mesmerized by the imposing figure sitting on the floor with an AK-47 strapped around his neck. Everyone seemed to regard him as royalty. He spoke in a voice so soft it would have been inaudible, except he was the only one making a sound in the large room.

"Until now," the Director had said, "you have only been learning the teachings of Allah from the Holy Quran. You have learned how all Muslims must unite for the nation of Islam, to defend against the evil infidels from the West who want to pollute our very souls with the decadence of capitalism, materialism, and pornography. You have learned your lesson well. Now, Allah is speaking directly to your soul. Now is the time to demonstrate to Allah the depths of your convictions to destroy the infidels."

Abdul, like the other young men in the room, hung onto every word the Director uttered while he continued in a slightly louder voice. "If there are those among you who have an everlasting love for Allah; if there are those among you who believe the promises of Allah as conveyed by the Mullahs and the Holy Quran; if there are those among you whose commitments are as strong as your beliefs, stand and follow me. I, with the grace of Allah, will take you to paradise."

The Director stood and without saying another word, turned and walked out through the back door. Somehow he didn't have to look back to know most of the young men in the room, including Abdul, were with him.

Abdul had followed the Director for years, training to be a soldier of Jihad in Syria and Yemen. Abdul was certain he had caught the Director's eye as being a very proficient and dedicated follower. On one clear spring morning when the entire expedition was preparing to move out for Afghanistan, Abdul was given a message from his brother informing him their father was extremely ill. With the blessings of the Director, who provided a private car and driver, Abdul returned to Dharma and his family for the first time since the day he left to visit the Mosque in Riyadh.

When Abdul stood beside the bedside of his dying father, the look of pride he saw on his face conveyed a message to Abdul which needed no words. He was glad to be home, even if it was to help bury his father, who died within a few days of his arrival. During that time, he had long talks about his cause and commitment with Ali, who seemed very interested, even though he had recently taken a beautiful young girl from nearby Duwadami as his wife. After another week passed, it was time for Abdul to return to duty. When he was saying his good-byes, Ali ran out to join him with his bag packed. Abdul was delighted and surprised. He and his little brother departed for Afghanistan.

Abdul remembered the day almost two years ago back in Afghanistan when he learned that he and Ali, along with Basil and Yusef, had become part of this fateful mission.

"You have been chosen," the Director had said to the dozens of men assembled before him, "to honor Allah by executing a very special mission. This mission is extremely secretive; the curse of Allah will forever be upon anyone who discloses any information about this mission or even the knowledge it exists. If there is anyone here who doesn't want to be a part of this, you may leave now." The Director gazed at them and was pleased but not surprised no one moved.

"The purpose of the mission is twofold: to kill many infidels and to demand the freedom of Sheik Omar." Everyone there knew Sheik Omar was the famous "blind Sheik" who had been convicted as the primary person responsible for the truck bombing of the World Trade Center in 1993. "We are going to train many teams," the Director continued, "so when the time comes, someone will be in position to accomplish the job."

The Director explained that the defenders of Islam, universally known as al-Qaeda, would train pilots to be among the fighters who would easily take over commercial airliners from the spineless American infidels. They would fly the passenger hostages to a predetermined landing strip and begin killing infidels until they released the Sheik. It will take at least a year to bring the plan to fruition. Go forth and train with supreme dedication, and may Allah be with you. Those of you selected for pilot training will be personally notified."

Within an hour, an aide to the Director came to escort Abdul and Ali to a modest house on the outskirts of a nearby village. When they approached the doorway, Abdul noticed some friends and fellow fighters leaving through a side door. Among them he recognized the other two brothers of the group, Maleed and Wail Alsheri, along with Mohammed Atta.

The brothers walked through the door. "Be seated, please," the Director said.

Abdul and Ali were very apprehensive while they sat across from the Director in the small room. It was only a few moments but seemed much longer before the silence was broken by the Director.

"I'll come directly to the point," he said. "Praise be to Allah, you two have been impressive." Then to Abdul he said, "I'm glad you invited your brother to join us." He leaned a bit closer to the brothers. "Ali, you're a great asset to the glory of Allah."

"Thank you, Emir," Ali said.

"Would you two like to be trained as pilots?" the Director asked.

"Yes! Yes!" the brothers exclaimed in unison.

"Then I have another question for you," the Director said. He paused a few moments for effect. "Would you like to join the brigade of Holy Martyrs?"

Abdul and Ali were surprised and shocked. They were very solemn when they stared at each other between quick glances at the Director.

"But, Emir," Abdul said with a whisper, "being a pilot on the mission you described doesn't involve being a martyr."

"What you say is true, but the mission I described this afternoon is not the real mission. Before I give you the details of the actual mission, I must ask you again. Would you like to join the brigade of Holy Martyrs?"

Abdul looked straight down at the floor in front of him, his eyes welling with tears. With a quivering lower lip, he raised his eyes to meet the gaze of the Director.

"I would be deeply honored to accept paradise in the praise of Allah." Abdul's voice registered deep conviction.

The Director looked to Ali.

"Yes," Ali said. He spoke softly. "Praise be to Allah."

The Director issued a personal decree to Abdul and Ali. "May all the blessings of Allah be your's. I will personally ensure you will want for nothing while you carry out Allah's will."

"Tell us, Emir, what is the real will of Allah?" Abdul asked.

"This must never be discussed with anyone. Do you understand?"

"Yes, Emir," Abdul said. Ali nodded.

"You have been chosen to cast the first stone for Allah in the final phase of the great war of Islam against the infidels. The war will last for many years, and you have been honored for martyrdom by being the tip of the spear, beginning the battle which we are destined to win."

The Director outlined the overall strategy which the most fervent of Muslim extremists had come to believe was the foolproof plan for Islamic superiority.

The plan was to take over American commercial airliners inflight, kill the pilots, and use the aircraft as weapons of destruction by flying them into specific strategic targets. These aircraft, specifically the Boeing 757 and the Boeing 767, were chosen because they shared a commonality of cockpit instrumentation. The cockpits were so similar that the Federal Aviation Administration allowed a pilot a common rating to fly both aircraft, by completing a single training course. Thus the martyr pilots would be familiarized with the largest number of aircraft with the least amount of training.

The 757 and 767 aircraft were also chosen because they were capable of carrying large amounts of jet fuel, a low-grade mixture of kerosene, guaranteed to explode into a tremendous inferno upon crashing into a target. Coast-to-coast flights would be selected for commandeering because they were sure to be fully loaded with fuel.

The American infidels were extremely naïve, the Director told them. Airport security was a sham. They were too afraid of offending someone to really search them. They also feared someone might file a discrimination lawsuit. They pretended to go to great lengths to keep weapons such as knives, guns, and explosives from being carried aboard their airplanes. It never occurred to the infidels that the most deadly weapon of all was the airplane itself. Such a possibility was inconceivable to faint-hearted westerners because they have never faced an adversary who would readily sacrifice his life for the will of his god.

Chapter 8

Tuesday, September 11 (Moon in Gemini to Cancer 12:07 p.m.) Be flexible. Embrace all options. Even the best of plans must often be refined to achieve your ultimate goals.

Abdul and Ali passed by the line of passengers at the counter at Gate 17. Abdul glanced at the marquee and noticed Flight 249 to Los Angeles was departing on time at 8:45 AM. Perfect.

"I don't see them," Ali said. He was trying not to move his lips and looked like a bad ventriloquist.

"There, over in the corner," Abdul said. He nodded his head towards the corner of the waiting area.

Basil Kabil and Yusef Utbak, the other two members of the team, were sitting together near the back of the waiting area. They were staring straight ahead, trying so hard to look inconspicuous they were conspicuous. At least that's the way they looked to Abdul, who thought they resembled a couple of Jihadist recruits who had flunked out of training and were waiting for a bus back to Kabul. Looks can be deceiving, Abdul reflected. He knew Basil and Yusef were chosen for the mission because they were deadly fighters in hand-to-hand combat.

While they were settling into two vacant seats on the perimeter of the waiting area, Abdul managed to catch the eye of Yusef, who was sharing a chuckle with Basil. Abdul was certain their amusement was at the expense of his brother and him, but he returned the smile and nodded his head indicating all was well.

"Ladies and gentlemen, may I have your attention, please," the diminutive lady at Gate 17 was saying over the loud speaker. "For those of you just arriving in the gate area for Flight 249 to Los Angeles, we're asking you to check in at the counter. We've had a change of equipment on this flight and you may have a different seat assignment. To avoid confusion, check in with us before boarding and we will make every effort to accommodate your requests for an aisle or a window seat. We should begin boarding in about ten minutes. Thank you."

Abdul rose to his feet after hearing the announcement, trying to figure out his next move. The term "change of equipment" puzzled him, but the more he thought about it, the more he was sure it meant trouble for the mission. Ali, Basil, and Yusef began to stir in their seats, sensing there was a problem.

"Could you help me please?" Abdul asked. He had hurried directly to the lady working the computer at the counter, failing to notice the long line of passengers in front of her.

"Sir, take your place in line and I will be glad to help you." The agent addressed him curtly with barely a glance. She was hardly five feet tall and in her late forties, but extremely efficient at her job. The lapel service pin she wore, wings with the Delta logo and a diamond in the middle, indicated she had spent twenty-five years, over half her life, working for the airline. There was no insult she had not heard or endured over that period of time.

Abdul persisted. "What do you mean, change of equipment?" The agent kept tapping on the computer, changing seats for the passenger at the counter, when a tall gray-haired gentleman in a red coat walked up.

"Good morning, Francine, how's it going?" The Red Coat asked the agent.

"Great, we're good for schedule, almost done with the re-seating," she said. The Red Coat was now standing beside her at the counter. She motioned toward Abdul and spoke in a discreet voice. "Could you see what's bothering this guy?" she asked.

"Sure," the Red Coat said. He walked toward Abdul.

"Is there a problem, sir?" The supervisor asked.

"What do you mean, change of equipment?"

"We originally had a 757 on this flight, but due to required maintenance on that aircraft, we substituted a 737-800 which does the job nicely."

"Thank you," Abdul said. He walked briskly away, motioning Ali, Basil, and Yusef to follow him.

Abdul scurried into the nearby men's restroom and observed it was empty except for one teenager washing his hands. He hurried over to one of many in a line of urinals hanging on the opposite wall to relieve the mounting pressure on his bladder. When he unzipped his fly and began urinating, he noticed how tender he was to the touch of his hand. He was distracted for a moment when he felt a twinge of excitement and firmness, being reminded of the all-night rutting of the infidel bitch prostitute.

When the teenager left the restroom, Abdul's three accomplices entered and went directly to join him at the urinals.

"What's wrong?" Basil asked.

Abdul spoke in a hoarse whisper. "We can't take that flight," he said. "We can't fly a 737. It must be a 757 or a 767."

"Why don't we wait and go tomorrow?" Basil asked. "It's not like the Sheik is going anywhere. He'll still be in jail tomorrow."

Basil and Yusef, not being members of the brigade of martyrs, did not understand the importance of the timing of the hijacking. Only Abdul and Ali knew their mission had nothing to do with Sheik Omar. Basil and Yusef did not know later on this day they would be in paradise, and the plane they were commandeering would kill many infidels. They did not know they were the tip of the spear.

"We cannot disappoint the Director," Abdul said. He glanced at the door to make sure they were still alone. "We must find another flight with the right airplane."

"How do we do that?" asked Yusef.

"Give me a minute to check things out. I'll meet you at the newsstand across from Gate 17." Abdul zipped his trousers and dashed out the door.

He walked quickly down the concourse from gate to gate looking out at the airplanes connected to the jetways. At Gate 18 to Raleigh Durham he saw an MD-88, a smaller jet with two engines on the tail. The same for Flight 649 to Cincinnati parked at Gate 19. The aircraft at Gate 20, a 757 to Chicago, was already being pushed back onto the ramp. Too late.

Abdul was becoming increasingly frustrated. He hurried to Gate 21, the last gate at the end of the concourse. It was Flight 121 to Atlanta departing at 8:50 AM. He dashed towards the window past the passengers who were beginning to board. It was a 757. Abdul was sure of it, even though he could only see one side of the fuselage, one wing and one engine.

"Continuing to board Flight 121, Boeing 757 service to Atlanta with passengers seated in rows thirty and higher; rows thirty and higher, welcome aboard," the young Tom Cruise look-alike agent was announcing. Abdul rushed to the counter.

"Can I get on this flight?" Abdul asked. His excitement mounted as he noted it was now 8:25, twenty-five minutes before departure.

"When your seat number is called, you're free to board," the agent said.

"That's the problem," Abdul said. He knew he had to think fast on his feet. "I don't have a seat on this flight. My ticket is for Los Angeles, but I want to go to... to Atlanta," he said. He had quickly confirmed the destination city on the board behind the counter.

"Sir, let me see your ticket," the agent said. He reached for the ticket Abdul was already handing him. "Mr. Itzack, we have plenty of seats on this flight, but you'll have to be rebooked and I don't have time to help you now because I'm busy with boarding. You'll have to go back to the ticket counter."

Abdul was perplexed, realizing it would be useless to argue at this point. "Thank you," he said. He quickly grabbed his ticket from the agent and ran down the concourse towards Gate 17.

Ali, Basil, and Yusef were thumbing through magazines at the magazine rack at the newsstand.

"We have to take the airplane to Atlanta! Let's go," Abdul said. He eagerly beckoned the three to join him.

"We don't have tickets to Atlanta," Ali said.

"The flight leaves at 8:50! We must hurry to the ticket counter to get tickets to Atlanta."

"Are you crazy?" Yusef said. "We can't risk going through security again, even if there were time, which there is not."

Abdul looked up and saw the Red Coat supervisor walking away from Gate 17, passing the newsstand. He knew this was their only chance. He had only twenty minutes until departure; he had to think fast.

Abdul said to other three, "Come with me, and let me do the talking." He dashed to catch up with the Red Coat.

"Sir! Sir! Could you help us please?"

The Red Coat turned to see four people chasing him and recognized Abdul as the passenger from Gate 17.

"Sir, you must board your flight immediately. We've already issued a final boarding call for Los Angeles."

"We've just learned our plans have changed and we need to go to Atlanta. Could you please help us?"

"What do you mean, Atlanta? That flight is also ready for departure, leaving in twenty minutes," the Red Coat said. He scrutinized the anxious group.

Abdul could tell the Red Coat was not happy with the situation and did not look willing to help them. He had to think of something fast.

"We are diamond dealers, and our most important client who was meeting us in Los Angeles was detained in Atlanta. Our only chance to make a presentation to him must take place today in Atlanta," Abdul pleaded. He glanced at the others who were nodding approval. When the Red Coat remained silent, Abdul knew he had to do more.

Abdul reached into his pocket. "We would be extremely grateful if you would help us," he said, pulling a roll of hundred dollar bills from his pocket.

"Let me see your tickets," the Red Coat said. He walked over to an empty ticket counter on the concourse. "We don't have much time."

The Red coat activated the computer and within five minutes had rebooked Mr. Itzack, Lachman, Abramovitch, and Schwartz on Flight 121 to Atlanta.

"Go immediately to Gate 21 and board the aircraft," he said. He shoved the tickets across the counter towards Abdul.

Abdul was very relieved. "Thank you very much," he said. When he picked up the tickets with one hand, he reached to shake hands with the Red Coat with the other. Without another word, Abdul and the others were dashing towards Gate 21. When the Red Coat withdrew his hand was holding in his palm five one hundred dollar bills.

"Have a nice flight," he called to them. They were already out of hearing, running like there was no tomorrow.

Chapter 9

Tuesday, September 11 (Moon in Gemini to Cancer 12:07 p.m.) Some days, conventional wisdom trumps conventional procedures. Today is one of those days. You may be of great aid to a stranger.

Jason pulled the blue light down from the dashboard and screeched the Crown Vic to a stop at the main entrance door of the Holiday Inn. They jumped out and Cassie flashed her badge to the Bell Captain and yelled, "Don't let anyone touch my car." They hurried through the front door.

Jason badged the desk clerk when he approached the front counter. "FBI," he said. "Could I speak with the manager, please?"

"In there," the clerk said. He nodded towards an open door across from the front desk. A middle-aged man with thinning hair sat in a small office working on a computer. He wore khaki Dockers and a wrinkled white shirt with curling collar tips and a clip-on tie. Jason and Cassie knocked and entered at the same time.

"How can I help you?" the manager asked. The proper introductions were completed.

"Do you have a Jacob Lachman in the hotel?" Jason asked.

After tapping a few computer keys the manager said, "No Lachman here."

"Anyone with the last name, al Din?"

A few more taps. "No."

"I didn't think so," Jason said. He flipped the pictures of the fully bearded al Din brothers on the manager's desk. "Do these guys look at all familiar to you?"

"No, not really."

"How about these guys?" Jason asked. He exchanged the pictures with computer renditions showing the brothers clean shaven.

"No, no. What did they do?"

"We want to ask them some questions," Cassie said.

"Excuse us for a second, please," Jason said to the manager. He motioned for Cassie to step outside the office.

"So much for your hot tip," she said. Jason duly noted the sarcasm in her voice and chuckled to himself.

"Let's think about this for a moment," he said. He saw the manager eyeing them from his office. "Why would Ali use the name Lachman?"

"Because he wanted to be known as Lachman, not al Din?"

"Why not Smith or Gonzales or Stenstrom?"

"Maybe he wanted to be perceived as Jewish, not Arab."

"Cassie, sometimes I think you're brilliant!"

"You mean like last night?" she asked. Another puckish remark.

"Especially last night," Jason said. "Maybe if it was Abdul registered at the hotel, he might be using a Jewish name also."

"You know, sometimes I think you're brilliant, too," she said.

"You mean like last night?"

"No, Casanova, I mean like now. Let's check the hotel for obvious Jewish names."

"Am I hearing here we should embark on a mission of racial profiling?"

"Why don't you leave the political correctness to the gender challenged member of this team? Do you want to find them, or not?"

"Let's get the manager to print us a copy of the hotel guest list," Jason said. He turned back toward the manager's office.

Muhammad, the bell captain, came through the door and approached the manager's office. He saw Jason and Cassie talking with the manager.

"Oh! There you are," he said. "I was going to tell my boss the car parked at the front door was yours. I don't want to get into trouble."

"I'm aware of the car, Muhammad," the manager said. "But thanks for telling me."

"You're welcome, sir," Muhammad said. He quietly turned to walk away.

"Wait a second, Muhammad." Jason beckoned him and looked closely at his nametag. "I'm Special Agent Lancer and this is Special Agent Reilly of the FBI. Could you look at these pictures and tell me if you have seen these people?"

Jason picked up the pictures from the manager's desk and showed them to the Bell Captain, beginning with Ali, bearded, then clean shaven. Nothing. He continued to watch Muhammad's face closely while he showed him the pictures of Abdul with a beard. Nothing. But when Jason handed him the computer image of Abdul clean shaven, he knew he'd hit pay dirt.

Muhammad appeared to be in shock. He acted as if he knew this guy. Jason wondered what he would do. He seemed to be speechless. Would he lie to the FBI?

"Well?" Jason asked.

"It looks like Mr. Itzack," Muhammad finally said.

Cassie whispered to Jason. "Now, there's an obviously Jewish name."

"When did you last see Mr. Itzack?" Jason asked.

"Last evening around eleven. He asked where he could find some food and I recommended the Brown Derby next door."

Muhammad was having to think fast. It wasn't food Itzack was looking for and he couldn't tell the FBI in front of his manager he was pimping. It was very smart, he thought, to tell them he sent Itzack to the Brown Derby in case they ever linked him with Sandra Thompson.

"Thank you, Muhammad; we may have some more questions later. If you see this guy again, call us immediately."

Jason turned to the manager who was already tapping on his computer.

"Room 201, the Honeymoon Suite," the manager said without being asked. "There are two adults in the room and they are supposed to leave today."

"Newlyweds?" Cassie asked.

"Oh, I have no idea. Anyone can stay there if they pay the price. It's a larger room with a sitting area and a king-sized four poster bed."

"Give us a pass key and point us to the room," Jason said.

Jason took the key card while the manager told them where to find the room. He pulled out his cell phone and started to dial.

"Who are you calling?" Cassie asked.

"Backup. I think it's time to roll out the cavalry. We'll stake the room until they arrive."

Cassie flashed a confident smile. "Oh! C'mon, Kemo Sabe, no need to bother Russo. We can do this."

Jason stopped dialing. He knew protocol for this situation demanded backup. Yet he could not disregard his mantra for the day. *Attention will be on you today so this is a time to shine.*

"Let's go, Jay, I'll take the lead," she said. She was now pleading.

Aires and Scorpio may be involved. Yes! Maybe that's it! Maybe the morning reading was making sense after all, Jason thought, remembering Cassie was indeed a Scorpio.

"Alright, you win," Jason said, folding up his cell phone. "Here's what we'll do."

After Jason briefed her on the plan of attack, they headed up the stairs to Room 201. The hallway was empty when they walked nonchalantly by the room, noticing a Do Not Disturb sign on the doorknob and no indications of activity. Jason returned quietly to the door and placed his portable listening device against the crack of the door between the hinges.

The PLD is a bundle of three tiny wires the size of a fishing line connected to a small box the size of a matchbox. On the end of one wire is the receptor microphone, about the size of a quarter. On the ends of the other two wires are insertable earpieces. Sounds from the mic pass through the box and can be magnified up to a hundred times.

Jason listened for a minute or so and heard nothing from the room but the fan from the air-conditioner. He nodded to Cassie down the hall, who used her cell phone to call the room. If anyone answered, she would pose as housekeeping and ask if they needed service. The phone rang and rang, but Jason heard no sound changes in the room. He once again nodded to Cassie, who stowed her cell phone and approached the door with the key card in one hand and her 9mm Glock in the other.

Special Agent Jason Lancer watched this stunning woman leaning against the wall by the door with her gun held high. He knew she was good, but how could she be so sure of herself? When she saw him staring at her, she looked him straight in the eye and gave him the slightest reassuring smile.

With Jason still listening at the door, Cassie slipped the key card into the slot and withdrew it. The green unlocked light came on and she pushed down the handle and cracked the door slightly. No sounds from the room. Jason quickly folded his PLD, pulled his Sig-Sauer 357 Magnum, and gave Cassie a quick nod.

In an instant, she was through the door of the darkened room with Jason close behind. Nothing moved. From the light spilling in from the open door, she could make out a human form on the bed across the room.

"Freeze! FBI!" Cassie shouted. She rushed toward the bed with her gun aimed and ready to fire.

Jason found the light switch by the door and turned on the overhead lights.

"Oh! God!" was all Cassie could say.

"Wait! Let me clear the room," Jason said. He saw Cassie was about to let her guard down.

Jason quickly inspected the bathroom, looking behind the shower curtain, into the closets, and under the bed.

"All clear," he said. Cassie holstered her gun and Jason focused his attention on the bed.

Sandra Thompson was naked, sprawled face down in the middle of the bed with each arm and leg tied to a bedpost. Her body was pale, almost white, except for her fingers and toes, which were the color of somewhere between laundry ink blue and purple. Blood covered her entire crotch area and spotted the sheet beneath her. Her ankles and wrists were raw from struggling against the ropes. She had given up the struggle.

"How revolting," Cassie said. She and Jason slipped on rubber gloves. Cassie felt for a sign of life in Sandra Thompson's carotid artery.

"I can't feel a pulse."

"And I don't see her breathing, either," Jason said.

"Wait! Her mouth is taped!" Cassie said.

"I'll cut her loose," Jason said. He took out the Swiss army knife which his mother had given him and slashed the ropes.

Jason rolled Sandra Thompson toward Cassie, who ripped the duct tape from her mouth. She still could not detect any sign of breath or heartbeat.

"I think she's gone, Jay," Cassie said. She stepped back and looked at Jason with resignation.

"Wait! Let me try this!" Jason said. He quickly removed the PLD from his pocket and turned up the volume. He inserted the earpieces in his ears, and placed the mic receptor gently between Sandra Thompson's breasts.

"There's a heartbeat!" Jason said. "It's faint, but it's a heartbeat!"

"I'll do mouth-to-mouth," Cassie said.

"I'll call the paramedics." Jason was already dialing his cell phone.

Cassie covered Sandra's mouth with her own and began to force air into her. It didn't seem to be working because she couldn't get much air to move at all. Moreover, she couldn't see Sandra's chest expand when she breathed into her. Jason finished his 911 call and could see she was having difficulty.

"Did you clear her airways?" he asked.

"Oh! I totally forgot."

She opened Sandra Thompson's mouth but couldn't see any obstructions. Like she had been trained, Cassie explored her throat with her fingers to make sure it was clear. She felt something. After much difficulty she was able to get a grip on an object which stretched out like a bungee cord. Finally it began to release, slowly at first, then popping out into her hand. That was when she realized she was holding a prophylactic.

"Oh! Dear God," she said. Her face reflected an expression of disgust. "Why on earth would someone want to swallow a prophylactic?"

"Maybe to keep from choking on it," Jason said.

Cassie completely lost it. She ran for a trash can sitting at a desk nearby and heaved violently, vomiting until there was nothing left. Without missing a beat she wiped her mouth on her sleeve and resumed her mouth-to-mouth on Sandra Thompson. This time, the rise and fall of her breasts was a sure indication to Cassie she was pushing air into her lungs.

By the time the paramedics arrived Cassie was able to induce a couple of weak coughs from Sandra Thompson who was trying to breathe on her own. Jason could see she was regaining some of her color and Cassie indicated she could feel a pulse in her neck. She showed, however, no signs of regaining consciousness.

The local police arrived about the same time as the paramedics. Jason told them to guard the area, but under no circumstances enter or allow anyone else to enter the room. This was a federal crime scene. He wanted all the evidence preserved for the FBI Crime Scene Investigators from Quantico, who were already enroute.

The paramedics immediately gave oxygen to the patient and started an IV. After radio consultation with a physician from the hospital emergency room, they switched her to a gurney for transport, covered her with a sheet and blanket, and started out the door. Cassie was leaning against the wall, completely exhausted, now that the adrenaline was subsiding.

"Good job, I think you might have saved her," the paramedic said to Cassie.

"Thanks, I hope she makes it," was all Cassie could say.

The hotel manager was there along with Jason and a couple of Mount Vernon policemen when they wheeled Sandra Thompson from the room.

"Do you recognize her?" Jason asked the manager. He motioned for the paramedics to slow down for a moment.

"You know, it looks like Sandy."

"Sandy?"

"Yes, Sandy, a cocktail waitress from the Brown Derby next door."

"The same place the bell captain recommended to Itzack?" Jason asked. He nodded to the paramedics to carry on.

"The same place," the manager said. He hurried to hold the elevator doors for the paramedics.

Cassie walked out of room 201 looking very dejected.

"Nice going, partner. I think you just sank a three pointer at the buzzer," Jason said. He raised Cassie's arm with one of his hands and high-fived her with the other.

"I'm sorry you had to see that," Cassie said.

"What, your mouth on her mouth, or you throwing up in the trash can?"

"No, those beautiful breasts on a dying girl. What a waste," Cassie said. She cut her eyes at him with a wry smile.

Chapter 10

Tuesday, September 11 (Moon in Gemini to Cancer 12:07 p.m.)
The admission of a problem is often the first step to a solution.
Simmering secrets cause the most damage. Mea culpa is the
mantra for today.

When the manager returned from the elevator, Jason
apologized for the inconvenience he had endured and was
about to endure from the onslaught of a federal investigation.
He told him the inquiry would be ongoing and would involve
dozens of law enforcement personnel from several agencies.
Jason warned him he would be required to provide a complete
list of registered guests during the time when Itzack was in the
hotel, as well as a list of employees and their work schedules.

Cassie tugged on Jason's coat sleeve. "I'm sorry to interrupt,"
she said, "but I need to find a place to clean up a bit."

"Hey! I can take care of that," the manager said. "The
housekeepers are finishing Room 211 down the hall. Why don't
you guys make yourself at home? In fact, we'll make 211 a
hospitality room for all your folks, for as long as you're here. I'll
make sure it always has plenty of soft drinks, snacks and fresh
coffee."

"That would be great," Jason said. He was impressed at the
manager's generosity and foresight.

"Thanks, that's very nice of you," Cassie said. She began walking toward the room.

When Cassie passed the housekeeper's cart in front of Room 211, she grabbed a bar of soap and several miniature bottles of mouthwash, as if she wondered if she would ever feel clean again. When she walked into the room, two housekeepers were standing there staring at the television. They were so intent they paid her little notice, and Cassie's attention was drawn to the screen. In a moment she appeared to comprehend the live picture she was seeing.

"Jason!" Cassie called down the hall. Jason was still chatting with the manager and the local cops. "You'd better come see this."

Jason hurried to Room 211, curious about what would precipitate such concern in Cassie's voice. He entered the room and his curiosity was soon replaced by anger.

Across the bottom of the TV screen, BREAKING NEWS was emblazoned in bright red and yellow. An off-screen announcer was describing the picture on the screen, black smoke billowing from the North Tower of the World Trade Center in New York City.

In case you've just joined us, what you're watching is a live picture of the Twin Towers of the World Trade Center in lower Manhattan. The plume of black smoke you see is coming from the North Tower. Still yet unconfirmed sources tell us this morning at approximately 8:46 AM, some sixteen minutes ago, a plane, believed to be a commercial airliner, crashed into the North Tower. Airline companies we have contacted have refused comment. Mayor Giuliani's office reports the Mayor is already near the scene and evacuations are under way at both towers of the World Trade Center."

When Jason edged closer to the TV, trying to digest the meaning of the picture he was seeing, a swift descending blur smashed into the South Tower causing a huge fireball and more black smoke streaking skyward.

The off-screen announcer was dumbfounded.

"What was that? Did you see that? I think another airliner hit the South Tower! Can we see that again? Line producer, can we see that again???"

Jason, standing beside Cassie, was speechless while the TV picture moved to split screen, showing a slow motion rerun of what had happened. There was little doubt. Clearly, a commercial jet with a United Airlines logo on its tail had flown directly into the building at a very high rate of speed.

"Son of a bitch," Jason said to no one in particular. "Son of a bitch."

In an instant, the pieces of the puzzle fit together in Jason's mind. It all made perfect sense. He knew Captain Ledford's intuitions about Abdul and Ali were correct. They weren't really interested in learning how to fly an airplane. They only wanted to learn how to crash it. They were absolute animals, instruments of an ideology, intent on sacrificing all their tomorrows for acts of hate today. And what acts of hate they were. Why would anyone do what they did to the girl in Room 201? Did these guys crash an airplane into a building?

"Wash up quickly. We're out of here." Jason said. He headed for the door and hit the speed dial on his cell phone.

"The Assistant Director's Office," the sugary voice said.

"Is he in, please?" Jason asked.

"Whom shall I say is calling?"

"Oh! I'm sorry. This is Lancer."

"Jason, Honey, I'm sorry I didn't recognize your voice. You don't sound like yourself."

"Who is themself this morning, Ashley? I really need to talk to Russo."

Ashley Banks was the quintessential all-American girl. She was attractive, but not beautiful; athletic, but not a jock; intelligent, but not a nerd; and Lord knows she was the sweetest thing ever to leave Birmingham. Jason could tell she liked him a lot. She was even a Virgo, a sign which would never disappoint as a lover or friend. He knew she could be his for the asking. Yet Jason knew he would never ask. Jason Lancer would never make a pastime of breaking hearts and leaving lovers, even if they were willing participants. Maybe the loss of his mother at such a young age instilled in him a subliminal fear of rejection by females. Or maybe seeing the unfair deal his mother suffered from the irresponsibility of his father caused a degree of caution in his relationships. Whatever the reason, Ashley Banks created no sparks, and Jason would be careful never to lead her on. Cassie Reilly, however, was different.

"Everybody wants to talk to Russo, Jason. Even the White House. In fact, he's on a conference call with them now, and I can't interrupt. Everything hit the fan here a few minutes ago and lit up the whole switchboard."

"That's what I want to talk to him about. Can you slip him a message?"

"You're trying to get me killed, aren't you Jason?"

"Not at all. Blame the intrusion on me. Slip him a note with my cell number on it and tell him it's an emergency."

Chapter 11

Tuesday, September 11 (Moon in Gemini to Cancer 12:07 p.m.) When unclear about what to do, do nothing. Conditions always change and a decision will be obvious. Cancer and Aires may surprise.

Abdul and Ali were sitting in first class in seats 3A and 3B. Basil and Yusef had economy seats further back in the airplane, all according to plan. The gravity of the moment was weighing heavily on Abdul. He realized the time had come. No turning back now. In less than an hour he and his accomplices would be in paradise and all the infidels surrounding him would be rotting in hell. He was so deep in thought he did not see the perky redheaded flight attendant in the aisle beside him.

"Could I get you guys something to drink, maybe a towel or something?" she was saying with a big smile. She had noticed they rushed on at the last moment so it was not unusual they were sweating profusely.

"Some water, please," Abdul said. Ali nodded.

"Flight attendants prepare for departure and crosscheck," the sultry voice on the PA directed. At the same time Abdul felt the slight movement of the aircraft and saw the open jetway drift forward past his window. The on time pushback was under way at 8:50. When he boarded he gave a quick look around and saw no police or military personnel, and all the flight attendants he had seen were female. Perfect.

Abdul mentally reviewed the plan while he sipped his ice water. A few minutes after takeoff, the Captain would cycle off and on the no smoking sign, indicating the aircraft had reached ten thousand feet. Soon after that the seat belt sign would be turned off. They would reach under the seat in front of them and remove the plastic blade holders from the handles of their carry-on bags. They would each go to a different restroom, retrieve the cutter blades from the heels of their shoes, and assemble the weapons. When they emerged from the restrooms, Abdul would grab the fight attendant closest to the cockpit and demand she open the cockpit door. She would refuse, and Abdul would slit her throat and slam her down on the floor to bleed out. While Basil and Yusef were making their way to the front of the aircraft, Ali would bring the next flight attendant toward the cockpit to witness what happened to the first one. She would then open the door, or they would repeat the process until all the flight attendants were dead or the door was opened. The passengers would be told to remain seated and they would not be harmed. They would not be a problem. The weak infidels from the west would either freeze or faint at the sight of blood.

Then they would proceed according to the plan they had rehearsed in the Boeing 727 they had used for training in Iraq. In fact, they were given a key to the cockpit door for that airplane which would fit all Boeing airplanes. They would try the key before they tore down the door.

When they entered the cockpit, they would lock the door behind them and depend on Basil and Yusef to control the passengers in the cabin. The pilots would be strapped in their seats making them easy prey. Abdul would grab the Captain and Ali would grab the First Officer. They would pull their heads back and slit their throats, making sure to cut both carotid arteries. The pilots would be unconscious within seconds and dead within minutes.

The brothers would drag the pilots from their seats and pile them against the cockpit door. Abdul would take control of the aircraft and make an announcement to the passengers telling them he was the Captain, to remain calm, and they would be on the ground very soon. He would turn off the radar transponder, making it difficult for Air Traffic Control to follow them on radar. He would type KDCA in the FMC, the flight management computer, push L-NAV to activate it, and the aircraft being flown by the autopilot would turn directly to Washington Reagan National Airport. He would set 3000 feet in the altitude window on the control panel and push Level Change. The aircraft would descend to 3000 feet. From over the airport at 3000 feet on a clear day, the entire city of Washington would be visible. Then Abdul and Ali would crash the 757 straight down into the dome of the United States capitol killing many infidels and leaders of infidels. Finally, they would forever be in paradise. Praise be to Allah.

"Delta 121, follow the Northwest Airbus, monitor tower," the Washington ground controller's voice crackled over the radio when he handed off control of the Delta 757 to the tower.

"Roger, Delta 121," Dusty Rhodes, the First Officer said into the mic.

"May as well sit'em down, Dusty. Looks like we're number three," Captain Tom Batten said. It was standard procedure for the First Officer to make the pre-takeoff announcement to the passengers, which also would alert the flight attendants to take their seats.

"Roger that," Dusty said. He switched his radio control panel to transmit on PA. "Ladies and gentlemen this is First Officer Dusty Rhodes speaking. On behalf of Captain Tom Batten and your entire flight crew, it's nice having you with us today on Flight

121 to Atlanta. We're currently number three for takeoff. We should be airborne in about five minutes. The flying time is a quick one hour and forty minutes and the weather is beautiful all the way. You've picked a great day for flying. We're glad you're with us, and we're working hard to make sure your flight is a safe and enjoyable one. Once again, welcome aboard. Flight attendants, please prepare the cabin for takeoff."

"The cabin is ready for takeoff," the perky redheaded flight attendant said to the pilots through the open cockpit door.

"Thanks, Nancy, we're out of here," Captain Batten said. The flight attendant closed and locked the cockpit door.

Abdul could barely contain his excitement. It's a great day for flying, the pilot had announced to the passengers. This confirmed the last and most critical piece of the puzzle had indeed fallen into place.

For the mission to have any chance to succeed, the weather had to be clear, with very few clouds to conceal their target.

The Director with the aid of his connections to a few international weather forecasters had finally given the go-ahead for today, 11 September. He had been very precise about the discreet communications to be used. When Abdul had his team in place and ready for the mission, he would log on to a wedding website for a wealthy couple in Kandahar. He would send this message: *May the blessings of Allah be with you forever and ever and ever.* Every day thereafter beginning the following day at noon Eastern Daylight Time, Abdul would log on to the Al Jazeera website and click on the weather link. When the next day's forecast for the high temperatures in the holy cities of Mecca, Medina, and Jerusalem all ended with a seven, the mission was a go for the following day.

On September 4th Abdul sent the discreet greeting to the couple in Kandahar. Each day at noon he checked the Al Jazeera website. Finally, on September 10 the attack order was given; the forecast high temperature for Mecca and Medina was 17 degrees Celsius and 27 degrees Celsius for Jerusalem.

"Delta 121, taxi into position and hold Runway One," instructed the Washington Tower controller.

"Roger, position and hold, Delta 121," Dusty transmitted.

"Before takeoff checklist complete, except for the lights, Captain."

"Thanks, Dusty," Captain Batten said. He turned the big jet from the taxiway to line up for takeoff on the runway. "You have the aircraft, I have the radios."

"I have the aircraft," Dusty said. He placed his feet on the brakes atop the rudder pedals and his left hand on the throttles.

"Delta 121, the wind is zero one zero at ten knots, depart northwest via noise abatement procedures, maintain five thousand, Runway One, cleared for takeoff." Washington Tower had issued takeoff clearance at precisely 9:06 AM.

"Roger, we're rolling, Delta 121," Captain Batten said. He turned the exterior lights on for takeoff.

"N1, TO/GA" Dusty said.

"Roger, N1, TO/GA power set." Captain Batten pushed the switch commanding the autothrottles to advance the engines to takeoff power.

The 757 raced down the runway.

In the passenger cabin Abdul and Ali were pinned back in their seats by the rapid acceleration.

"Allah is great, Allah is great," Abdul chanted softly. He tapped Ali's arm with a clinched fist and a look of determination on his face.

"Eighty knots, throttles hold, engine instruments checked," Captain Batten said. This indicated all was well with the aircraft while it accelerated through 90, 100, and 110 knots. Then they heard a desperate transmission from the control tower!

"Delta 121, Washington Tower, cancel takeoff clearance! Delta 121, cancel takeoff clearance!"

Captain Batten was taken by surprise. The aircraft was almost ready to fly, but the urgent call from the tower was very explicit.

"Abort, I have the aircraft!" he commanded. He snatched the throttles to idle, placed his feet on the rudders for directional control, and extended the ground spoilers which killed all the lift on the wing.

"Roger, you have the aircraft," Dusty said. He relinquished control of the aircraft. "All engines in reverse, speedbrakes extended," he said. Normal procedures for a rejected takeoff were being followed. With tires smoking, the huge mass of metal, fuel, and people screeched to a stop near the end of the runway.

"Delta 121 aborting, Runway One," Dusty transmitted.

Captain Batten made an announcement on the PA after he brought the airplane to a complete stop. "Ladies and gentlemen, this is the Captain speaking. We have discontinued our takeoff. Please remain seated and await further instructions."

Abdul, Ali, Yusef, Basil, and all the other passengers were thrown forward against their seat belts amidst the deafening noise of the engines. Fear gripped Abdul when he looked out the windows to the right and saw the Potomac River getting closer and closer. Were they going to slide off the end of the runway and into the river?

Abdul unbuckled his seat belt preparing to get out of his seat when Ali grabbed him by the arm and held him down.

"What are you doing, Abdul?" He asked.

"We have to take the airplane, you camel-brain," he said to Ali in a whisper. "The Director must not be disappointed."

"Are you crazy? We could never takeoff from this airport in this airplane. Don't you remember anything from training?"

"I remember how easy it is to kill infidels and take command of the airplane."

"I'm talking about pilot training in the simulator in Florida not our commando training in Afghanistan and Iraq. We never became proficient in anything but airborne flying because we knew we'd never have to takeoff or land."

"We could do it," Abdul said.

"What if they aborted because an engine failed? What if they have hot brakes? Be calm, my brother, don't be a fool."

Abdul was usually the clear-thinking one, the steady one. So close to paradise, and this abrupt stop on the runway caused him to lose his wits for a moment. Ali was making complete sense and Abdul began to settle back down in his seat. When he did, he turned his head around and looked towards the back of the airplane to see Yusef and Basil rose up in their seats looking directly at him. He knew what they were thinking and they were looking to him for a signal. Abdul gave him a very slow negative shake of his head and turned around.

"Tower, Delta 121, what happened?" Captain Batten asked.

"Delta 121, are you able to clear the runway?"

"Delta 121, that's affirmative, but why the clearance cancellation?"

"Delta 121, I'm not sure. All I know is Center put an emergency stop on all departures. When able, taxi clear of the runway and contact ground 121.7."

"Roger, Delta 121."

"Dusty, check the manual for the brake cooling time while I taxi clear of the runway and away from the terminals."

"Roger, I have it right here." Dusty was already checking the manual, anticipating the request for the brake cooling time.

"Not too bad, Tom, the cooling time is 30 minutes."

"Thanks, Dusty, that would take us until 9:40 before it's safe to continue. Contact ground and get clearance to an area we can hold for about thirty minutes, and then call the company."

"Washington Ground, Delta 121, clearing Runway One."

"Delta 121, Ground, do you need any special assistance?"

"Ground, Delta 121, that's negative. We need a place to wait for about thirty minutes for brake cooling."

"Delta 121, taxi to the far right side of the ramp and hold there facing north as long as you like. The airport is now closed."

Dusty contacted Delta Airlines via the company radio and asked to speak to dispatcher #31, Huckabee. The dispatcher was the person in flight control who shared the responsibility for the flight planning and monitoring the progress of the flight.

"Delta 121, this is Dispatcher Huckabee, how do you read?"

Captain Batten indicated to Dusty that he would take the radio. "Delta 121, loud and clear. What's going on?"

"Delta 121, are you airborne?"

"Negative. Tower cancelled our takeoff clearance, and we rejected the takeoff."

"Thank God you're on the ground. We have a national security emergency underway. Two commercial airliners have crashed into the twin towers of the World Trade Center. This cannot be an accident or a coincidence. It's believed multiple flights have been hijacked by terrorists to be used as weapons against strategic targets. The entire U.S. airspace system is being shut down."

"Do you believe we have hijackers aboard our flight?"

"We have no idea. But to play it safe, I would not mention to the passengers we have a security problem. When you are able, taxi to the gate and deplane because your flight is definitely cancelled. I have to go now to deal with airborne flights."

"Delta 121, roger. Thank you."

"Incredible," Captain Batten said to Dusty. He glanced at the cockpit door to make sure it was locked. "No American pilot under any circumstances is going to fly an airplane into a building. That would never happen. That means the hijackers were foreign pilots. Incredible."

Captain Batten signaled for the flight attendant to pick up on the interphone and motioned for Dusty to listen in.

"Hi, this is Nancy,"

"Nancy, this Tom. Is everyone okay back there?"

"Everyone's fine, just a little nervous about the sudden stop."

"Good. Nancy, what I'm about to tell you is for flight crew only. There have been a number of hijackings this morning and the entire national air route system is being shut down. We aborted the takeoff because the tower cancelled our takeoff clearance. We'll be at the gate to deplane in approximately half an hour. If any passenger makes any threatening move whatsoever, call me immediately. We'll keep the cockpit door locked, and I'll make an announcement shortly. Would you tell the other flight attendants, please?"

"Do you think we have hijackers on board?"

"No, but I want to play it safe."

"Thanks, Captain."

Captain Batten began talking on the PA. "Ladies and Gentlemen this is the Captain speaking. We had to discontinue our takeoff because of a problem with one of our engines. After our brakes cool for about half an hour, it will be safe for us to return to the gate. At that time, please deplane and take all your personal items with you. We apologize for any inconvenience. Thank you."

'See, I told you we might have engine problems," Ali said to Abdul. Ali sighed, like the weight of the world was off his shoulders. Abdul always believed Ali missed his wife more than he looked forward to the seventy-two virgins.

Abdul stared out the window. "Yes, you did."

Captain Batten looked at his watch. "This is very strange," he said. "It's 9:37 AM on a clear day at Washington Reagan National Airport and not a plane is flying. Nothing. Very surreal."

Finally, the brakes were cool and Captain Batten was about to ask Dusty to call for clearance to the gate when a blur out his left window caught his eye.

"Jesus Christ!" he said. "Look at that 757. Did you see that?"

Dusty looked in time to see an airliner streaking low and fast dive straight into a large building to the northwest of the airport.

"Oh, my God," Captain Batten said. "A plane just hit the Pentagon."

Delta 121 arrived back at Gate 21 with a planeload of confused and concerned passengers. Some of them had been using their cell phones, and word had spread among them about the planes hitting the Twin Towers and the concern for other planes being hijacked. Abdul, Ali, Basil, and Yusef, appearing uneasy amidst the apprehensive passengers, deplaned quickly and slipped away into the crowded terminal.

Chapter 12

Tuesday, September 11 (Moon in Gemini to Cancer 12:07 p.m.) In matters of the heart, the heart matters. Listen to it. Do what must be done, even though it may break your heart.

The Crown Vic with its blue light blazing raced northward on US 1 with Cassie at the wheel. Jason wanted her to drive because he needed time to think. He had to decide what and how he would tell Russo, when he called back. He had to think about why the al Din brothers would emerge on this particular day in Mt. Vernon, Virginia, after disappearing several months ago in Florida. He had to think about the fact airplanes don't accidentally crash into buildings on a clear day. They must be flown into the buildings by pilots. And these pilots must be ready and willing to die for a cause they deemed to be more relevant than themselves. Or for a reward in the hereafter to which they thought they would not otherwise be entitled. They were modern day kamikazes, not for a homeland, but for an ideology.

Suicide pilots, one part of the modern-day equation which had never been seriously considered. There had been suicide bombers in the Middle East for decades, but never suicide pilots. Yet here they were. Jason felt sick to his stomach. He hadn't foreseen this scheme, even after meeting these dudes in Florida. He felt as if he had been bluffed into laying down a full house by some arrogant punk, who then flipped over a non-suited two and a seven.

"O.K., we're headed north. Where to?" Cassie asked. She still looked queasy.

"Hooverville, I guess," Jason said. That was the nickname he sometimes gave the J. Edgar Hoover Building, headquarters of the FBI.

Cassie remained silent, encountering heavier traffic which was still hanging on from the morning rush hour.

"Lancer," Jason said quickly into his cell phone. He answered it the moment it rang.

"This had better be damn good, Lancer. Where the hell have you been?" Russo asked. His mood was not pleasant.

Jason knew he was already skating on thin ice. He didn't need the obligatory good morning slap in the face from Russo to remind him. As carefully as he could, he explained the early morning trip to Mt. Vernon to check out a tip the al Din brothers might be there at the Holiday Inn. He reported the bell captain had identified Abdul as a Mr. Itzack, a guest in the hotel. But a check of the room revealed the brothers had already departed, leaving behind a badly abused woman clinging to life.

"Was she a working girl?" Russo asked.

"I'm not sure. The manager identified her as a cocktail waitress at the Brown Derby, a restaurant next door," Jason said.

"Is she talking?"

"No, she's unconscious. I'm not sure she'll make it."

"You mention 'brothers.' Are you sure Ali was there?"

"Oh! I'm positive he was there," Jason said. He remembered it was Ali who made the intercepted phone call that started all of this. "At least he must have been there because the brothers always travel together. Always."

"Who's the tipster?"

"Anonymous."

"What's the name?"

"If I told you, it wouldn't be anonymous," Jason said. He chuckled, hoping a little levity would cause Russo to move on to more pressing business, like airplanes hitting buildings.

"Don't fuck with me, Lancer! I'll have your ass in Billings by Friday."

Jason said nothing, aware that anything he said at this point would be a sign of weakness. What he was thinking was, Oh! Please, please don't throw me in that briar patch. Jason was curious, however, why Russo thought he could threaten him by banishing him to a simpler, quieter life.

Russo finally broke the silence. "Alright, alright," he said. He had softened his tone. "If the al Din boys aren't there, where do you think they are?"

"From what's happening in New York, I'm afraid they're aboard a commercial airplane preparing to attack us," Jason said. He tried to sound professional and businesslike.

"That's what we're thinking, too. What's worse, there are at least two more airliners who aren't responding to calls. We'll check the passenger lists of those flights to see if they're aboard."

"A better idea would be to check the flights that haven't been hijacked. If you can find them, you can warn the pilots they may have terrorists on board."

"You're right, Lancer, we'll get on it," Russo said. "We have a couple of agents arriving now at the FAA Air Route Traffic Control Center."

"Also," Jason said, "to save time, only examine this morning's departures form Dulles or National on 767 or 757 aircraft.

"Won't they use an alias?"

"More than likely. You might try Itzack, the name Abdul used at the Holiday Inn. And Ali has been known to use Lachman," Jason said. He failed to mention the late night phone call intercepted by VORS.

"I gotta go, Lancer. Get in here and work this case. But don't think you're out of the woods yet. When the dust settles around here, you're coming in for a little 'come to Jesus meeting.' I already heard about the poker party."

"Poker party? What's that supposed to mean?"

"Save the crap, Lancer. You've deviated from protocol so much they're starting to call you 'Free Lancer.'"

"Listen, I work for you. If you don't like the way I'm doing something, I would expect you to tell me. Hello … Hello …" The line was dead.

"What was that all about?" Cassie asked. She seemed especially curious about the poker party remark.

"Russo never passes up an opportunity to bust my chops about something. He said he heard about the poker party, whatever that means."

"It means he heard about us. That's what it means," Cassie said.

The tone of Cassie's voice sent a jolt through Jason's entire body. Why was it the very moment their relationship accelerated past friend and co-worker she seemed resigned to the fact that it was over. It was a recurring theme for Jason. As soon as a woman became important in his life, she left him. The fact that death caused his mother to leave him didn't make it any easier. With his mother gone, Jason had been cared for by his grandmother for seven years, until one night she died in her sleep. He took it very hard, and the fear of desertion and the fear of rejection grew stronger. These fears resulted in Jason's current state of mind: a heart never given is a heart never broken. *But what about hearts that are stolen?*

Jason cut his eyes towards Cassie for a moment. He was drawn to this very attractive woman. Especially when she had her game face on, like she did now. She swiftly maneuvered the Crown Vic in and out of traffic. Her purposeful, diligent manner on and off the job and her secretive nature only deepened Jason's enchantment. Was this going to be one of those 'better to have loved and lost than never to have loved at all' situations? Jason was always convinced the loving was never worth the losing. But now, especially after last night, he wasn't so sure.

"Jay." Cassie said. She sounded apprehensive. "I need to talk to you."

"Is this about us or them?"

"It's about us."

Jason knew the answer to the question before she answered. He was beginning to read her nuances. He wondered if it was because they spent so much time together at work, or because wherever the heart goes, the brain eventually follows. Nonetheless, he knew this was a conversation he did not want to have.

"Cassie, you've got to be kidding. I can't talk about us right now in the middle of all this."

"I wanted you to know ... last night ..."

Chapter 13

Tuesday, September 11 (Moon in Gemini to Cancer 12:07 p.m.) Ghosts of the past appear. Smokescreens clear to reveal clarity. Emphasis on vocation is paramount.

A shadow flashed over the busy highway accompanied by a deafening roar! A large commercial airliner flying at a very low altitude and still descending streaked northward toward the city and was quickly dropping out of sight over the horizon.

"Holy Christ!" Jason said. He watched the plane disappear ahead. His attention was drawn to events unfolding on the road in front of them.

"Watch out, Cassie!" Jason shouted. He braced himself and pointed ahead to a jack-knifing eighteen wheeler slamming into an old Lincoln which had stopped in the road. They tried to avoid the chain reaction of cars crashing ahead of them, all distracted by the low flying plane.

"Hang on! I got it!" Cassie screamed. She skillfully steered the Crown Vic into a side skid, avoided the wrecked semi, and came to a stop off the side of the road. Thankful that she had avoided an accident, Cassie closed her eyes, took in a deep breath, and exhaled slowly. "Are you okay?" she asked.

"Yes, I'm fine. Good job. Let's see if anyone's hurt over there," Jason said. He nodded towards the Lincoln a few feet away.

When Jason and Cassie jumped from the Crown Vic, they were met by the sound of a tremendous explosion coming from the north where the plane had disappeared. A mammoth cloud of black smoke began drifting skyward.

"The plane crashed!" Cassie said. "Oh! My God!

"It didn't crash, Cassie. It attacked."

Jason instructed Cassie to check on the passengers of the Lincoln while he pulled out his cell phone and hit a speed dial number.

"Assistant Director's Office," the always sweet voice said.

"Ashley, it's Jason. I need to talk to Russo."

"Jason, Honey! Twice in one day. I'm honored. But he asked not to be disturbed."

"Now! Dammit, Ashley, put him on now!"

Jason regretted his tone and demeanor as soon as the words left his mouth. He was trying to muster an apology when he heard a click on the line.

"Russo."

"It's Lancer. I wanted to…."

"Lancer, a plane just hit the Pentagon!"

"I was afraid of that. It flew right over us and we heard the explosion."

"Where are you?"

"We're caught in a multiple car accident on US 1, south of National Airport."

"You saw the plane?" Russo asked.

"Yes, it looked like American Airlines and I think it was a 757."

"We think it was American Flight 77 out of Dulles Airport."

"You think the al Din's were flying it?"

"I have no idea. There's another plane we think is headed towards Washington; the White House and the Capitol are being evacuated."

"You want us in the office?"

"No, it's a zoo here. Get to National. If the brothers don't surface, you can begin the investigation there. How's Reilly holding up?"

"She's great," Jason said. He looked over at Cassie attending to the couple in the old Lincoln. "She's a real pro."

"Good."

"How're we doing here?" Jason asked. He put away his phone and walked over to the Lincoln.

"Not too bad. The lady's leg is injured. It might be broken."

Jason attempted to call 911 to report the location of the accident and the fact there were injuries, but couldn't get past the busy signal of the jammed switchboard.

"Let's go. We're out of here."

"We're gonna leave this accident scene?" Cassie asked. She surveyed the scene around them.

"We're under attack, Cassie," Jason said. He noted her reluctance. "We don't have time to mess around with a traffic accident. Let's go."

"You still want me to drive?" Cassie asked. Jason had jumped back into the passenger side of the car.

"You haven't scared me yet. Code 3 to Reagan National."

Off they went, blue light flashing and sirens blaring, toward Washington Reagan National Airport, a few miles away.

Jason's mind was like a runaway slide show, flickering repulsive images from a projector which would not turn off: the North Tower burning; a plane hitting the South Tower; the al Din brothers in the simulator in Florida; Sandra Thompson tied spread eagle to a four poster bed; the airliner zooming overhead; a skeleton in medieval black armor on a white stallion, the tarot card of Death; a red rose lying on a mahogany casket.

Jason remembered going through his mother's belongings after she died in the plane crash like it was yesterday. In the top drawer of the kitchen cabinet next to the silverware he had found the two decks of cards which had meant so much to her. One was the well used deck of Bicycle playing cards and the other was her frayed Rider-Waite deck of tarot cards. When Jason removed the tarot deck from the box, the card of Death was on top, the very card she pulled for her reading on the day of her ill-fated flight. The thought of the card still sent shivers down his spine.

At this moment Jason felt extremely vulnerable. He had been plowing through this day, feeling like he was flying blind. He would give anything to have the guidance of tarot right about now. He wished he could pull another card to balance the Five of Swords and garner further wisdom from the deck to bolster his confidence.

Jason's thoughts were interrupted by a buzzing sound from Cassie's cell phone. She pulled her foot off the accelerator to slow down a bit while she answered her phone. She listened intently, occasionally glancing at Jason, then replied to the caller in a few words of Arabic before closing her cell phone.

"Who was that?" Jason asked.

"One of my informants was checking in," Cassie said.

"Informants?"

"Yes." After a few moments she added, "Anonymous informants".

"Oh," Jason said. He could see where this was going, but he couldn't let it go so easily. "Did they inform you?"

"They informed me," Cassie said, trying to repress the grin, "that they had no information for me."

"Sometimes the best information from an informant is no information," Jason said. He chuckled to himself.

Cassie told Jason that after she received the call from him this morning, she had made a couple of inquiries about the latest on the al Din brothers, and this was a response to one of those calls. Jason thought it interesting that her informant spoke Arabic. He wondered to which side of the ocean she was talking? Was her informant also someone in the CIA? Despite his curiosity, he understood sometimes the identity of contacts must remain secret, so he didn't press her on the issue.

Cassie began working her way toward the inside lane when they sped under the sign indicating the next exit was Washington Reagan Airport.

"Which terminal?" she asked.

"Head for the control tower. The airport manager's offices should be nearby. Maybe we can start there," Jason said. He was still trying to figure out what to do next.

When they approached the control tower located near midfield, Jason's cell phone vibrated.

"Lancer," he said. He saw a number he did not recognize.

"Special Agent Lancer, this is Agent Lacy Jamison."

"Oh! Yes. I remember meeting you at the office," Jason said. He recalled the scuttlebutt said her pistol and her bra size were exactly the same, "38".

"I'm over at the ARTCC working passenger lists from today's flights out of Washington. I got a hit on Itzack and Lachman."

"Really?"

"Yes, they're on Delta Flight 121 out of DCA to Atlanta which departed on time at 8:50."

"The pilots must be notified immediately. Where are they now?" Jason asked. Cassie listened intently.

"That's what's strange about this. The flight information computer shows them 'out' at 8:50, about an hour ago, but it doesn't show an 'off' time."

"Maybe they're still on the ground."

"Could be. All Washington departures have been cancelled as of 9:06. But who knows, things are pretty wild around here."

"Yes, I can imagine. We'll be at the Delta terminal in a couple of minutes. Thanks, Agent Jamison for your quick heads up call."

"You're welcome, Jason. See you soon." Jason was amazed she remembered his first name.

Jason instructed Cassie to continue down the row of terminals to the Delta Airlines complex, which was the last commercial terminal at DCA. He updated her on the information provided by the phone call from '38's.' They were there in minutes, despite the heavy traffic congestion. They parked in front of a local police cruiser sitting in front of the drop off area with lights flashing and an officer sitting behind the wheel. Leaving the Crown Vic locked with the blue light flashing, they badged the officer in the cruiser and rushed inside to investigate the status of Delta Flight 121.

The flight information board over the Delta ticket counter showed Flight 121 was scheduled for 8:50 and had 'departed'. Jason identified himself to a Red Coat supervisor. When he asked if Flight 121 was airborne, the Red Coat excused himself to place a call to flight operations.

"Jason, I need to be excused, also," Cassie said. She nodded to the nearby ladies' room.

"Can't it wait until we check this flight?"

"No, it can't," she said firmly. Changing her tone she said, "For some reason, I feel like a morning after honeymooner. I can't imagine why."

"Oh, alright. Hurry."

As soon as Cassie disappeared, the Red Coat hung up the phone and turned to Jason.

"Flight 121 didn't get airborne. It's been back at Gate 21 for about ten minutes," the Red Coat said. He pointed past security down the concourse.

"Would you do me a favor?" Jason asked. He glanced at the ladies' room. "When my partner comes out, would you please tell her to meet me at Gate 21?"

"Sure."

"Thanks," Jason said.

When Jason approached the security checkpoint, he encountered a large convergence of passengers and several extra policemen. No flights were being allowed to depart and they weren't allowing any passengers through security. When he finally made his way past the crowd, he flashed his badge and was directed to the lieutenant over in the corner who waved him through.

The concourse had a glass divider which stretched for about fifty yards separating the arriving and departing passengers. There were no passengers on the departing side where Jason was hurrying toward Gate 21, but his eyes were scouring the arriving passengers. Then he saw them! They appeared differently with no beards, but it was definitely them.

Abdul and Ali, in a crush of people, were walking steadily towards the exit followed closely by two other men, who also appeared to be of Middle Eastern descent. Jason stopped in his tracks while trying to figure out what to do. He felt totally exposed, being the only person on his side of the glass. It didn't matter. Ali had already seen him and was elbowing Abdul to get his attention. For an instant, Abdul and Jason had direct eye contact, separated only by the dividing glass. The expression on Ali's face appeared to Jason to be somewhere between surprise and desperation.

"Hi!" Jason shouted through the glass. He tried to appear friendly and happy to see them. Maybe, he thought, they would believe he really was with the FAA. The brothers and their accomplices seemed puzzled by Jason's reaction to their seemingly chance encounter, but only for a moment.

"Wait!" Jason said. "I want to talk to you." They started walking faster, then running toward the exit end of the concourse.

Jason sprinted back toward the security checkpoint and the throng of people waiting there.

"Stop them! Stop them!" He yelled to the police officers ahead. It was too late. The four terrorists were charging toward the terminal doors, flattening any unsuspecting man, woman, or child who got in their way. He saw them dash through the exit doors to the outside as he fought his way through the crowd at the security checkpoint.

Cassie was leaving the red coat at the ticket counter when Jason tore through the people jam and ran for the doors.

"Jason!" she yelled. "Wait!"

"Come on! They're running!"

Cassie was at fast break speed within two steps following Jason out the door and into a very volatile and dangerous scene. The terrorists were jumping into the police cruiser which had been stationed at the drop off area. The officer lay writhing in the street clutching his throat, trying in vain to stop the blood spurting from both his severed carotid arteries. His service revolver was missing from his holster.

Jason and Cassie raced towards the curb with guns drawn. The cruiser, with Ali behind the wheel, began to pull away.

"Watch out! A gun!" Jason shouted. He and Cassie dove behind a bench and a mailbox. A revolver protruded from the passenger window of the cruiser. Jason maneuvered his body into position to fire. Two shots rang out. Abdul had flattened both tires on the driver's side of the Crown Vic and the police cruiser sped away with lights flashing and sirens blaring.

Jason made the call for help on the radio of the Crown Vic while Cassie rushed to aid the officer. She saw it was hopeless when she tracked through the large pool of blood surrounding the body. His heart was no longer beating. Seeing the bloody, slashed throat, Cassie, for the second time in one morning, appeared ill. She ran to the small hedge past the curb and heaved, surrendering nothing but embarrassment.

Several law enforcement types were running out from the terminal and two patrol cars screeched to a stop at the scene. Seeing the situation was under control, Jason walked over to check on Cassie.

"How're you doing?"

Cassie pooched her lips downward in an expression of repugnance and resignation, while she searched for words.

"I can't believe it," she said finally. "This is insane."

"I think we've had enough excitement for one morning, Cass," Jason said. He placed his arm around her shoulder reassuringly. "Let's get out of here."

Chapter 14

Monday, October 15 (Moon in Virgo to Libra 1:25 a.m.) Reflect. Review. Regroup. Recharged batteries energize efforts. Evening disappointment may delight. Scorpio intrigues.

Buster's was jumping! The upscale sports bar phenomenon sweeping the country was also sweeping Washington. It was as if the pulled pork crowd and the high tech crowd had joined forces and decided to go into the restaurant business. Large screens were mounted on every wall. Smaller TVs, all tuned to a different sporting event, filled every empty space.

Jason was surprised there was already a wait for a table at 6:00 p.m. on a Monday night. He gave his name to the hostess and headed to the bar. He had arrived early to be alone and allow some time for the brain cells to settle. Cassie seemed reluctant to join him this evening, which troubled him a great deal. He was troubled because lately she appeared reticent to spend any personal time with him at all. He was certain she would not have agreed to meet him this evening had it not been October 15th, his birthday. To sweeten the deal, he reminded her that the Lady Huskies were playing the Lady 'Dores from Vanderbilt in a rare televised pre-season game. After leaving the office early in the afternoon Cassie agreed to meet him at Buster's in time for the seven o'clock tip-off.

The Monday night football/poker game parties at Jason's bungalow had been placed on hiatus since nine-eleven. In fact, everything except work had been placed on the back burner. All energies were directed to the investigation of countless leads involving possible terrorists and their activities. All vacations at the FBI had been cancelled until further notice. Twelve-hour days were the norm, especially at the JTTF, which shouldered the brunt of the workload.

Russo, more than anyone else, was showing signs of fatigue. As Assistant Director, he was responsible for operational control of the JTTF. And he felt constant pressure from his boss, the Director of the FBI, who had to answer the daily questions of everyone from the President to the press as to why we hadn't known about the terrorists and why we couldn't catch the rest of them. The good news was Russo was totally immersed in his job and had no time to address any personal concerns he might have had about Jason. Maybe all of that was water over the dam. Maybe.

The events of September 11, 2001, rocked the nation like nothing since Pearl Harbor. Never had American citizens died within the borders of the continental United States as the results of an enemy attack. And the most heinous aspect of this attack was the use of our own commercial airliners filled with innocent civilians as weapons to kill thousands of other innocent civilians.

On that morning, nineteen terrorists successfully commandeered four of our planes. American Airlines Flight 11 from Boston to Los Angeles destroyed the North Tower of the World Trade Center. United Airlines Flight 175 from Boston to Los Angeles destroyed the South Tower. The Pentagon, the headquarters of the United States military was badly damaged by the Washington Dulles to Los Angeles American Airlines Flight 77. The only hijacked aircraft which did not hit its target was United Airlines Flight 93 from Newark to San Francisco. After some of the passengers mounted a gallant attempt to retake the aircraft, the terrorists aboard this flight were forced to crash the plane into a wooded area of northern Pennsylvania.

Jason sat by himself on a stool at the bar reliving these extraordinary events and slowly sipping a Coors Light. Lined up above the bar were five TV screens. Jason's attention was naturally drawn to screen number three which was showing a game of Texas Hold 'em. Having had a life-long interest in the game, he was excited to see poker had finally been discovered by the American public through television. The development of the poker table with the mini-camera in the side rail allowed the viewers to see everyone's cards yet keep them hidden from the other players. This device exposed each hand and the game itself to allow the television audience to share the intrigue and nuances of every bluff, call, raise, and re-raise. Watching millions of dollars being won or lost on the turn of a single card was addictive.

It wasn't only the game which captured Jason's interest on screen number three. He couldn't take his eyes off the saucy auburn-haired girl sitting at the end of the table behind a huge stack of chips with her legs crossed in the chair beneath her. Her engaging smile revealed straight, white teeth and accentuated deep dimples in her cheeks which would melt the heart of any man. Except perhaps her lone opponent who sat behind a much smaller pile of chips. He had the appearance of a middle-aged malcontented athlete who had lost his gym privileges. He was dressed in a black warm-up suit with a black baseball cap pulled down over dark sunglasses. When a poker tournament was down to the last two contestants, the prize money was displayed on the table. In this case, there was a tremendous pile of cash, with so many stacks of hundred dollar bills that a shopping cart could not possibly hold them.

The pocket-cam showed the girl holding an ace, three, of diamonds and the guy in black had suited connectors, the nine and ten of clubs. The dealer flipped over three cards divulging the flop: a rainbow king, jack, and nine. Jason increased the volume on the speaker in front of him so he could listen to the commentary.

"What's she gonna do, Vince? The action's on Annabelle Duquemin, but she got no part of that flop."

"You're absolutely right, Mike, but she's been riding Bill Helling like a park pony. Will she give him any slack now?"

Annabelle tapped her fingers on the felt, indicating a check.

"She checked quickly, Vince. Was she not happy with the flop, or did she pick up something from Helling? He flopped bottom pair and the way things have been going he may try to force the issue here."

Bill Helling pushed two hundred thousand dollars worth of chips forward.

"That's what he's doing, Mike. He must have thought Annabelle showed weakness with that check. He has bottom pair and a gut shot straight draw, so he's trying to take the money right here."

Annabelle became very serious, continually shuffling a short stack of chips with her right hand and staring at Helling. After a few moments, she methodically counted out chips, stacking them near the rail and watching her opponent.

"She can't be thinking about calling two hundred thousand dollars, Vince. She has nothing. She could only win this hand with another ace or she would have to catch runner, runner, for a straight or a flush."

"Raise," Annabelle said. She pushed forward several large stacks of chips. "One million".

"She's not calling, Mike. She's raised it a cool one million dollars more on a stone cold bluff!"

Bill Helling jumped up and turned around with an expression on his face like he was running from a foul odor.

"You're killing me, Annabelle," Helling said to everyone and to no one at all, while he paced between the table and the spectators.

The engaging smile returned to Annabelle's face while she watched him rant.

"*Raise, raise, raise,*" Helling continued. "*You have no idea who you're playing with. Every time I bet, you raise. You've got to be bluffing. I know you're not that good and you can't possibly be that lucky.*"

"*Well, Bill,*" Annabelle said, looking him straight in the eye, "*if you think I'm bluffing, why don't you call?*"

Bill Helling sat back down and stared at his cards for a few moments. He tossed his cards into the muck.

"*I don't believe it, Vince. Now you're seeing power poker. Annabelle Duquemin made the legendary Bill Helling lay down the best hand. If she keeps this up, she'll soon be a champion on the World Poker Tour and two million dollars richer!*"

Jason continued to watch with amusement when Annabelle Duquemin did, in fact, win the Champion's bracelet and the money only a couple of hands later. Annabelle raised one million again after the flop and again Helling ranted. Thinking he was being pushed around and still tilting from the previous hands, he went all in with a pair of tens. Annabelle called with a set of queens and won the title.

"Wow," Jason thought. "Two million dollars. How difficult can this game be?" He had been to Las Vegas a couple of times, but FBI business always kept him away from the poker tables. Someday, he promised himself, he would take a vacation and go play with the big boys. He was usually the winner when he played poker with the guys, and, after all, the cards don't know how much money is bet on them. If he really worked at it, why couldn't he be successful? Someday.

Jason and Cassie were tasked with heading the investigation of the al Din brothers. They were also charged with the responsibility of tracking them down and bringing them to justice. Easier said than done. How could the brothers simply vanish into thin air?

The cop car used by the would-be hijackers to escape from the airport had been found abandoned a couple of miles away near a rapid transit station. It would have been easy to spot four civilians in a stolen police cruiser, so finding the car nearby was no surprise. The subway was a logical means for them to flee the area, especially due to the traffic bedlam around National Airport and the Pentagon after the attack by the airliner.

Jason and Cassie interviewed hundreds of people who worked at the airport and the rapid transit line in an effort to identify the terrorists and get a lead on where they went. They divided the tedious tasks of reviewing security tapes between them with Jason taking the airport and Cassie scouring the tapes from the train stations.

Jason was able to positively identify Abdul and Ali al Din from their images on several security cameras at the airport. He was the only law enforcement person to have actually laid eyes on the two accomplices. Even though he saw them for only a few seconds at the airport, he still remembered them very well. The identification of the two accomplices, however, remained a mystery.

Cassie had reported she found nothing after several hours of reviewing the train tapes. Unlike the airport tapes where Jason knew the perps were there and it was only a matter of finding them, the transit tapes were a random shot in the dark. Hours and hours of grainy pictures of a cross-section of society. Jason, while disappointed, was not surprised Cassie was unable to spot them.

The FBI promoted the brothers and their accomplices to the head of the class. They installed them on the "Ten Most Wanted" list and posted their pictures on the Bureau's website and in every federal building throughout the world. The list posted the aliases of Abdul and Ali as Abraham Itzack and Jacob Lachman respectively. The accomplices, Basil Kabil and Yusef Utbak, were identified only by the names they used to purchase airline tickets: Aaron Abramovitch and Benedict Schwartz.

Jason noticed the basketball game had replaced the poker tournament on screen number three and that meant it was past 7 p.m. Still there was no sign of Cassie. He downed the last slug of his warm beer and decided to check the crowd waiting at the hostess stand.

When Jason approached the front door, he saw Cassie getting out of a navy blue BMW convertible across the street. The driver, an attractive brunette, waved goodbye and gave Cassie the peace sign. Cassie nodded to her then glanced in the direction of Buster's while the BMW sped away.

Who's the girl? Jason wondered. Nonetheless, he was relieved Cassie had not stood him up. He was about to tell the hostess he was ready to be seated when he saw Cassie turn away and dash into the Hilton Hotel across the street.

Five minutes. Ten minutes. Fifteen minutes dragged by with Jason getting more apprehensive with every passing second.

When he opened his cell phone to call her, she emerged from the hotel and hurried across the street into Buster's.

She beamed when she spotted Jason. "Hi," she said. "I'm sorry I'm late."

"Oh, no problem," Jason said. He was trying not to show concern. When he was able to look beyond her smile, he saw she was wearing a black cocktail dress and stilettos.

"Wow! You are beautiful," Jason said.

"Thank you."

"I thought you knew Buster's was a sports bar," Jason said. He gazed around at the casually dressed patrons.

"I did."

"Well, let me say you'll be the most smashing female eating BBQ tonight."

"Not tonight."

"No?" Now Jason was really confused.

"Jay, it's your birthday. It's very special. I've made dinner reservations at the Hilton."

"Oh! Cass, I came straight here from work. I haven't been home to change or anything."

"I know. We've all been working too hard for too long. Come with me."

Cassie took Jason by the hand and led him directly out the door and across the street into the Hilton.

This girl constantly surprises me, Jason thought. The challenges of nine-eleven had not only strained their relationship but had also placed it on the back burner. Cassie's recent reticence toward him personally only reprieved him from having to make difficult decisions. Maybe she was comfortable enough to take it to the next level. Maybe. He would do whatever had to be done with Russo to dissolve his professional partnership with Cassie and make way for a private one. Finding a new partner at work would be fairly easy because of the Bureau's exceptional training and standardization of procedures. Partners in life, however, were much harder to find.

"This isn't one of those office surprise things, is it?" he asked. Jason turned toward the restaurant off the lobby.

"I think we can say it's not one of those office things." Cassie held his hand tightly and redirected him into a waiting elevator. She inserted a card key into the slot beside the elevator controls and pushed the button for the concierge floor. "This party is a little more private."

This is finally beginning to make sense, Jason thought. He remembered sitting at the breakfast table performing the daily ritual. *Go with the flow today and you will be taken to heights never before experienced.* His horoscope had been interesting, but it was especially intriguing after he had pulled the Two of Cups from the deck of tarot cards. The card showed a young man and woman pledging their cups to one another.

Cassie opened the door to a deluxe suite and they entered a large sitting area with a table for two set exquisitely, including a white tablecloth and three candles. Separating two wine glasses was a bottle of '01 Caymus, already open and breathing. In the background the haunting raspings of Rod Stewart emanated from the entertainment center. Jason could see a king-size bed and an oversized bathroom, accented by a hot tub.

Cassie pulled out the chair for Jason and he sat down in amazement. She poured a splash of wine into Jason's glass and stood there waiting. Finally Jason realized what she was doing. He grabbed the glass, swirled it around, gave it the obligatory sniff, and took a sip.

"Very nice," he said. He looked at her approvingly. "And the wine is also very nice."

Cassie smiled, then filled both wine glasses and started for her chair. Jason quickly jumped up and pulled out the chair, and they both giggled like school children.

The dinner arrived about a half hour later and was magnificent. Cassie had ordered everything in advance and arranged for Jason to have grilled halibut, his favorite. She had a very rare petite filet.

With every sip of wine, Jason could feel the tensions of the past month draining from his body. It was nice to let it go, and talk the small talk, and enjoy the presence of the beautiful creature across the table. Johnny Mathis was finishing "Misty" when Cassie savored the last few drops of her second glass of wine.

"Are you ready for dessert?" she asked.

"I usually don't have dessert. Besides, I don't see how things could get any better."

"Well, it is your birthday."

"Are you having dessert?"

"I think I will."

"Did you order it? I didn't see dessert with the room service."

"No, I brought it with me. Let me get it," Cassie said. She rose from the table and started for the bedroom. "You sit tight for a moment."

Jason thought he knew what was coming next on this night of pleasant surprises. Cassie always thinks of everything, so she probably had his favorite, a chocolate on chocolate birthday cake, in the other room. He remembered telling her his mother always made that for him on his birthday and now he could almost taste it.

"Almost ready," she called from the other room. "I hope you like it."

Here it comes, Jason thought. She's probably lighting the candles and getting ready to sing. He would have to act surprised and grateful.

"Happy birthday, Jay," Cassie said.

Jason turned around in his chair to look and immediately liked what he saw. She was standing in the doorway completely nude.

CHAPTER 15

Monday, October 15 (Moon in Virgo to Libra 1:25 a.m.) Someone old, someone new. Someone borrowed, someone blue. Following your heart can be a bumpy ride. You may need to fasten your seatbelt.

Cassie was carrying a single dish covered with condoms and wearing nothing but a smile. It was absolutely the most scrumptious dessert and the most unforgettable birthday present he could ever imagine.

They ravaged each other like untamed animals unleashed on a fresh kill after months of hungering in the wilds. Again and again their passions raged, finally yielding to a caring tenderness. Jason was enthralled by the way she seemed to anticipate his needs. Her whimperings gradually crescendoed into a primal orgasmic scream at which time he also blissfully lost control. Was she feeling it or was she faking it? Jason wondered. Oh! Hell. Who cares? This is incredible.

Finally, Cassie led Jason into the hot tub for a little relaxation and recuperation. The warm water swirling around his body was soothing, and the feeling of contentment increased while Cassie sat straddling his lap. With only their heads above water, she pressed her firm breasts into his chest, held his head in her hands, and kissed him softly.

"Jason," she said. "You know that talk we've been trying to have?"

Jason nodded.

"I think now is the time."

"You have me at somewhat of a disadvantage here," Jason said. "I don't see how I can talk when I can't even think."

"Maybe that's the point," she said.

"Well, regardless of all the wonderful things pressuring me at this very moment, I'm not too rattled to express exactly how I feel about you."

"Shh, shh." Cassie placed her index finger first against her lips, then against Jason's. "First, there's something I want you to know, and there's really no easy way to say it. Jason, this thing happening here between us is not going to work."

"What do you ... ?"

"Shhhh." She shushed him again. "There's no denying the unbelievable chemistry between us. But this must end before our careers are compromised any further and we have regrets."

"I'll talk to Russo. I'll get a transfer. I'll do anything."

"Do anything you want, Jason, but somebody has to be strong here and I have to be the one. I can continue working with you if you like, and for the good of the mission I'd like to do that. But there are issues here which will not allow us to have a personal relationship. You can do whatever you want, but this is the way it has to be for me."

"What about tonight?" Jason said. "What was this all about?"

"I wanted you to remember I really do care about you. Good night, Jason."

Cassie kissed him softly on the lips. In barely a moment she stepped out of the hot tub, dried off with a towel, slipped her bra and panties into her purse, donned the black cocktail dress, grabbed her coat and was out the door.

Chapter 16

Tuesday, October 16 (Moon in Libra) In critical matters, there are no do-overs. Take whatever steps necessary to survive. As they say, the night is darkest, just before the dawn.

"Ring ... ring ..."

The ringing of a cell phone shattered the silence and fractured the deep, tormented sleep of an exhausted Jason Lancer. He opened his eyes to see he was still in the Hilton hotel suite. He didn't have to look at the other side of the bed to know Cassie wasn't there.

"Ring ... ring ..."

Maybe she was calling to tell him she had changed her mind. Finally, he found his cell phone in the pocket of his hastily discarded trousers.

"Hello," Jason said. He didn't bother to check the caller ID.

"Lancer, it's Russo. Did I wake you? I called your home phone and you didn't answer."

"Of course, you woke me," Jason said. "I guess I didn't hear the other phone." His mind was racing trying to figure out what would precipitate such an early morning call. Surely Cassie hadn't talked to him. Not this soon. "What's up?"

"Mount up, Lancer. It's time to charge. We got lucky. We found our guys."

"Where are they?"

"St. Louis. A postal inspector at a post office south of the airport recognized Abdul from our top ten list when he was applying for a post office box. He tailed him until we could get our guys involved. We think the four of them are still together and we've got 'em covered at the Webster Groves Best Western."

"Why not take 'em down?"

"That's the idea, but the boss wants you there because you're the only one of us to actually lay eyes on these guys, especially the two mystery guys."

"Let's do it. What's the plan?"

"An FBI jet will be waiting for you and Reilly at Reagan at 0900. That's three hours from now. We'll bust 'em at noon. Call me when you get on the ground in St. Louis. Good luck. I'm calling Reilly now."

Jason quickly donned his wrinkled clothes which were scattered around the suite and ran to retrieve the Crown Vic from Buster's across the street. He knew he had to hurry back to his house. Performing on very little sleep was one thing, but he had to shower, shave, and put on a clean suit to be at his best for this high profile arrest.

The morning paper was waiting for Jason on the front steps. When he picked it up and tapped the heavy dew from the plastic wrapper, he wondered what the headlines would read tomorrow. The President had declared war on the terrorists, but there had been no victories. It was hard to find an enemy to fight. These arrests would be a welcome sign of progress to a nervous country.

A glance at his watch reassured Jason he would have time for a quick breakfast. He was hungry and extremely thirsty, the aftermath of an unforgettable night.

Hungry, thirsty, and heartbroken. How did it ever come to this? Jason wondered. Maybe after these arrests things would be different for Cassie and him. Maybe. At least now he didn't have time to brood over the situation. He tossed the paper on the kitchen table, started the coffee pot, and ran to the shower.

While he wolfed down a cup of coffee, a bowl of Cheerios, and two large glasses of orange juice, Jason felt relieved Russo had said he would call Cassie. If Jason had to make the call, he had no idea what he would say to her. It was just as well when he next saw her it would be on the plane to St. Louis where they would be totally consumed with the mission at hand.

When he was finished his breakfast, Jason, out of habit, grabbed the paper and turned to the sports page. After glancing at the headlines, he turned to the comic section to check his horoscope.

Libra. September 23–October 22. Leave nothing to chance today. Keep both feet on the ground in mind, body, and spirit.

Jason became very still. With his heart racing, he read it again. Leave nothing to chance today. Keep both feet on the ground in mind, body, and spirit.

The words and vision of his mother during his last few moments with her over twenty years ago pounded his mind.

"It's just that I'm flying to Jacksonville today for a luncheon. I'll balance it out with a reading from the tarot deck. I'm sure I'll be fine. Hey! It's time for you to go. Don't want you to miss your bus."

Jason breathed rapidly and perspiration beaded on his face. He leaned over in his chair, elbows on his knees, and with his face resting in his hands. Suddenly he lunged towards the junk drawer by the sink and grabbed the tattered deck of tarot cards. Hesitating for a moment, he collected his thoughts. He knew he had to do this, and he had to do it right. Calmer, he shuffled the cards three times and cut them once. With his hand resting on the deck on the table in front of him, he closed his eyes, took several deep breaths, and turned over the top card. He opened his eyes.

DEATH!

Chapter 17

Tuesday, October 16 (Moon in Libra) Short term actions may produce long term consequences. Do not confuse a fork in the road with a dead-end. Libra may be in peril.

Jason felt pain on the right side of his forehead when he opened his eyes. He felt groggy, weak, and confused. He was sprawled on the floor beneath the kitchen table with tarot cards scattered all around him. He realized he must have passed out and bumped his head when he fell. The shock of his horoscope and tarot card matching those which had foretold his mother's death was more than he could take. He slowly rose to his feet and righted the fallen chair.

Jason glanced at his watch. 7:35. He was relieved to learn he had been out for only a few minutes. He sat motionless, pondering a situation which needed no pondering. The signs could not be clearer. There was no way he was going to get on an airplane today. His fear was not only for himself, but how could he be responsible for the death of Cassie and the others on the flight?

Jason reached for his cell phone and dialed a number.

"Assistant Director's office."

"Ashley, it's Jason. I need to talk to Russo."

"Jason, Honey, I'm putting together the contacts and the rundown on St. Louis, but it'll take me a few minutes," Ashley said. She sounded like she was making an apology.

"Never mind that. Ring Russo."

"Oh! Alright, Sweetie Pie. You be careful out there in St. Louis now, you hear?"

"What 'chu need Lancer?" Russo asked. His tone made it obvious he was busy with something or someone else.

"I need to … I would like to … Sir, I can't go to St. Louis today, could we do this tomorrow?"

"No! We can't do this tomorrow, Lancer. We're at war here. What the hell are you talking about?"

"I, uh, I have a problem and I need a day of personal leave. Just one day."

"What's the problem?"

"I said, it's personal," Jason said. He knew horoscopes and tarot cards would never be something Russo would understand.

"Lancer, I've had enough of your bullshit. If your problem is not a cerebral hemorrhage or a coronary, at 0900 your ass had better be sittin' on that airplane or sittin' in my office and right now I don't give a flying fuck which. Do you understand?"

Dead line. Dial tone. One way Russo was always sure to have the last word was to hang up immediately after saying something. It worked every time and always left Jason angry and frustrated. Now, in addition to the anger and frustration, he felt a deep sense of desperation.

How could anyone with a college education and years of training and experience with the top law enforcement department in the country be held hostage by horoscopes and tarot cards? That's what people would think. But Jason, like his mother, felt these mediums were valid. His mother had done her duty, even though it resulted in her death. Why couldn't he? If only he could talk to someone. A few hours ago, he was convinced Cassie was that person, but not anymore.

And Russo was no help. Jason had tried to talk to him and Russo had brought the hammer down. So much for a little understanding. Russo had suddenly become the problem. Jason asked him for understanding and instead got an ultimatum. Ass in airplane or ass in office. Would he be this difficult if he knew Jason was wrestling with the psyche of the card of Death? He must make a decision because it was obvious this situation was never going to resolve itself. Consequences be-damned. A drastic set of circumstances required drastic measures. Leaving his personal .357 magnum under the mattress Jason grabbed his badge and his ID, and holstered his service revolver.

Jason's colleagues looked puzzled when they saw Jason exiting the elevator on the top floor of the Hoover building. They had to be thinking he should be on his way to St. Louis? The clock on the wall read 8:45 and now all eyes were on him while he steadfastly walked toward the open door of Russo's office. When Jason entered the office, Russo was sitting at his desk with his back to the door talking on the phone. He ended his conversation and swiveled around in time to see Jason enter the room and pull his service revolver from its holster.

"What the hell are you doing?"

The loud bang could be heard by everyone on the top floor when Jason took his gun and slammed it down on Russo's desk, followed by his ID and his badge.

Jason turned and walked out of the office as quickly as he had walked in, amidst a sputtering of protests from Russo and startled stares from everyone.

Chapter 18

Tuesday, October 16 (Moon in Libra) In order to face the future, you must acknowledge the past. Pandora's box, like a box of chocolates, produces surprises. But not always so sweet. Cancer and Aires play dominate roles.

The deafening noise from the passing jets was disconcerting to Cassie while she waited for Jason to join her in the Bureau's private jet. She would never expect Jason to be late for an assignment as important as this one, regardless of what might be happening to their personal relationship. She was so deep in thought she barely heard her cell phone ringing.

"Reilly, it's Russo. Have you talked to Lancer?"

"No, we're waiting for him. The pilots are all set. As soon as he arrives, we're out of here."

"Go to St. Louis and make the bust. Lancer won't be joining you. He turned in his badge."

"He did what???"

"He walked in and quit. That's it."

"Why?"

"I don't know, Reilly. I was hoping you could tell me."

"Well, I can't. I'll call him."

"Go to St. Louis and do your job, Reilly. Somebody around here has to." And Russo hung up.

Cassie dialed Jason's cell phone, not really knowing what to say if he answered. She disconnected when it switched to voice mail.

"Let's go," she said to the pilots. "No one else is coming."

Confused and exhausted, Cassie fastened her seatbelt and slumped into her deep leather seat. Maybe last night was a mistake. Did she hurt him so badly he resigned? Men. Who could figure them out? Fortunately for her, Cassie thought, she no longer had to try. With the door closed, the noise of the other planes was replaced by the constant hum of the FBI jet's engines while it inched along towards the active runway. Cassie was sound asleep long before they were airborne.

My Dearest, Precious, Cassandra,

If you are reading this, it means your father and I have passed on. I hope the circumstances of our deaths, whatever they were, caused you as little pain and grief as possible. You were always our shining star and we did everything possible to protect you from anything unpleasant from the day we signed your adoption papers in Riyadh. It is my prayer these words do not distress you, but finally I want to set the record straight. Please forgive me for not having the courage to tell you the whole truth before now.

Your father and I told you we had no idea who your biological parents were. Actually, we did. He knew, and I knew. But strangely, he never knew that I knew.

We desperately wanted a child, but because of severe endometriosis, I was never able to conceive. This caused tensions in our marriage. I felt so guilty it was easy for me to forgive your father for having a tryst with our nineteen-year-old Saudi housekeeper. Cassandra, your biological mother's name was Ghaada Haady, but we called her Golly, a nick-name she liked and continued to use. She was a beautiful, sweet, girl from Dharma. And your father, well, you really were "Daddy's girl", just like he always told you. Golly, being an unmarried girl in trouble in an unforgiving culture, disclosed the affair quite innocently to me, pleading for my confidence and my help. I made the best decision of my entire life, and in return for absolute confidentiality, offered financial support for her and a home for her baby. And there you were. Answered prayers. Your father couldn't believe I really suggested we adopt you. He was so happy, and as far as I know, he never strayed again.

Golly returned to Dharma and married a merchant named al Din. Sadly, she died giving birth to her second son. That's the other thing I wanted tell you, dearest one. You are sharing blood with a couple of half-brothers somewhere on the planet.

So now you know, my darling. May God bless you for all your days, because indeed you were a blessing for us.

— Your Loving Mother

Cassie woke briefly from her deep slumber when the plane encountered an area of mild turbulence. Since the sudden death of her father two weeks ago, she had dreaded sleep. Disturbing dreams always accompanied even the briefest naps. And the dreams became even more intrusive after the attorney for her parents' estate presented her with the letter from her mother.

Being an only child adopted by parents who had no brothers or sisters, Cassie accepted the fact she had no family other than her parents. And she was content with that. She felt loved and happy and had never had a desire to search for her biological mother or father. When she read the letter, Cassie felt no betrayal or animosity toward her parents. How could she? They had committed their lives to her from the time she was born.

But now she was curious. She had real, live brothers. Half brothers, but brothers nonetheless. Where did they live? What were their occupations? Did they have families? Maybe she was an aunt. Did she dare open Pandora's Box and delve into the unknown? Was she prepared to live with the consequences, good or bad?

It was apparent to Cassie almost immediately she would try to find her siblings. After all, being with the Bureau had its advantages. With favors from a few friends and her ability to speak fluent Arabic, it should be fairly easy to find some answers. It did not go unnoticed by her that her brothers were named al Din. But al Din was a fairly common Saudi name, so she should not fear such a coincidence. Regardless, this was a private matter, and she saw no reason to inform Russo, or even Jason, of these new revelations.

The telephone rang several times before someone answered.

"Hello," a female voice finally said.

Cassie had asked her successor in Riyadh to run a confidential search with the information provided by her mother's letter. Soon she was dialing a phone number in Dharma.

"Hello," Cassie said, now speaking Arabic. "Could I speak with Mr. al Din, please?"

"He's not here," the woman said.

"When would be a good time for me to call him?"

"I don't know. Who is this?"

Cassie thought she heard a child crying in the background.

"My name is Cassandra Reilly and I'm a friend of the family."

"I've never heard of you."

"I know. Are you Mrs. Al Din?"

"I have to go now. Goodbye."

"Wait. Mrs. Al Din, when your husband returns, please have him call this number and reverse the charges."

Cassie recited the number twice but got no confirmation that the woman had written it down.

"What's this all about?" the woman asked.

"Tell him it's about his mother."

"His mother? You are crazy. Goodbye." And the line was dead.

Cassie was sitting at her desk in her cubicle. Jason was out chasing other leads concerning the two brothers. The DNA results from the lab at Quantico had confirmed Abdul and Ali al Din were brothers, and indeed they were the perps who attacked Sandra Thompson. Additionally, the lab returned a positive match with the samples collected by Jason on his visit to the simulator in Boca Raton.

Cassie couldn't resist. She had to know. She pulled a long black hair from her head, placed it in an evidence container, and expedited it back to the lab, asking her friend there to compare the sample with the markers from the brothers.

"Hello, Cassie?"

"Yes."

"This is Jim from down at the lab."

"Hi. Thanks for getting back to me so quickly. What do you have?"

"Oh! I got matches all around on the sample you sent me. First of all, your sample matched the DNA lifted from Sandra Thompson's mouth. When I compared it to our base markers from the crime scene investigation, the sample revealed it was a perfect match with your DNA, but we already knew that because you gave her mouth-to-mouth reviving her. But then it gets puzzling. When your samples were compared with the ones from the brothers, it revealed there is an 80% chance the three of you are siblings."

"Really? How ridiculous. How could that happen?"

"The percentages reflect what we sometimes find with siblings who share only one parent, but obviously that's not the case here. Maybe some samples were mixed when they were collected or something crazy like that. When I have time, I'll start from the beginning and run the tests again to see where we went wrong."

"Oh! No need to do that, Jim. I wanted to be sure the base sample which was sent to the lab was the correct one. And it was, so now my questions are answered. Thanks for your help. Bye, Jim."

...She went into the bedroom and soon returned carrying a single dish covered with condoms.

...They ravaged each other like untamed animals unleashed on a fresh kill after months of hungering in the wilds. Again and again their passions raged, finally yielding to a caring tenderness.

..."Go to St. Louis and make the bust. Lancer won't be joining you. He turned in his badge."

"He did what???"

"He walked in and quit. That's it."

"Why?"

"I don't know, Reilly. I was hoping you could tell me."

The plane bumped along in another stretch of turbulence. Cassie subconsciously checked to see that her seat belt was tight and settled back down into the posh leather seat.

"Is this Cassandra Reilly?"

"Yes, who's this?"

"My wife is very upset you called asking for me. My name is Ali al Din."

Cassie shuddered at the sound of the voice on the phone. She knew she was finally talking to one of her brothers, who happened to be one of the vicious terrorists who headed the top ten list.

"Hello. Are you there?"

"Yes," Cassie finally said, speaking Arabic. "I'm here. I'm sorry if I upset your wife."

"I don't care about that. Who are you and what's this about my mother?"

"There's really no easy way for me to tell you this," Cassie said. "My name is Cassandra Reilly, and I was born in Riyadh. My mother's name was Ghaada Haady."

"Do you think I'm stupid? You're with the FBI aren't you?"

"Yes, I am, Ali, but..."

"I knew it. Good bye, you infidel sow."

"Wait. Ali. I am with the FBI, but that doesn't change the fact my mother was your mother. Ali, I'm your only sister.

"I don't believe anything you say."

"I will never lie to you, Ali."

"So what name did they call my mother?"

"They called her Golly, and she died giving birth to you."

Cassie knew from the documents Jason had collected that Ali was the youngest brother.

"How do you know this?"

KARUMMP!

Chapter 19

Tuesday, October 16 (Moon in Libra) Secrets are stressful to keep, and to reveal. Family member surprises. Don't try to act alone. Even the Lone Ranger had Tonto.

Cassie was jolted awake when the G-5 touched down at Lambert Field in St. Louis. Her body was damp with sweat, not so much from sleeping against the leather seats, as from the nightmare involving her fugitive brothers. She had begged Ali to give himself up. She tried to reassure him she would do everything in her power to spare his life while his case progressed through the court system. She even tried to appeal to him by talking about his wife and his young child. Ali dismissed her pleadings, saying he would slay many Jews and infidels and would not again be denied his rightful destiny with Allah.

Fortunately, it would soon be over, Cassie thought. She gazed out the window to see the sleek jet had taxied to a stop at a private ramp on the west side of the airport. She deplaned and jumped into the waiting Crown Vic for the short trip to the Webster Groves Best Western.

Senior Field Agent David Fuller began briefing the swat team assembled in a crowded rental van across the street from the motel. Cassie realized how much she missed Jason. Since her first day in the field, he had always been there giving her guidance and leadership. He was the one person who always had her back. She could not stop thinking about the last time she and Jason had followed this pair into a hotel and found poor Sandra Thompson. Then she had found out she was related to these savages. Soon it would be over and the truth could come out. She didn't dare tell Russo before the brothers were captured, or he would snatch her off the case immediately.

During the briefing, Cassie noticed a large brown linen company truck arrive at the loading dock around the side of the motel. A short, dark-complected man in a white uniform and a white busman's hat went into the building pushing a large canvas hamper cart filled with clean linens. Senior Agent Fuller completed his briefing and announced the raid would begin as soon as the linen delivery truck departed the premises.

"Where's the nearest restroom?" Cassie asked Fuller. She knew it might be a few minutes before the truck left.

"Use the one in the lobby," Fuller said. He pointed across the street, not even trying to hide the 'rookie girl is nervous and has to relieve her bladder' grin on his face. "It's through those doors and to your right. We won't start without you."

Cassie dashed across the street without acknowledging the half chuckles from the others in the van. When she approached the rest rooms, the linen delivery man came out of the men's room pushing his hamper, filled with soiled linens. For a moment, their eyes met. The man turned down the hall toward the delivery doors and Cassie went into the ladies' room.

Before going into the stall, Cassie stopped and stared into the mirror behind the sinks. What was wrong with the picture she had seen? What was it about the man pushing the cart? Was it strange his hat was pulled down so far over his eyes? Maybe. But not as strange as what she remembered seeing when the man walked away. His pants were skin-tight and were so short you could see the top of his socks. Oh! My God!

Cassie rushed from the ladies' room and peered around the corner, in time to see the man make a turn out of sight toward the service entrance where the truck was parked. Pulling her Glock from its holster, she sprinted down the carpeted hallway. Glancing around the next corner, she saw the man stop and walk around the hamper cart to open the rear doors of the truck.

"Freeze! FBI!" Cassie shouted. She bounded around the cart to be within a few feet of the man. "Get on the ground! Get on the ground!" she said in Arabic.

The man turned around slowly with his hands in the air and Cassie knew she was staring directly into the eyes of Ali al Din. Her intuition was already telling her she had made a big mistake when she heard a slight rustling behind her.

"Don't move, infidel bitch! Prepare to die." Cassie knew it was the gravelly voice of Abdul al Din. He emerged from beneath the soiled linens in the hamper cart with a gun aimed at Cassie.

"Shoot me and your brother dies!" Cassie said. She steadied her aim at Ali's head.

"Perfect. My brother dies, he's with Allah and the virgins. Then you die and rot in hell with pigs. It's a beautiful thing."

"Wait!" Ali said to his brother. His stare remained locked on Cassie and the muzzle of the Glock. "Look at her."

"What?"

"She's Cassandra Reilly."

"How do you know who I am?" Cassie asked.

"Because," Ali said. He measured his words carefully. "I recognize your voice from the telephone. And you look exactly like the picture we have of our mother."

"Well, what do you know, we're having a family reunion," Abdul said. He got out of the cart and moved closer.

"It doesn't have to be this way, guys. No one has to get shot here. I can help you."

"Help us spend the rest of our lives in prison? Never." Abdul said. He moved closer, glaring into Cassie's eyes. He was so close he could hear Cassie's deep, deliberate breathing. Her trigger finger tightened on the Glock.

Chapter 20

Tuesday, October 16 (Moon in Libra) When the winds of change blow, enjoy the breeze. And hoist a mighty sail. Nothing ventured, nothing ventured. Scorpio awaits.

Jason left the Crown Vic parked in the FBI parking garage with the keys in the ignition and took a taxi to go home. Within minutes of leaving Russo's office, his cell phone rang. The caller ID indicated it was Cassie, no longer a call he had to take. Was she wondering what was going on with him? Some questions are better left unanswered. Maybe this was one of those questions.

"Stop," Jason yelled to the taxi driver. "I'll get out here." The driver curbed the taxi and stopped the meter at $9.50. Jason handed the driver a twenty and told him to keep the change. He exited the cab under a huge sign which read, "Georgetown Cadillac."

Having had the use of the Crown Vic for several years, Jason really hadn't needed to own a car. When in Washington, he was usually working, and when out of town for vacation or leisure, he found it more convenient to fly. It was not that he could not afford to own a car in D.C. In fact, it was more like he could afford to not own one, a fact which escaped his colleagues at the FBI.

Jason never advertised to anyone he was financially quite comfortable. No one knew there was a million dollar settlement from a wrongful death lawsuit filed on Jason's behalf after his mother died in the plane crash. The trust fund became his at age twenty-one with nearly a half million left after attorney fees, college, and the costs of Jason's upbringing, were paid.

On the day Jason received the check for the funds he was frantic about suddenly having so much money at his disposal and not having a clue about what to do with it. He handled it the way he handled all major decisions: he consulted his horoscope and the tarot cards.

Libra. September 23–October 22. Waste not today what you may be in need of tomorrow. Three quick shuffles and a cut of the tarot deck exposed the Wheel of Fortune card which supported the meaning of the horoscope. After considering what the readings revealed to him, Jason entrusted his nest egg to a financial advisor in Tallahassee, a friend of his mother's, with instructions to compile a portfolio slanted towards maximum growth. The market in general and his stocks in particular did well in the nineties, and Jason, even though he was without a job, was worth over a million dollars.

After the obligatory haggling, Jason bought the car he wanted and was soon driving home in his new 2002 bright white Cadillac Escalade with all the bells and whistles. It was big and rugged like a truck, but smooth and luxurious like a Cadillac. And it hadn't gone unnoticed by Jason that all the Washington Redskins and half of all rock stars seemed to have one.

Jason drove along allowing himself to be wowed at all the gee whiz features of his new car. He fidgeted with the six-way heated and air conditioned power seat while flipping through the seemingly limitless channels on the satellite radio. All the while, he followed the voice instructions of the new GPS navigation system while it directed him to the nearest IHOP. Whenever he was nervous or tense, there was nothing like a stack of banana nut pancakes to make things right: comfort food extraordinaire, the first step toward making all things right.

Jason was experimenting with the sun roof and driving across a bridge when the cell phone rang again. Without checking the caller ID, he grabbed the phone and tossed it through the open sun roof into the rushing waters of a creek which emptied into the Potomac; another step toward making things right.

It was almost noon by the time Jason wheeled "Pearl," the name he had given his new car because of the white luster of her paint job, into the driveway of his bungalow. His body was sinking slowly, mentally and physically. The life altering events of the past eighteen hours were taking their toll.

Jason poured four fingers of Makers Mark on two cubes of ice in a tumbler and gravitated to the bedroom. Sipping and thinking, he found himself staring at the phone on the night stand as if it were an intruder. He reached down and disconnected it from the wall and sat on the bed. Sipping and thinking. Thinking and sipping.

How could someone's life disintegrate so quickly? Jason was having an anguish attack. This time yesterday he was point man on a critical case for the top law enforcement department in the country. He had high hopes for deepening a relationship with the most interesting woman he had ever met. But that was yesterday. Pangs of guilt were beginning to seep into Jason's thoughts. Sipping and thinking.

What have I done? Do I have no sense of responsibility at all? What about commitment to duty? What would my mother have thought? More pangs of guilt, sharper now. He knew his mother had given her life rather than shirk her responsibility. She boarded that airplane knowing the consequences. She knew, because it was in the stars and in the cards. Yet, she ignored the signs and did what she had to do. Why did she? Why couldn't he? Jason shuttered. What does that make me? A quitter? A deserter?" Thinking and sipping.

Regardless of what was going on between him and Russo, or even him and Cassie, his country needed him, and he had shirked his duty and quit. No way to sugarcoat it. He took the last sip, rattled the ice cubes around the glass for a moment before placing it on the nightstand. Lowering his head to the pillow, Jason yielded to the solace of sleep.

After more than twelve hours of continuous rest, Jason opened his eyes to the total darkness of the very early morning hours. Laying awake listening to the stillness, it was all very clear to him what had to be done. He had to move on.

Jason had experience at moving on and he was good at it. What choice did he have? Like when his mother died, he had to move on.

After a quick shower, he put on the most comfortable outfit he owned, his favorite tennis warm-up suit. He filled a single suitcase with an assortment of clothes from his dresser and grabbed a few hanging clothes and threw them into Pearl's back seat.

A car whisked by and the morning paper hit the driveway with a thud. After standing there and staring at it for a moment, Jason removed the wrapper and read the headlines under the lights of the carport.

TERRORISTS KILLED IN ST. LOUIS

TWO OTHERS ESCAPE

The FBI along with state and local authorities shot and killed two fugitives from the FBI's ten most-wanted list in a noontime shootout Tuesday in St. Louis. The deceased men were known only as Aaron Abramovitch and Benedict Schwartz. Two others, brothers Abdul al Din and Ali al Din, considered the ringleaders of the terrorist cell, somehow managed to escape in a linen truck, after overpowering FBI Special Agent Cassandra Reilly. She was found handcuffed to a stair rail at the Webster Groves Best Western, but was otherwise unharmed...

Jason was so overcome with guilt from abandoning his partner and the Bureau, he could not bear to read any further. He turned the page to the comic section and the horoscopes.

"Libra. September 23–October 22. A door never closes unless another one opens. Change is inevitable. Embrace it, and you will see new horizons."

Tossing the paper into the nearby recycle bin, he pulled the tattered tarot deck from his pocket. After three quick shuffles and a cut, he placed the deck on Pearl's hood. Methodically he turned the top card, the Knight of Wands, depicting a young warrior on a mighty stallion passing pyramids or mountains on a great traveling adventure. Tarot, tarot, how do you know?

With an inner peace, Jason turned off all the lights, locked the door to the house and programmed a new destination into Pearl's navigation system, 2438 miles away. Slowly he backed out of the driveway.

PART II

Chapter 21

Saturday, October 20 (Moon in Sagittarius) Renew friendships. Water over the dam always goes downstream. Look for timeless beauty in natural wonders. Aquarius plays role.

Jason was momentarily blinded by the setting desert sun when he topped the hill on Route 93 looking down on Hoover Dam. Beyond, already succumbing to the dusk, was the city of Boulder. Off to his right, stretching as far as he could see were the deep blue waters of Lake Mead. Below the dam to the south, the Colorado River trickled along the bottom of a colossal canyon and seemed insignificant compared to the mammoth lake and dam. Jason tightened his squint thinking he might see the lights of Las Vegas, a futile effort against the furnace-colored glare from the Valley of Fire. The reddish purple rays gleaming through the western clouds made a convincing argument the valley had been named appropriately.

The digital clock on the controls of the satellite radio read 9:28 p.m., allowing Jason to relax a bit from the grind he had been laying on Pearl for the last few hours. The satellite radio was another new toy Pearl offered, and he loved it already. He could listen to the same channel across the country or flip through a selection of over two hundred choices, anything from Bach to Broadway to Brownsville. Perfect for Jason, who liked all kinds of music, especially the stretch from Broadway to Brownsville. The radio also reminded him to change his clock to Pacific Time. The impromptu detour he had taken to the south rim of the

Grand Canyon took longer than expected, but was very impressive and offered an unexpected perspective on life. Gazing at the captivating beauty of this vast trench in the desert, created by millions of years of a river running through it, had made him feel extremely small and insignificant. Perched on the rim of the Grand Canyon, Jason had realized whether or not he kept his government job, in the overall scheme of things, didn't make any difference. Yet, the guilt remained.

He didn't want to be late for his seven o'clock dinner rendezvous at Padre's, a legendary bordello turned Tex-Mex saloon 4.2 miles west of the dam on Highway 93. Jason was meeting Clayton Spaulding, the only person he knew in Vegas. Clayton was a retired agent who got out while the getting was good after twenty years. Actually, Jason always thought Clayton had known his days were numbered.

Jason also had the feeling that Clayton had expected one of the new age supervisors who was long on schooling and short on experience to pull the book and nail him with a procedural technicality or a sin of political incorrectness. He was considered to be somewhere between a real character and a real loose cannon. Maybe that's why Jason liked him, and he couldn't help but smile thinking about the phone call he had placed to Clayton a couple of nights ago.

"Jay! You ole sumbitch! How's it hanging?" Clayton had asked.

"It's hanging, Clayton. And I always wondered, is 'sumbitch' one word, or two?"

"Actually, it's four words," Clayton said. He laughed. "Unless it's a term of unabashed affection, then it's only one. Sumbitch! It's good to be hearing from you rather than about you."

"Oh, you've heard."

"Of course, hasn't everyone? Actually our buddy Ashley told me what, but she didn't know why. I figured if she didn't know it was none of my business. Still feel that way."

"Thanks, Clayton. I'm coming out your direction and thought it might be nice to touch base."

"Absofuckinlutely! You lookin' for a job?"

"Oh! Heavens no. I thought you might buy an old out-of-work ex-nobody a drink."

"I'll do better than that. I'm good for dinner, too! And the whole thing'll be cheaper'n any drink you could get anywhere around Hooverville. When'er you comin'?"

"I'm driving out. Be there day after tomorrow."

"Padre's, 4.2 miles west of the dam on 93 on your right. It's an old whorehouse turned Mexican restaurant. See you at seven. Be hungry, horny and thirsty."

"Maybe two out of three," Jason had said chuckling. "See you then."

Jason wondered when he recalled Clayton's comments if there might be something from the old bordello still on the menu.

He had to hit the brakes when he rounded the final curve before crossing the dam. All traffic ahead was stopped. Probably an accident, Jason thought, while the cars crept along. So much for making Padre's at seven. When he progressed to the front of the line, he saw there was no accident at all, but a highway patrol checkpoint, complete with sniffer dogs and mirrors to look underneath the cars. Jason realized this was not merely a license check. They were worried about explosives being near the dam, a legitimate concern because Highway 93 crossed over the top of the dam. Welcome to the world of post nine-eleven.

"Sir, may I see your driver's license and registration, please?"

"It's a new car," Jason said. He handed his license to the no nonsense Tommy Lee Jones look-a-like.

"Could I see your sales contract, please?"

Jason knew that was coming because he still had the usual cardboard license plate on the back of the car from the dealer.

"Long way from home, aren't you?" the Tommy Lee type asked. He glanced over the sales contract.

"It's all relative," Jason said. His tone implied he couldn't care less.

"Are you carrying any weapons?"

Jason thought about it for a moment. "No," he said. He was glad he had left his longtime companion, Mr. SIG SAUER under the mattress at the bungalow, and his service revolver on Russo's desk.

"May we search your vehicle?"

"Of course," Jason said. He watched three other officers and a dog looked under and around the SUV.

They opened every door and compartment and Pearl endured a thorough sniffing from the large German shepherd. Jason desperately wanted to tell them to cut the crap because he was a Special Agent of the FBI. But he was no longer an agent with the FBI and there was certainly nothing special about him. Regrets? Guilt? This was going to take some time.

Out in the West Texas town of El Paso; Marty Robbins was blaring from the purple bubble-tube juke box in the back of the large open room known as Padre's. When Jason walked through the front door, he glanced back at the scattered cars in the parking lot. He saw everything from an old Chevy, with the trunk tied down with a piece of rope and so completely covered with dirt and rust you couldn't tell what the original color was, to a brand new yellow Jaguar. Then there was Pearl, which Jason had parked near the front door to minimize the vulnerability to a break-in. The only thing missing from the parking lot scene was a posse of Hell's Angels' choppers scattered about.

"Jay! Jay! Over here!" Clayton Spaulding hailed Jason from the last of a row of booths along the wall on the opposite side of the room. It had been almost a year since Jason had seen Clayton and he was surprised at the full, yet neatly trimmed blue-gray beard. The blue sport coat, Comanche string tie, and snakeskin cowboy boot ensemble was also vastly different from the standard attire of the Bureau. Obviously, dress codes west of the Pecos were more imaginative and relaxed.

"Hey! Kenny Rogers! What are you doing here, and what have you done with my buddy Clayton?" Jason always enjoyed teasing his old friend.

"You've got to know when to hold 'em, know when to fold 'em, know when to walk away, KNOW WHEN TO RUN!" Clayton crooned the old Kenny Rogers standard.

"Ouch! That hurts!" Jason winced, feigning offense.

"Welcome to the West, Old Buddy. Have a seat and take a load off." Clayton extended a warm handshake. He glanced at the petite brown-eyed cutie coming to take their order. "Would you like a little Mexican, or would you like to start with some food?"

"Oh! Stop it, Clayton. I knew it was you."

They each ordered a couple of Coronas with a slice of lime and the "Broncbuster," an all you can eat sampling of everything hot and Mexican. After attacking the beer and the never- ending servings of chips and salsa, Jason began to relax from the long drive across the country.

"So how's the business?" Jason asked.

When Clayton retired from the FBI, he had accepted a position heading up a struggling security firm in Las Vegas. The firm offered security to non-casino concerns and was owned by a young widow who had no clue about running a business. In only a few months, Clayton, with the utilization of a few organizational skills and some hiring and firing, was not only turning a profit but also growing the company.

"Business is fandamntastic! Things are poppin' 'round here like a balloon blower in a cactus patch. In fact, I got the perfect job for you."

"I'm not looking for a job," Jason said. He reiterated what he had told him on the phone.

"Southwest Security Advisory Board," Clayton said. "You can be on that board quicker than a Dallas debutant. Ever'body out here's queer for a resume with FBI on it."

Jason listened while Clayton rambled on about his adventures in Vegas. He remembered how he had missed his bantering at the Monday night poker games. Regardless of how crazy he was, you couldn't help but like him. Good ole boy or not, he was a true friend.

Continuing the hard sell, Clayton relayed to Jason that after running the security firm for a few months, he had been picked for the SSAB. He was assigned the project of overseeing the security of the Hoover Dam, which was lax even before nine-eleven. The primary concern was the way in which employees were allowed entrance to the control room of the dam. They simply flashed an ID at a minimum wage security guard and walked directly into the most vulnerable part of the facility. Once past the guard, they had access to the entire area, even the elevators down into the bowels of the huge power generating facility. The water driven turbines provided electricity to all of Nevada and most of Southern California, including Los Angeles.

Clayton had convinced the Bureau of Reclamation, a branch of the U.S. Department of the Interior with administrative responsibility for Hoover Dam, to install the new PRINTSCAN system to control access to the dam. PRINTSCAN, the very latest in technology, uses a combination of a thumb print and identification card scan to open the door. An employee walks halfway into a circular revolving door of bars, known as a cheese grater, where he places his right thumb on the device and simultaneously swipes his ID card through the device. The device instantly recognizes the readings, if they are stored in the data base, and opens the lock to allow the cheese grater to revolve and allow entry. Clayton was proud of having this system in place before nine-eleven.

"You're very kind to offer to help, Clayton, but I'm not looking for work right now." Jason smiled, trying not to diminish his enthusiasm.

"Hells bells, Jason. You quit your job in the middle of your career and drive all the way 'cross country for no apparent reason. What do you want?"

"I want a change."

Jason knew he could never explain even to Clayton that when the force of the stars and the mission of the FBI collided, he had been conflicted to the point of not being able to do his duty. Just because nothing happened to the airplane on the flight he was supposed to take to St. Louis doesn't mean it wouldn't have, if he had been on the flight. Therefore, his actions saved Cassie and airplane. Didn't they?

"And I could really use some hints on a place to live near the strip," Jason said.

Clayton, excited he was finally going to be able to do something to help, flipped a business card out of his pocket and wrote something on the back.

"The Desert Stars," Clayton said. He pushed the card towards Jason. "A new building I'm securing on Koval, south of Flamingo. It's close to everything. You can rent it by the month, buy it, lease it, or lease it to buy it."

"Thanks, Clayton, I'll check it out."

"So you're lookin' for a place to stay, but you're not lookin' for work. Do you know how you're gonna' make a living?"

"I'm going to play poker."

"Then maybe you should rent only for a week." Clayton grinned as he guzzled down the last slug of his Corona.

Chapter 22

Tuesday, October 23 (Moon in Capricorn to Aquarius 9:26 p.m.)
Domestic matters require attention. Establish routine. The dust
always settles at the end of the storm.

The poker room at the Bellagio was filling rapidly with eager
patrons hurrying to get the last seats at the few remaining
tables. The regulars can always tell a poker player when he
enters the casino, because he knows exactly where he is going
and proceeds toward the action with purpose. What a cross
section of society this is, Jason thought. He mucked his two
cards, nine, three off-suit, and looked around the room. One of
every kind is here, a virtual Noah's Ark of mankind right here in
this room.

Even at Jason's table of $5-$10 Texas Hold 'em, an assortment
of characters sat at every position, mostly tourists on their
pilgrimage to Sin City. At the number one spot, to the
immediate left of the dealer, was a young guy in a ten gallon
cowboy hat and a Hook 'em Horns football jersey. His
appearance reminded Jason of a young Doyle Brunson, the
legendary poker star and author of the first legitimate "how to"
book on poker, *Super/System – A Course in Power Poker*. Jason
remembered someday he must get around to buying that book.
"Tex" was an affable soul who liked to see a lot of flops, bully
the table with a lot of raises, and drink a lot of beer.

Number two was a grey-haired elderly lady with a slight German accent. Jason looked for a numbered tattoo on her arm wondering if she was a survivor of the holocaust. She would survive here, too, if the blinds didn't eventually break her, because she only played locks and cinches. Jason decided he would not be in any pot with "the Rock," the name he had given her, if he didn't have the absolute nut, a hand which could not be beaten.

Jason reviewed in his mind what his mother had taught him about poker. In Hold 'em, the blind bets are placed before the cards are dealt. The player to the left of the dealer posts the small blind and the next player to his left posts the big blind, which is twice the amount of the small blind. The button, a marker which denotes the player which is the dealer, rotates clockwise to the next player after each hand.

Jason was in position three at the end of the table, a position he really liked in this game. Not only did he have loosey-goosey "Tex" and "the Rock" sitting to his right, but he could look directly down the table at the other players. He also had a view of the high-limit area which was located adjacent to, albeit a half level up from, where Jason was playing.

Around the table at the other positions were the usual doctors, lawyers, and Indian Chiefs; freeloaders, fakers, and candlestick makers, all vacationing and having fun. This is the perfect game to hone poker skills and make a little money at the same time. It was also the perfect situation to put some distance between him and the FBI. Maybe.

Jason folded an ace of diamonds and six of spades and tossed them into the muck. He called cards like those ace, crud. Such a hand should not be played in a game like this with a full table because someone usually had an ace with a bigger kicker. And that could be expensive. Jason pushed his chair back, and reflected on the events of the afternoon.

The Desert Stars condo building, complete with parking garage, had turned out to be even better than Clayton described it. The manager had showed Jason a unit on the ninth floor with a northern view of the Vegas strip. It was a new two bedroom for sale or rent and very nicely furnished. Jason liked it a lot, once he got through the front door. He almost didn't go in because when he saw the front door it made his skin crawl. This was unit 911.

Jason looked at the condo and stared at the numbers again on the way out the front door. He flashed on the Twin Towers, Abdul, Ali, Sandra Thompson, Russo, Cassie, his mother, the horoscope, the tarot cards, DEATH!

The manager thought he had offended Jason or perhaps his client was suddenly ill, when Jason abruptly excused himself and left. He ran to find Pearl in the visitors parking place in the garage. He quickly opened the newspaper and read his horoscope. *Libra. September 23– October 22. Make a fresh start with a bold move. Discard old baggage. Domestic fears, if confronted, are obstacles which are easily overcome.*

Several minutes passed before Jason began to calm. He grabbed the tattered tarot deck from Pearl's glove compartment. Three shuffles and a cut left him staring at the top card on the deck. Slowly, he turned it over: the Knight of Wands. Again, the Knight of Wands, reprising so soon. A Knight carries a wand and gallops past pyramids on a high-spirited stallion. Jason was relieved. He interpreted the reappearance of the card to mean he should complete his transition and establish his new domicile.

Jason walked to the office to tell the manager he had decided to buy Unit 911. Regardless of Clayton's admonishment to rent for a week, Jason was determined to look toward the future. He knew with the way real estate was booming, especially in Vegas, he couldn't go wrong with ownership. And as for the demons of nine-eleven, he now felt he had the courage to fight them, if that's what he had to do.

"Call," Jason said. He pushed a five dollar chip forward after peeking at his hole cards and finding a pair of fours. Not the best of starting hands, but it would be nice to see a flop. Maybe another four might appear.

The other players folded and the action was back on Tex, the big blind, in seat number one.

"Mount up, all you bulls and heifers; price of poker's goin' up." Tex bellowed at the table and splashed another ten dollars into the pot.

The Rock sitting between Tex and Jason sat motionless, as if she had heard or seen nothing at all. Slowly, she pushed in her chips, calling Tex's raise. Jason quietly mucked his cards. If this lady called the raise from the Hook 'em Horns cowboy before the flop, he knew his two fours were no good.

Jason reflected on the short ten minute walk he had taken from his condo to the poker room at the Bellagio. Distances out here could be deceiving. The hotels are bigger than life and appear very close, but actually are miles away. Appearing like a mirage, the fantasy of the next jackpot and unlimited wealth can be seen all around. They seem so close. Not really.

The flop was ace, queen, seven, rainbow, cards of different suits. Tex tossed in a bet and the Rock raised, again slowly pushing chips into the pot. Finally, after some grumbling to himself, Tex called. The turn card was the four of clubs, which made Jason second guess himself for a moment, but only for a moment. Tex had finally gotten the message and checked. The Rock bet the max, ten dollars, on the turn and the river. Tex called. Jason was not surprised when the Rock took down the pot with three queens, beating Tex's pair of aces.

Walking over to the casino, Jason had realized he had never played poker for the purpose of making money. He had played since he was a kid, and even though he usually won and considered himself good at the game, it had always been just a game. Now, he was sailing into uncharted waters and thought it was only prudent to start small with the tourists and the five-ten games while brushing up on basic strategy. It was obvious to make any real money, he would have to play and win at the larger cash games. But first, he would get his feet wet without risking too much.

"Raise," Jason said. He glanced at his two hole cards and found 'pocket rockets', two aces. He pushed two five dollar chips into the pot. Everyone folded around to the Hook 'em Horns jersey.

"Back at'cha , pod'ner," Tex growled. He tossed in two chips and grinned after guzzling half of his mug of suds in one gulp.

Finally. Jason tossed in a chip to call. Regardless of what the fool had, he couldn't beat his aces.

The flop was the five and jack of spades and the ace of diamonds. Sweet. Jason savored the fact he had three aces.

"Five," Jason said. He pushed in the max bet, confident of his set of aces.

"And five." Tex never tried to hide his excitement.

"Raise," Jason said.

The smile left Tex's face and he appeared almost sober for a moment before splashing in a call.

The turn card was the three of clubs. No help.

Jason bet ten. Tex called.

What on earth could he have over there, besides money? Jason reviewed the betting in his mind.

The river card was a worrisome seven of spades. Jason tapped the table softly, indicating he was checking.

"I didn't come in here checkin', pod'ner," Tex said. He tossed a ten dollar chip into the pot.

There was too much money in the pot for Jason not to call, so he flipped in a ten dollar chip, knowing what was about to happen. As expected, Tex turned up the king and queen of spades, giving him a spade flush. Jason wished this had been a no-limit game. Then he could have gone all in to protect his hand and prevent even drunks and fools from drawing to straights and flushes.

So much for getting his feet wet. Jason needed a break after such a bad beat so he stood up to stretch and look for the men's room. He again glanced up to the high-limit section above his table at a group playing $60-$120 Hold 'em. They were all very serious, except for an auburn haired girl with a quick smile. Why did she look so familiar?

Chapter 23

Monday, November 19 (Moon in Capricorn) To swim, you must first get your feet wet. Proceed boldly but watch for sharks. Keep one hand on your wallet and the other on your heart. Scorpio makes appearance.

During the next few weeks Jason settled into Desert Stars Unit 911 and tried to develop a routine which resembled a lifestyle with some degree of normalcy. Residents of Las Vegas could pace themselves and play poker whenever they wanted, without feeling they were working against the clock. Most tourists felt like they had to see every flop until it was time to run for the airport.

Knowing he was in this for the long haul, Jason figured the only way to really make this work was to act like a professional in his new job. He set limits for himself, never allowing himself to lose more than a certain amount in any given session. He never played when he was tired, hungry, angry or feeling mentally down, and avoided anything which kept him from feeling the force, the energy. He knew all his life he had had one decided advantage over most of the other players, the force of the stars. With the guidance of his horoscope and his tattered deck of tarot cards, he would ride the force to a better life.

What happened to fall? Jason wondered. He zipped up his jacket and quickened his gait on the crosswalk which spanned Las Vegas Boulevard. Overnight, the gale-force wind had switched to the north and suddenly had a bite to it. Another three minutes and he would be in the friendly confines of the Bellagio. He had enjoyed playing at the Mirage and several other hotel casinos, but still favored the Bellagio. They catered to the poker crowd. And they always had several games in progress, a very important fact for someone looking for a game, especially a high stakes game.

Jason had toiled at the $5-$10 game and had usually done well. Still, when he won, he could only squeeze out a couple of hundred dollars, certainly not enough to sustain the lifestyle to which he would like to become accustomed. After the morning readings, he knew it was time to test the waters of the high limit games.

Libra. September 23–October 22; Broad steps will take you toward your goal; greater horizons are visible from the next step up the ladder.

Three quick shuffles, a cut, and a flip of the top card from the tarot deck revealed The Wheel of Fortune. Four winged guardians surrounding the wheel which indicated all fortunes come from on high. Could there be a clearer sign? It was show time. It was time to venture outside his comfort zone, to find out if he could play the game successfully when the stakes were substantial enough to make a difference in his bank account.

"Good morning, Mr. Lancer," Fred called out to Jason when he approached the poker room of the Bellagio.

"Good morning, Fred," Jason said.

Fred had the appearance of a svelte Jackie Gleason with a full head of wavy gray hair which cried out for another dose of Grecian Formula. He was the day manager of poker operations and always addressed Jason as "Mr. Lancer", despite Jason's insistence otherwise.

Even though Jason had given his last name to Fred only once, from that moment on he was "Mr. Lancer".

Jason remembered the day he met Fred. It was about a month ago. He had played at the $5-$10 table for ten hours straight and had been up and down all day. Finally, Jason, on the button, caught the hand he was looking for, a pair of pocket kings. He raised the bet after three calls and a raise in front of him.

The cast of characters at the table were right out of central casting. There were a couple of locals and the garden variety of tourists having a good time, including the obligatory liquored up Hispanic who pumped the pot at every opportunity. This one said he was a road builder from Columbia. Perfect. Easy pickings. Right? Wrong. The flop was king, seven, three, rainbow, giving Jason a set of kings. Everyone dropped out except Jason and the road builder, who raised to the max and hit a six in the gut on the river for a seven high straight. Why did this seem like a recurring theme? This fool had put all that money into the pot with a four, five, off-suit. Jason felt like he had been sucker punched.

Standing behind the dealer with a rack of assorted chips, Fred had been watching the hand, waiting to replenish the dealer's tray when the hand was over. Jason picked up his few remaining chips and started walking towards the exit.

"Sir." Fred called to Jason. "Would you allow me to treat you to dinner?"

"I may have lost my appetite on that one," Jason said. He knew comps were sometimes given by the casinos, but had never received one.

"That's poker, sir. You played that hand perfectly. Sometimes good hands produce bad results. What's your name?" Fred asked. He pulled card and a pen from his coat pocket.

"Jason."

"And your last name?"

"Lancer."

Fred scribbled Jason's name on the card and handed it to him.

"Here you are, Mr. Lancer. Take this to Jasmine across the atrium from the main lobby and enjoy a nice meal. The Maine lobster and the New York strip are both excellent."

Jason squinted to read the nametag on the jacket. "Thank you, Fred. I really appreciate that."

Jason recalled that great meal as he approached the podium of the poker room. Since then, he had learned to appreciate Fred while he watched him work his magic on the players. He knew how to strike the perfect balance of being friendly and businesslike, a seldom mastered art.

 "The five-ten tables are full right now, Mr. Lancer. I've got you on the list," Fred said. He jotted down Jason's name. "We should be kicking off a new table in a few minutes."

Jason peered up at the high limit area. "What about thirty-sixty?"

"Thirty-sixty? Absolutely. One seat available," Fred said. His tone was both questioning and encouraging. "Thousand dollar buy in."

"Are they all pros in that game?" Jason asked.

"No, there are a couple of out-of-towners up there."

"I think I'll give it a try," Jason said. He pulled a stack of hundred dollar bills and handed it to Fred. "After all, the cards don't know how much is bet on them, do they?"

"No they don't, Mr. Lancer." Fred nodded to the high limit area. "But up there, the players sure do."

Jason settled into spot four at the table and endured several skeptical looks from some of the players.

Fred placed a rack of chips in front of him and Jason looked at his first two hole cards, a pair of queens. Wow. Welcome to the big time. He raised thirty dollars. The man in spot five wearing a Hogan golf hat was short on chips, but that didn't stop him from throwing in a thirty dollar raise. Everyone else folded and Jason called, wondering if the guy had aces or kings. The flop was queen, jack, three, rainbow. Jason bet, only to be raised. Jason re-raised. The Hogan hat guy to his left was all in. They flipped their cards face up and the fourth and fifth cards, the turn and river cards, revealed trash. Jason saw he had won the pot with three Queens over Hogan Hat's three Jacks.

"I've enjoyed this game about as long as I can stand it," Hogan Hat lamented as he got up to leave the table. "Good luck, guys."

Jason mucked a pair of trash cards and was stacking his chips when he saw Fred escorting a new player to occupy spot five beside him.

The auburn haired girl looked at Jason and smiled. "Hi."

"Hi," Jason said. He was so struck by her youthful beauty it was the only response he could muster.

Who is this girl? Jason searched his mind while most of the other players acknowledged her presence as if they knew her.

He tried not to be conspicuous but could not prevent himself from glancing in her direction. When she rose and crossed her legs in the chair beneath her, he knew. She was the girl from screen three at Buster's. He was sitting next to Annabelle Duquemin, the multi-millionaire champion on the World Poker Tour.

Chapter 24

Monday, August 27 (Moon in Sagittarius to Capricorn 8:01 p.m.) Travel may be necessary to garner power. Faith and trust are tested. Today is not the day to avenge prior harm. Taurus provides strength.

Months earlier.

The dark green, dirt covered Range Rover lumbered down the lightly traveled farm road across a lush expanse of meadowland. The scene resembled something seen on the Travel Channel, chronicling the adventures of yet another African safari. But appearances can be deceiving. There were no lions or elephants or giraffes being stalked by city-slickers with large cameras in this picture. This was not Africa. This land was mainly forests with an occasional farm gnawed into the landscape. This was southeastern Uzbekistan.

"There." The man in the passenger seat shouted. "There it is." He pointed to an old rusted-out tractor covered with weeds, a landmark on the crude map they were following. Their trip seemed to last forever, twelve hours on bad roads across Afghanistan from high in the mountains near the Pakistani border. But for the man in the passenger seat, the journey was only beginning. His face sported a week-old Don Johnson scruff, the remnants of a thick, black beard which he never shaved completely. Not only did it enhance his persona as a man who must be taken seriously, but it also helped hide a wicked scar which ran from below his right eye to his collarbone. This was a wound which had never been seen by a doctor and had left him marked for life. At least he still had a life, which was more than could be said for the Russian soldier who had slashed him with a bayonet during the Russian invasion of Afghanistan. "Scar Face" had wrestled the gun away from the Russian and impaled him on his own weapon. He established himself as a favorite with the Emir when he stayed to fight rather than be evacuated to safety for treatment.

"Turn here," Scar Face said. He gestured toward a small trail leading into the forest. "This should be it."

The driver down-shifted the Range Rover into four wheel drive and turned down the trail which was still muddy from the recent rains. There was grumbling from the man bouncing along in the back seat holding an AK-47. He had been sent on the trip as a bodyguard. But Scar Face knew he was really the money guard. Also in the back seat was a large metal Halliburton suitcase filled with ten million U.S. dollars. The Emir respected Scar Face but trusted no one, especially with such a large amount of cash.

They soon exited the forest and entered a clearing exposing a farm house with an old barn off to the side. Everything looked deserted. They sat in silence surveying the situation for a moment before Scar Face stepped out of the Range Rover and walked toward the front door. Before he reached the front porch steps, the silence was broken by a low screeching noise from the direction of the barn. The door swung open, straining against the rusty hinges.

A small man in a dark green uniform stepped into view. A sudden chill ran down Scar Face's spine at the sight of a Soviet style uniform, and he felt the urge to kill again. Not now. Be calm. There's other work to be done here. When the man in the uniform took another step into the daylight, Scar Face recognized Ille Ivanov from the pictures he had been shown.

Ivanov had been a general in the army of the former Soviet Union. When the cold war ended and the Nuclear Reduction Treaty was implemented, Ivanov was given the demoralizing task of accounting for, disarming, and destroying all designated nuclear weapons in the southern half of the Soviet Union. He had made no secret of his disappointment of the fact all of these powerful armaments would be destroyed and never make a beautiful mushroom cloud. Maybe not all of them.

After the breakup of the Soviet Union, Ivanov had been appointed as the chief of all armed forces of Uzbekistan, a position which did little to assuage his disenchantment. Moreover, his greed and hunger for power were without boundaries.

"You have no luggage," Ivanov said. He spoke in broken Arabic, peering at Scar Face and the Range Rover. He knew it was the party he was expecting because in the windshield of the Range Rover were two signs. One sign said "PRESS", and the smaller one said "AL JEZEERA," precisely as the guard had relayed to Ivanov from the checkpoint at Termiz.

"It's in the car," Scar Face said. He motioned for the bodyguard to bring the Halliburton.

"You bring it," Ivanov said. "Only you, the others stay in the vehicle."

Scar Face appeared uneasy. Ivanov knew he had no choice but to obey. One wrong move would be his last. A Soviet General would never allow himself to be vulnerable.

"The Director sends his greetings," Scar Face said. He approached the barn door where Ivanov stood.

"Please give him my warmest regards," Ivanov said. Scar Face returned a suspicious smile.

"Don't you have something for me?"

"Here, on the workbench," Ivanov said. He motioned for Scar Face to follow him to the counter built against the inside wall of the barn. He flipped a light switch. A single bare light bulb dangling from a cobweb shrouded cord illuminated a small aluminum suitcase resting on a blanket. Ivanov knew Scar Face could see the group of armed men huddled in the shadows. He placed the large silver Halliburton on the counter beside the smaller one and flipped it open, exposing the cash. Ivanov opened the smaller case. Both men looked at each other and smiled.

"How does it work?" Scar Face asked.

"Just a key and a code. Here's the key, and the code is Chairman Lenin's birthday: 04221870." Ivanov pointed to a slot in the device and handed him what looked like an ordinary credit card with the usual magnetic stripe on the back. Scar face nodded he understood and zipped the card into his fanny pack.

"Do you need instructions?" Scar Face asked.

"No, I know how to spend money," Ivanov said. "I think I'll go to Disney World." He paused for a wry smile. "That is, unless you're going to Disney World."

"No, I'm not going to Disney World," Scar Face said. He laughed and closed the small case and carried it to the Range Rover. He appeared anxious to begin the journey which would take him halfway around the world.

Chapter 25

Monday, November 19 (Moon in Capricorn) There's more to a Trojan horse than meets the eye. Employ all senses to seek the truth. A craft is crafted on experience. What's easy on the eyes is often expensive.

Jason was both excited and apprehensive having Annabelle Duquemin occupying the seat next to him at the poker table. He was excited because he had been intrigued with her from the first moment he saw her on TV. He was reminded of that when he saw the gold bracelet she was wearing on her left wrist, indicating she was a World Series of Poker Champion.

Jason was concerned because he had such a great player sitting behind him in the clockwise rotation of the game. He felt extremely vulnerable, and not just because of his table position. He realized most of the players in the high-limit games were not only skilled at poker and liked to gamble but also had the bankrolls to back them up. If there were such a thing as a comfort zone at a poker table, this was not it; not for Jason, not now.

Annabelle occasionally traded quips with some of the others at the table, but, for the most part, she just sat there and smiled. At least she always flashed a quick smile when she caught Jason looking at her, which was often. She also smiled when she raked in a winning pot, which was also often. Jason felt increasingly intimidated. He wasn't only afraid of losing money. He also didn't want to embarrass himself in the presence of this poker star, this very attractive poker star.

Jason didn't play a hand for what seemed like an eternity. He couldn't catch any suitable cards with which he felt like he could jump into this game. Finally, he limped in from the small blind with ace, ten, off suit. It would be nice to see a flop.

"Raise," Annabelle said. She pushed in thirty dollars from her position in the big blind.

Two others, who had previously called, folded and the action was back on Jason. What was she doing? Was she protecting her blind or did she have a legitimate hand? Oh, well, Jason thought, it's only money.

"Call," he said. He tossed in thirty more dollars in chips.

The flop was ace, ten, ace. Wow! Jason thought. He leaned forward slightly and glanced down at his chips. He had flopped a full house. He wanted to be careful and not scare Annabelle out of the hand. Maybe he could trap her.

"Check," Jason said. He tried his best to appear dejected.

Annabelle smiled and quickly tapped the table indicating she was also checking. So much for entrapment.

The turn card was a three, which didn't matter at all to Jason because his hand was already made. He refused to look at Annabelle and slowly pushed sixty dollars worth of chips into the pot. Without saying a word, she tossed her cards into the muck. Jason made a monster hand but didn't make any real money because no one would call his bet. Did she not have any cards worthy of a call, or did she sense she would be walking onto a trap?

One thing Jason noticed about the poker superstar was when she was in the game after the river card, the last card turned face up in the game, she usually won the money. Maybe she was having a lucky day. Some of these professional gamblers are lucky most of the time.

The afternoon dragged on while Jason watched his stack of chips dwindle. He won an occasional pot, but was down several hundred dollars. Jason peeked at his hole cards to find suited connectors, the nine and ten of diamonds. Maybe it's time for my luck to change.

"Call," Jason said. He was sitting on the button after everyone else folded around to him. He confidently pushed thirty dollars of chips into the pot.

Annabelle limped in from the small blind, and the guy to her left in the big blind tapped the table, indicating a check. The flop was the two of hearts and the jack and queen of diamonds. Jason had flopped an open-ended straight flush draw. How sweet was that?

"Thirty", Annabelle said. She beamed the usual infectious smile. Was she also on a flush draw or even a straight draw? Did she pair something? She certainly would not have limped in if she had started with a pair. It didn't matter. No one can throw away an open-ended straight flush draw.

"Call," Jason said. The big blind had already mucked his cards.

The turn card was the six of spades. No help.

"Sixty," Annabelle said. She slid a stack of chips forward.

This girl doesn't let up, Jason thought. How could the six of spades have helped her? It doesn't matter what she has, it won't beat a straight flush.

Jason firmly plopped his chips into the pot. "Call, he said.

The river brought the ace of clubs and another sixty dollar bet from Annabelle. Now Jason was in a real quandary. He didn't make his straight flush or a flush or even a straight for that matter. He had nothing and he had pumped all that money into the pot. Maybe Annabelle didn't have a very strong hand and could be bluffed. Maybe the ace on the river would make her think he had aces again. After all, she had folded when he bet at her with the full house of aces. It might work.

"One twenty!" Jason said. His bravado was louder than usual as he firmly planted two stacks of chips on the table in front of him. He had doubled Annabelle's bet on a stone cold bluff. He stared at her, as if daring her to call.

"Call," she said. She flashed another smile.

Jason knew he had been had, when he turned over his cards. Annabelle won the pot with a pair of jacks, turning over the ten and jack of clubs.

"Don't you know it's not nice to steal?" she said. She appeared to enjoy teasing Jason while she raked in the chips.

"I do now," Jason said. He wondered how she could call his raise with only a pair of jacks, especially with two over-cards on the board. She never appeared to consider his having an ace or even a queen in his hand. How did she know? Could she tell?

It was as if Annabelle was conducting a poker clinic the way she was dominating the table. Jason was enjoying her performance but was not sure he could afford the lesson.

"I think it's dinner time," Jason said to the other players. He picked up his few remaining chips, having no need for a rack to carry them. "Good luck, everyone."

Jason knew he had a lot to learn about the game, so he wasn't really discouraged by today's performance. Well, maybe a little. At least he knew enough to walk away when he was having a bad day, rather than continue to send good money after bad.

The first swig of Coors Light on draft went down easily for Jason while he settled into a small booth in the back of Jasmine. He told the waitress he needed a few more minutes to decide on his entrée. What he really wanted was a little time to nurse his brew and unwind and reflect on his experience at the table.

Jason heard footsteps behind him.

"Would you allow me to buy you dinner?" a female voice asked.

Chapter 26

Monday, November 19 (Moon in Capricorn) Be still thine heart. Lessons learned, no matter the pain, are lessons learned. Dinner is a treat. Scorpio rules.

Jason was surprised to be looking directly into the emerald blue eyes of Annabelle Duquemin. Not wanting to exhibit poor manners, he rose to his feet.

"Oh! Were you expecting someone?" Annabelle asked. She sensed Jason's awkwardness.

"No, no. Please join me," Jason said. He stepped around the table to pull out her chair.

"I'm Annabelle Duquemin," she said. She extended her hand and put him at ease with her alluring smile. "My friends call me Belle."

"I know," Jason said. He couldn't hide his blush. "I'm Jason Lancer. Jay Lancer."

Jason held her firm handshake a moment longer than necessary, trying to decide if his heart was racing because of electricity or chemistry. Whatever it was, he liked the feeling.

"It's very generous of you to offer to buy me dinner with my own money," Jason said.

"Oh, I would never spend your money on dinner. Actually, I'm going to let Fred buy dinner for both of us." She flashed the comp card Fred had given her from the poker room.

"That's wonderful. Fred seems like a very nice guy."

"That's funny. That's exactly what he said about you."

"You asked him about me?"

"Sure, you were the only one at the table I hadn't seen before, so I asked Fred who's the cop at position four."

"You're kidding."

"My exact words," Belle said. Her smirk indicated she knew she had nailed him. "Are you a cop?"

"Not exactly. I was with the FBI, but not anymore."

"Oh, FBI. I guess I should apologize for trying to demote you to a cop."

"Not at all. Have gun, wear badge, chase bad guys. It doesn't matter what they call you. It's all good." When Jason spoke the words he felt a pang of uncertainty about where he was and what he was doing there. Was he going to be able to continue down this new career path? Maybe Clayton's comment about renting for a week was more truth than humor. Or maybe he was still tilting from the costly decisions he had made at the poker table.

"Isn't an FBI agent just a rich man's cop?"

"Maybe, and you knew right away. But, how could you tell?"

"'Telling' is what I do best."

Every minute Jason spent with Annabelle Duquemin only confirmed he was dealing with a rare and special person.

"So you knew I had aces full."

"Yes."

"And you also knew I didn't hit my flush."

"Absolutely. I can read you like a book, Jay."

I can read you like a book, cutie pie. The words spoken by his mother on the last day of her life reverberated in Jason's mind. Was this the basis for his attraction to this girl? She was attractive and loved poker. Is this someone he should like, someone who reminds him of his mother and reads him like a book? In any case, it's hard to fight the power of chemistry or electricity or whatever it is.

"So if you can read me, the others can also."

"Sure, at least the better players can."

Jason felt very discouraged. It was as if he was driving down a road where he thought he knew his way, and suddenly realized he was lost. The first instinct is to quickly turn around and find familiar territory.

"It looks like I should stick to chasing bad guys," Jason said.

"Oh, don't be so hard on yourself." She gave him a sympathetic look. "So where are you based with the FBI?" She asked, trying to change the subject.

"I'm no longer with the Bureau."

Belle stared quizzically.

"It's a long story," Jason finally said. "I'd rather not get into it."

"Works for me, Jay," Belle said. She reached across the table and placed her hand on his. More electricity.

Chapter 27

Friday, January 11 (Moon in Sagittarius to Capricorn 12:18 p.m.)
An important journey continues. Confidences must be guarded.
Dinner may prove unsettling.

The night was dark and the sea was choppy with swells from four to six feet from a west wind on the lower side of a low pressure area centered over the Gulf of Mexico. The tiny shrimper tossed about with the salty old captain, Pablo Mendez, wrestling the tiller to maintain his course.

Pablo Mendez had enjoyed a good life in Castro's Cuba, having distinguished himself during the Bay of Pigs invasion. He had been a young gunner on a gunboat patrolling the northern coast. Soon after the attack began, his captain and the two other crewmembers were killed by a grenade launched from an insurgent's boat. Pablo assumed command, steering the craft and firing the bow-mounted machine gun. He promptly sank the intruder's boat and raked the surface with bullets until there was no longer life in the life jackets. His actions made him a favorite with Castro, and especially with his brother Raul. Since then, he had been allowed to own his own boat and had become a successful shrimp fisherman.

On occasion through the years, Pablo was given the opportunity to do a 'favor' for the government. The extra money was good and he was always honored to be of service. Tonight, however, the old Captain seemed uncertain about his assignment. The request was easy enough. He had been asked to take a passenger across the Yucatan Channel and deliver him to a charter boat near the coast of Mexico, north of Cancun, and far enough south of Brownsville, Texas, so as not to raise the suspicions of the U.S. Coast Guard.

Pablo appeared noticeably concerned about his passenger. According to Raul's friend, who always asked him to do these 'favors,' he was supposed to be some low-level diplomat. Maybe Pablo couldn't figure out why a diplomat would do a night crossing into Mexico on a shrimper rather than on an airplane? Maybe it was the wrinkled suit or the fanny pack he was wearing. A diplomat wearing a fanny pack? Perhaps it was the shiny piece of luggage he was clutching as if it were handcuffed to his wrist. Or was it the vicious scar on the right side of his face and neck which his scraggly black beard could not cover? When a person has the feeling something is wrong, there is usually something wrong. But Pablo pressed on. He was, after all, performing a favor for his government, which had been good to him.

This was the part of the journey Scar Face dreaded the most, and not because he was afraid of being detected, captured, or shot. He could deal with that. His greatest fear, motion sickness, was weighing heavily on his mind. And with each pitch of the boat, it was beginning to weigh heavily on his stomach. Being from a part of the world covered with sand, rocks and mountains, Scar Face had been in a boat on only a few occasions, and had never been out to sea.

Scar Face was becoming leery of the frequent stares he was getting from Pablo Mendez. The only light in the small wheelhouse was from the minuscule peanut lights of the compass and tachometer, and from the cigarette which perpetually hung from the side of Pablo's mouth. Still, he could see the subtle glances.

The El Viajante Special, Palomino steak with zesty marinade and diced onions, the plantains, and the black beans and rice Scar Face had gobbled down in Havana, were rebelling against him. The cabin was devoid of conversation, perhaps because the two men could share only a few words of English. The only sounds were the constant hum of the diesel engine and the monotonous lapping of the waves against the sides of the boat.

The Director had arranged passage for Scar Face from Bagdad to Havana as an Iraqi diplomat with full diplomatic immunity. Therefore, Iraqi and Cuban officials would examine only his papers and would not be allowed to search his person or his luggage.

Scar Face knew he could delay it no longer. He grabbed the Halliburton, burst out of the wheelhouse, and with two quick steps reached the side of the boat. Gripping the railing with one hand and the Halliburton with the other, he thrust his head over the side, feeding El Viajante's special to the fish. He emptied his stomach and heaved some more.

"Better now, my friend?" Pablo asked. Scar Face stumbled back into the wheel house, wiping his mouth on the sleeve of his suit.

"Better now," Scar Face said. He was embarrassed but surprised at how quickly he really did feel better.

"Sleep, my friend, sleep," Pablo said. He pointed to a small space on the floor in the rear of the wheelhouse.

Knowing they had several hours before reaching the coast and with a renewed sense of well-being, Scar Face succumbed to the rigors of the days of travel. He stretched out on the floor and with a hand on his fanny pack and his head on the Halliburton, he fell asleep.

In what seemed like only a few minutes, Scar Face was awakened by the sound of the engine slowing. In reality, he had slept for several hours and they were approaching what looked like a small sport-fishing boat. He stood up and unzipped the fanny pack attached to his waist.

The old captain, weary from the long journey, maneuvered the shrimper alongside the sleek sport- fisherman.

"Who goes there?" Scar Face shouted in Arabic.

"The defenders of Islam!" One of the men answered in perfect Arabic across the transom of the sport-fisherman.

Perfect. Scar Face felt relieved when he recognized the unmistakable voice from the other boat.

"Muchas gracias, my friend," Pablo said. He extended his hand to Scar Face, grateful to have completed his mission.

"Have a pleasant journey." Scar Face smiled and extended his hand.

In the predawn light the old captain could not see the hand Scar Face was extending was not the hand of friendship.

Pablo Mendez was dead before he hit the deck falling backwards into the wheel house.

Scar Face methodically replaced the handgun in the fanny pack and retrieved the mini-grenade with the five minute time delayed detonator. Before zipping the fanny pack he fingered the contents to make sure everything was there.

Scar Face pulled the pin on the grenade and dropped it into the hatch containing the fuel tanks. With a tight grip on the Halliburton, he bounded over the side of the shrimper to his friends in the other boat.

"Abdul, my brother," Scar Face said. They embraced with a hug.

"My brother, God is great! Do you have everything?"

"Everything!"

"Including the instructions?"

"Everything," Scar Face said. He patted his fanny pack and triumphantly held up the Halliburton. Then he turned to the other man. "Ali, my brother!"

Ali hugged him tightly and whispered into his ear, "God is great, my brother, God is great."

Those were the last words Scar Face would ever hear. When Ali embraced him, Abdul fired a small caliber hollowpoint bullet into the base of his skull with one hand and grabbed the Halliburton with the other.

Ali cut the strap to retrieve the fanny pack. Together the al Din brothers heaved Scar Face back into the shrimper and sped away toward the coast. They never looked back when they heard the thunderous explosion.

Chapter 28

Saturday, January 12 (Moon in Capricorn) Keep your affairs in order, especially affairs of the heart. Commitment to cause bears fruit. A masterpiece was once a clean slate. Scorpio impresses.

"Right turn ahead," the female voice said.

Jason tapped the brakes to disengage Pearl's cruise control and glanced down at the moving map of the navigation system.

"Turn right," the voice instructed. Jason veered onto the US 95 exit ramp. "Left turn ahead."

Jason smiled to himself and piloted Pearl onto Nevada 157, Kyle Canyon Road, and started the climb up Mt. Charleston. He had not been to Mt. Charleston before but had heard some of the poker players talking about a fabulous restaurant and lodge near the top of the mountain. He had not used Pearl's navigation system since arriving in Vegas and was amused at how the female voice always reminded him of Cassie. He recalled how she would often sit in the passenger seat with a map and bark out directions when they were chasing bad guys back in D.C. Did he miss those times? Maybe. Did he miss Cassie? Absolutely. He missed her professionalism and self-confidence on the job. And off the job, he missed everything about her, especially her body and the incredible sex it provided. Fading memories, Jason thought, mercifully fading memories.

Jason looked in awe at the picturesque vista of the valley behind him when he climbed the winding road. The lights of the strip were beginning to invade the twilight while the setting sun dipped behind the top of the mountain. To the east, Lake Mead sprawled toward the horizon like a turn of the last century Charles Partridge Adams landscape. Equally surreal was the ever present string of lights dotting the sky from beyond Hoover Dam down to McCarran Airport. Air traffic was almost back to normal following the aftermath of nine-eleven.

Jason recycled the events of the day, beginning with his morning ritual.

Libra. September 23-October 22. Explore new horizons. If opportunity knocks, answer. Listen to music, dance; loosen the strings of your heart.

After eating his oatmeal, Jason had pushed aside the newspaper and quickly shuffled the tarot deck three times. After cutting the cards he flipped the top card over exposing The Star: a naked woman on bended knee pouring water into a rippling pool and onto the earth while she meditates. What does this mean? Was he a star? Was he meeting a star? Once again the combination of the horoscope and tarot left Jason confused as to what to do. When that happened he did nothing but remain vigilant and watch events while they unfolded.

After breakfast, Jason had walked over to the Bellagio where Fred had an immediate opening in the 60-120 game. The usual sharks were there, local pros out to make their daily bread, along with a couple of whales from back east. Jason had thought a lot about what Belle Duquemin had told him when they had dinner during the holidays. He knew he had to get with the program if he were to have any chance at all of surviving as a poker player. He was trying very hard not to give away the strength of his hands. And also he was beginning to study other players for "tells." There was so much to learn, so many aspects of the game Jason had never considered before.

Jason had played for a couple of hours and was down a few hundred for the day when he noticed Belle had entered the room and was watching him from an unoccupied table nearby. He smiled. She smiled. Jason was on the button. Looking at his hole cards he found the eight and nine of diamonds, suited connectors. He raised, thinking if someone called, he at least had a respectable drawing hand. And if no one called, he would wind up stealing the blinds, which is exactly what happened.

While Jason gathered and stacked his chips, he got a big smile and a thumbs-up from Belle. He pushed back from the table to take a break and walked over to where she was sitting.

"Nice move," she said. "But I told you it's not nice to steal."

"I wasn't stealing," Jason said. "I had suited connectors."

"Like I said, it's not nice to steal," she said with a giggle. "Hey, how about dinner?"

"How about lunch?" Jason asked? He looked at his watch to see it was almost noon.

"No, I can't today, but I'm good for dinner."

"Sure. Jasmine?" Jason asked. He thought about the comp meals provided by Fred.

"No, Mt. Charleston," Belle said. She wrote an address on a napkin. "Do you need directions?"

"I think I can find it."

"I thought you could," Belle said. She beamed the usual smile as she walked away. "See you at seven."

"Approaching destination," the female voice had monotoned, bringing Jason back into the moment. He was surprised to be arriving at his destination so soon, because he was only half-way up the mountain, nowhere near the mountaintop lodge. He checked the address Belle had given him to make sure he had entered it properly into the system. He had.

When Jason rounded a hairpin turn, he was headed straight into a driveway which stretched through a gate and down to a flat lot whittled into the side of the mountain. The area was covered with juniper, aspen, and Ponderosa pines. At the very back of the lot, a chalet style bungalow perched on the edge of the cliff. On the post which held the mailbox there was a picture of two queens, the queen of hearts and the queen of diamonds. This must be the place, Jason thought. He shifted Pearl into four-wheel drive and traversed the gravel road down to the bungalow.

When Jason exited the car, the entire world seemed at peace. The quiet was disturbed only by a lone woodpecker calling in the distance. When he closed the car door, a large dog barked and bounded off the porch toward him.

"Whoa, big fella!" Jason said with all the firm friendliness he could muster. He knew from growing up on a farm that if a dog charged you, and you showed any signs of being afraid, you were about to be bitten. On the other hand, if you were firm, yet friendly, the dog would usually acquiesce and make nice.

"Nice boy," Jason said. He slowly extended his hand toward the huge black Labrador retriever. "I mean, nice girl," he quickly added, noticing it was a female. The dog sniffed, and licked his hand and within moments they were best friends, with Jason rubbing her head and massaging her ears.

"Hi there," Belle called. She came around the deck from the back. "I see you found it."

"Of course, never in doubt."

"And you've already met my roommate."

"Your roommate?"

"Yes, your new best friend there is Duchess," Belle said. She reached down and gave her a pat on the neck. "Some kind of watchdog you've turned out to be." Then to Jason she said, "Although, she usually is a good judge of character."

"I'm glad Duchess thinks I'm a character," Jason said.

"Come on in." Belle led the way into the bungalow.

Jason followed her though the door into a great room which encompassed the living room, an entertainment area, and kitchen. Although the décor was a decorative dichotomy, it worked very well. The furniture and the walls were rustic western wood, while the rugs and accessories were the pastels of country French. The back of the room was all sliding glass doors leading onto a lower deck, providing an incredible long mountain view of Mt. Charleston to the south and the city of Las Vegas to the southeast.

"What could I get you to drink?"

"Anything wet. A beer would be great."

When Belle walked toward the kitchen, Jason noted how well she looked in her faded, tight-fitting jeans. He tried not to stare when she returned with a Corona, but he couldn't help noticing how she filled out the light blue cashmere sweater. Jason couldn't decide if she looked better coming or going.

"Come outside with me. I need to check the ribs."

Jason followed her, and noticed a picture on a lamp table of Belle in the arms of a young man. He wondered who it was, but didn't ask.

Jason stepped out onto the deck to the sounds of Bobby Darin's "Mac the Knife" emanating from the outside speakers. He was surprised to see a bright fire in a fire pit in the center of the deck, providing a buffer from the chill of the mountain air. A screen covered the blaze to prevent escaping embers from being a fire hazard.

"I hope you like baby-backs," Belle said.

"Ummm! My favorite. Wow! Does that smell good," Jason breathed the aroma from the barbeque grill. "What's your secret?"

"Low heat, long time," Belle said. She raised the lid of the grill. "And lots of secret sauce." She painted the baby-backs with a layer of mystery paste from a large bowl. With the adroitness of a veteran short order cook, she stirred the baked beans simmering in an iron skillet and rolled the ears of corn which were cooking in tin foil.

A table was set in the corner of the deck, complete with a white tablecloth, fine china and silver. Two candles glowed from antique candelabras, illuminating an already breathing bottle of Kendall Jackson Merlot which protruded from a centerpiece of small flowers.

Jason began to get a feel for what this girl was all about. The décor, the table setting, the menu, were all a mixture of contrasting styles like a Western shabby chic'. Rustic, yet elegant. Rustic elegance. Unusual and very refreshing.

Jason assumed the address Belle had given him was for the restaurant at the lodge on Mt. Charleston. He had no idea she lived on the mountain. And then to go to all this trouble. She seemed to think of everything. Jason wondered, did she really think of everything?

Chapter 29

Saturday, January 12 (Moon in Capricorn) Be receptive to wise counsel. Your life can change in the skip of a heartbeat. A violin played as a fiddle is no less beautiful. Life is a gamble. Take a chance.

Conversation was very easy and natural with Belle. Even though she would occasionally lob in a zinger, she always followed it with a disarming smile. Jason liked the repartee with women who have the self confidence for jousting. Not many do.

"So how did you do today?" Belle asked. She attended to the grill and the needs of the meal. "Did you get 'em?"

"No, they got me again," After a long silence, Jason said, "I couldn't catch any cards."

"Well, at the money level you're playing now, you really don't need any cards."

"What do you mean?"

"Don't get me wrong. It's nice to make a hand now and then, but the cards aren't nearly as important as the people. Over the long haul, no matter how many bad beats it seems like you're taking, the cards will average out. So, like I told you that night at the restaurant, the bottom line of your bank account depends on your ability read people."

"You mean like you 'read me like a book.'"

"Exactly. But you have to allow me to do that."

Jason was impressed with Belle's grasp of the game, and grateful she was sharing it with him. Even though he felt a little foolish and inadequate, he knew he was getting a lesson in poker here that would cost him a fortune to learn at the tables.

"Whether you know it or not," Belle continued, "you are always 'telling' your opponents whether your hand is weak or strong. So you must discipline your actions at the table so you act the same way every time, regardless of whether you have rags or rockets. Basically, it comes down to this: if I know you are weak, it doesn't matter what cards I have; if I place a large bet, you will most likely fold. So the only pots you win are the ones in which you have a strong hand. And even then you don't win much, because I can 'tell' you have good cards, and, therefore, I will fold."

"I never really thought of it that way," Jason said.

"So, can't you FBI guys always tell if someone is telling the truth?"

"Absolutely, if we hook them up to a polygraph machine."

"Then playing poker should be easy for you. All you have to do is continually give everyone at the table a polygraph test, without the machine."

Belle moved the corn-on-the-cobs to the warming rack.

"Piece of cake," Jason said. He knew it really wasn't. Finally he asked, "So what are these 'tells' you look for?"

"First of all, a poker player is always trying to portray his hand the opposite of what it really is. So the first basic 'tell' is if he acts strong, he's weak, and vice versa."

Belle discussed with Jason some of the more obvious "tells" of poker and how to take advantage of them. She included the importance of body language, facial expressions, especially the eyes, the manner in which they bet, conversation and others sounds, shrugs, etc. They also talked about 'actors' at the table who try to give you false tells, and how to detect and deal with them.

"Thanks for the education," Jason said, when they were about to sit down for dinner. "But why are you helping me?"

"I guess I've always had a soft spot in my heart for G-men."

"You mean FBI guys?"

"No, guys who lose a grand a day."

"I don't lose a grand a day," Jason said. He secretly knew, however, that lately it wasn't far from the truth.

"Just kidding, Jay. Just kidding," Belle said.

The ribs tasted every bit as good as they smelled and the accompanying corn-on-the-cob, baked beans, and cole slaw were scrumptious. Sinatra was singing "New York, New York" while Jason freshened the fire, although the merlot did not disappoint and was providing plenty of warmth of its own. Belle stepped into the kitchen and returned with a crystal tumbler filled with Breyers' coffee ice cream, covered with toasted shredded coconut and splashed with Kahlua.

"Are you chilly?" Jason asked. He couldn't help but notice the obvious protrusions through her cashmere sweater. He was embarrassed that his downward glances had not gone unnoticed.

"No, I'm just happy to see you," Belle said, doing her best Mae West impersonation. She clinched her arms together to stave off the shivers, which only accentuated the obvious.

Ever the gentleman, Jason took off his denim jacket and stepped around the table toward Belle.

"Here, this might help." He placed his jacket around her shoulders and found he had no desire to remove his arms. He pulled her gently to him. She offered no resistance and slowly melted into his chest.

"I'm feeling warm already," Belle said. She placed her arms around his waist and held him closer, pressing the endowments of her blue cashmere against his body.

Sinatra switched to "All the Way," which didn't give Jason any ideas he didn't already have. They started to gradually sway to the music. When he placed his cheek against the top of her head, he inhaled the aroma of her hair, something like Herbal Essence with a strong hint of smoked barbeque. Very apropos.

Within moments and without warning, Jason felt the firmness in his groin expanding uncomfortably against the buttons of his jeans. He knew Belle was feeling him against her firm abs, and she began applying some pressure of her own, with every beat of the music.

"I'd say you're happy to see me, too," Belle said, Mae West again.

Sinatra crooned to another song, but Jason was no longer aware of the music. He was tuned in only to Belle as she turned her mouth upwards to his, lips slightly parted. They kissed. Their tongues were in each other's mouth, searching, yearning. Jason wasn't quite sure who was leading this dance, but soon they had sashayed and kissed their way inside the house, through the great room, and into the master bedroom, dropping the denim jacket along the way.

They were still kissing and gasping for breath when they reached the plush king-size bed with Belle tearing at the buttons on Jason's plaid flannel shirt while he was exploring her back, confirming his earlier thoughts that she was sans bra. When she unfastened the last button, Jason pulled the blue cashmere sweater over her head, threw it into the corner along with his shirt, and dropped his jeans and underwear, kicking them to the side of the room. He was staring at her like a deer caught in headlights, and, in this case, the headlights were a couple of more than ample breasts, with nipples still erect and pointing slightly upward. Belle didn't notice because she was gazing at his impressive appendage, standing at full attention, now that it was finally freed from his tight jeans.

"I sure hope you're not bluffing, Jason said.

"Bluffing? I'm gonna put you 'all in.'"

And she did.

Duchess, who was curled up in the corner, lifted her head and began whimpering, showing concern,

"It's okay, Duchess," Belle said. She was trying to catch her breath, lying quietly on Jason. "I won."

"If that's losing, I don't ever want to win, "Jason whispered.

"I think maybe we chopped that one."

"If you say so. I don't remember much of what happened."

"Here's what happened. We both anted up; you had big slick and I had a pair of queens," Belle said. She pointed to the small queen of hearts and queen of diamonds tattoo she had, one on each cheek, at the top of her buttocks. "After the flop, you pushed with big slick and I came over the top with my queens and you smooth called. When you saw the turn, I knew you were pot committed, and put you all in. We both got there on the river and chopped the pot. What do you think?"

"I think I like this passion poker," Jason said.

"Yea, me too."

Over objections from Belle, Jason brought everything in from the deck and helped with the dishes. It was late and he knew he should be going. He didn't want to wear out his welcome, or anything else. Belle was beginning to look very intriguing again in those jeans and that sweater.

Standing by the sliding glass doors in the great room, they kissed. Duchess came in and rubbed her head against Jason's leg.

"Nice meeting you, girl," Jason said. He reached down and rubbed her neck and ears. He noticed a small tag on her collar depicting the queen of hearts and the queen of diamonds. "Hope to see you again soon, Miss Queen of Hearts."

"Wow! How did you know?" Belle asked.

"Well, you're both sweethearts, but I have a feeling you like diamonds better than she does," Jason said.

"Great read. I think you have potential here."

"I'll be playing at the Bellagio tomorrow. Will you be there?"

"No, I'm in a tournament at the Mirage, but I'll come by to check on you if I can."

"Thanks. And thanks for an unforgettable evening."

Jason kissed her softly on the lips again and reached down to give Duchess another pat on the head. When he did, his eyes were drawn to the picture on the table. Belle hesitated for a moment.

"That's my fiancé," she said.

Chapter 30

Sunday, January 13 (Moon in Capricorn to Aquarius 9:41 p.m.) Concede not to boundaries. There's no hill that can't be climbed. Be wary of water sports. Cancer lends support.

The Milky Way glittered the evening sky. It was the type of South Texas night which was a threat to inexperienced aviators because it is difficult to discern the horizon. With the bright stars above and the burn-off fires from the natural gas wells below, it is easy to become confused; the sky and the ground look the same. More than one pilot has paid the ultimate price after becoming spatially disoriented on nights such as this.

According to the World Almanac, the nights at this time of the month are supposed to be dark, with the moon nowhere in sight. Still, the stars provided enough light allowing the two dark figures wading in the river to be easily seen.

"Do you think there are alligators in this river?" Ali asked. "There were monsters in Florida. Remember when we were there and the alligator ate the schoolboy?"

"Shhhh! Stop it Ali. Do you think if there were alligators in this river the Americans would be talking about building a fence? Be quiet and listen for trucks and helicopters."

Abdul, with the Halliburton resting on his head, followed closely behind Ali. If they happened upon a deep hole or an underwater log, Ali would take the fall and Abdul and the silver suitcase would remain safe.

Moments later the brothers were back in the USA, sloshing northward out of the Rio Grande, a few miles southwest of McAllen, Texas. When the sand firmed beneath their feet, they began jogging towards the cover of the mesquite forest.

Suddenly they heard the sound of an engine.

"Is that a boat on the river?" Ali asked.

"No. It sounds like a motorcycle," Abdul said. He peered to his left as the noise grew louder. "Hurry!"

They sprinted to the tree line and dove into the bushes. Ali retrieved a camouflaged cloth from the duffle bag he was carrying and spread it over them while they lay flat on the ground. This was a drill they had rehearsed many times in training. The noise grew even louder. The brothers, peeking from underneath the cloth, watched a Border Patrol Officer on an all-terrain vehicle zoom toward them. Had he seen them? He was scanning the bushes with a high beam spotlight. He passed them, stopped suddenly, and turned off his engine and his light. Abdul knew what he had to do, and already his finger was tightening on the trigger of his weapon.

The next minute seemed like an eternity. They heard the officer close the lid on his cigarette lighter and exhale his first drag. The next sound was the unmistakable pattering of piss pooling in the sand. Was he showing disrespect, or was he really unaware of their presence? Abdul thought about shooting the infidel in the gonads, just because he could. Although since becoming the keeper of the Halliburton, he was trying to keep things more on an even keel.

Fortunately for the officer, he zipped his pants and was on his way, not knowing he had been given a new lease on life.

Abdul huddled quietly beside his brother in the sand for a few minutes. What strange turn of events had brought him to this point lying in the sand soaking wet, listening to frogs and worrying about alligators and snakes? He was especially concerned about the snake called the sidewinder, an ill-tempered rattler which leaves a series of arcs in the sand rather than the usual slithering curves.

I should not even be here, Abdul thought. Long ago he should have been with the virgins, in the splendid way of Muhammad and the others on that glorious day when buildings collapsed and infidels died by weapons of their own making. Abdul became excited thinking about it, although he was ashamed he had failed the Emir.

"Be not dismayed," the Director had consoled Abdul in the message left on his special private number in Dharma. The phone line had been established as a last resort for the brothers should they be out of contact with the network. A call was placed to a number in Paris, which forwarded the call to Dharma. The recording, while not the voice of the Director, contained the words of the Director. "It is the will of Allah that you give yourself and your service to an even more glorious cause. Go to Mexico . . ."

The message had instructed the brothers to cross the border into Mexico and proceed south to meet Scar Face and receive the ultimate gift. They were ordered to receive the gift and then pre-martyr Scar Face, because his identity was known by the former Russian general. Scar Face was the only person able to connect them to the ultimate gift, one of the few nuclear weapons secured by the network. Abdul was grateful for the confidence placed in him by the assignment of the new mission. Lying in the wet sand, he wondered if someone at this moment was planning a pre-martyr event for him. Surely not. "I have the greatest respect for you, my brothers," the message had said. "You will be the greatest of all martyrs."

Chapter 31

Sunday, January 13 (Moon in Capricorn to Aquarius 9:41 p.m.) Narrow escapes lead to broad horizons. Restraint can be the strongest force. Schedules should be maintained.

Fortunately for the brothers, the night was cool as they scurried northward away from the Rio Grande. Their clothes had dried from the crossing but were soaked again with sweat. In the distance they could hear occasional traffic on a highway they were approaching. Abdul knew it had to be US 83, which paralleled the border between Rio Grande City and McAllen, Texas.

Abdul retrieved a cell phone from a waterproof bag in his fanny pack and turned it on. Almost immediately it had a signal and he dialed a number.

"We're here. Thirty minutes? Everything OK? Yes, I have the money. Hurry. We're hungry and thirsty."

Abdul had contracted with a one-stop, full service smuggler to pay twenty-thousand for passage back and forth across the border to Mexico, as well as transportation to and from Cancun and the rental of the fishing boat. Abdul was holding out ten-thousand until the smuggler fulfilled his promise to pick them up in a car he had agreed to rent for them with the forged drivers license they provided him. So far, so good.

Traffic was light when they approached the highway, with a big semi going by every five or ten minutes. Ali took the red bandana from around his neck, tied it around a golf ball sized rock, and placed it in the middle of the eastbound lane of the highway. The brothers remained out of sight behind the mesquite bushes.

A large truck zoomed by, followed by a Winnebago camper going so fast it appeared as if he were trying to catch the speeding truck. After a few minutes, a car approached going no faster than the speed limit. When the lights of the car illuminated the red bandana, the brake lights came on and the car pulled over to the side of the road.

Abdul and Ali waited. When the car came to a complete stop, the lights flashed off and on twice.

"That's it. Let's go!" Abdul shouted.

The brothers ran to the car.

"Pop the trunk," Ali shouted to the driver. Abdul remained out of sight at the rear of the car. The trunk opened, and the Halliburton was inside the trunk before the one-stop smuggler could see it. Abdul grabbed the cooler out of the trunk and threw it into the back seat with Ali before jumping into the front seat with the smuggler. Ali opened the cooler and let out a howl!

"Beer or Gatorade?" Ali asked.

"Both!" Abdul shouted. He grabbed a Gatorade and swigged it down. "You're a good man, my friend, a good man," he said. He took a can of beer and rubbed it all over his head and the back of his neck, relishing the refreshing coolness of the can. "How did you know what I wanted?"

"As they say, this is not my first rodeo, my friend," the smuggler said in broken English.

"Rodeo?"

"Yea, rodeo."

"Oh! Yea, rodeo." Abdul said. He had not a clue what he was talking about.

They drove east for a few miles.

"You have the money?" The smuggler asked.

"I have the money," Abdul said. He felt his fanny pack and reached back for another beer from Ali.

They rode in silence for about half an hour. When they approached McAllen, the road changed to four lanes. The smuggler turned into a Motel 6, directly across the street from an all- night truck stop.

"This is where I leave you, my friend," the smuggler said. He glanced at Abdul, as he stopped the silver Toyota Camry in front of a room about halfway down the parking lot.

"Yes, I know," Abdul said. He felt for the zipper on his fanny pack and glanced back at Ali.

"My brother, pay the nice gentleman," Ali said. His voice was kind, but was accompanied by a stern look toward Abdul.

"I have rented this car for you. These are the keys. The rental agreement and your license are in the glove compartment. I have rented this room for you," the smuggler said. He was beginning to feel uncomfortable. "Here is the key. Could I please have my money?"

"Yes, you can," Abdul said. He unzipped his fanny pack and reached in, feeling the money, and also feeling his handgun.

A police cruiser drove into the parking lot and parked beside them on the driver's side. The officer was staring at them. Abdul glanced at the officer and looked back at Ali who was still giving him the evil eye. He pulled his hand from his fanny pack and thrust it at the smuggler.

"Thank you, my friend," Abdul said. He handed him a wrapped stack of one hundred dollar bills.

The smuggler quickly dropped the car keys on the seat and jumped into the police cruiser.

"Be careful, my friends," he shouted. The cruiser slowly backed away. "Have fun in Los Angeles."

Chapter 32

Monday, January 14 (Moon in Aquarius) Monetary matters rise to the surface. The learning curve tightens. Clouds fade to reveal a clearer picture. Pisces surprises.

The upper level room at the Bellagio was relatively quiet with only one table hosting a game. Jason sat down reluctantly because they were playing $100-$200, still a little rich for his blood. He was also wary of the game because he didn't know any of the players, except for Birmingham Bernie, whom he knew by reputation only.

Bernie was in the timber business in Alabama and a Vegas regular, frequenting the strip every month or so. He was a big man, whose stature appeared even larger because he always wore the same high-heeled cowboy boots and big black broad-brimmed hat. Fred said he had played some football for the Bear back in the late sixties. He also said not to fall for the Gomer Pyle character Bernie always played, because he could also play some very good poker.

"What 'chu got there son?" Bernie probed for information after the flop. He chomped an unlit cigar from the side of his mouth while he squinted sideways at Jason beneath the brim of his hat. As was his style, Jason remained silent and motionless, refusing to engage in repartee with the players during a hand. He was afraid he would give more tells than he would get from mixing it up with these old codgers.

Jason was sure he was second best in this hand. He had noticed in the short time he was at the table that the more Birmingham Bernie talked, the stronger was his hand. Jason was on the button and held the king and queen of diamonds before the flop. Bernie tossed in a raise after the obligatory soliloquy of syrupy slang. Jason really wanted to see a flop with his suited connectors, and he wasn't convinced Bernie wasn't trying to do a little blind stealing. The two others had folded, so Jason called. The flop was ace of diamonds, jack of clubs, and the eight of diamonds.

"I say, what 'chu got there son, a pair of mules?" Bernie asked. He stared first at the flop and then again at Jason, hinting Jason might have a pair of jacks. "I can't believe the frog-eye helped you. Maybe you got a little ole wallerhorn and a thousandleg in the hole and now you're trying to sweat out a little straight on me." Jason remained the frozen mute while Bernie recounted the possibilities of the hands Jason might hold, in a language which seemed foreign even to a born and raised Southerner. "Maybe you got yourself a little flush draw," Bernie continued. He had finally nailed Jason's hand. "One time I seen a man lose five sawmills drawing to straights and flushes," Bernie said. He paused to pontificate the moment. "Then he finally made one, and lost the other two. Two hunnerd!" Bernie splashed the pot with two black chips.

"Call." Jason's calm reply drew a sinister look from Bernie.

The turn card was the six of diamonds, giving Jason the nut flush. Jason didn't see the card hit the table because he was watching Bernie for a reaction.

"Hot dammit! Check. You're gonna call anyhow. Check!" Bernie said. He slapped the table with his hand.

"Check," Jason said.

"Sum bitch. I knew you were in there barefooted and I gave you a free card. Sum bitch!"

The river card was the two of spades, no apparent help to anyone.

"I can't believe I gave you a free card." Bernie continued to rant and slammed two hundred into the pot.

Jason sat quietly for a moment, elated that Birmingham Bernie had fallen into the trap. "Raise," he said finally. He slid four hundred into the pot.

"You messin' with me, son? If that black duck on the river helped you, I got 'chu beat. Four hunnered!"

Jason couldn't believe his good fortune. There was no pair on the board, so there was no possibility of a full house or four of a kind. A straight flush was not possible; therefore Jason's hand could not be beaten.

"Raise," Jason said. Again he pushed forward four hundred.

"Hot damn sum bitch!" Bernie shouted, throwing two hundred more into the pot and turning over a pair of jacks, giving him a set. "I'm holdin' trip mules from the turn. What I'm talkin' 'bout is Johnny J. Jones, and this shoe clerk runs me down with a flush and then traps me on the river." Bernie fumed to no one in particular.

Jason raked in his biggest pot of the day noting he was up over five thousand dollars. Meanwhile, Birmingham Bernie harangued on. "Can't protect your hand in this piss ant game. We need to play some real poker. How 'bout a thousand, two thousand? What the hell, how 'bout we play no limit?"

The dealer looked to Jason and the other players for objections and observed none. Jason had always wanted to try his hand at no limit Texas Hold 'em. No better time, he thought, than when he was on a hot streak and Bernie was on full tilt.

The dealer motioned for Fred, who came over to the table and announced a no limit game would start with a new dealer after a ten minute break. Jason turned to leave the table for the break and saw Belle walking in.

"Wow!" Belle said. She stared at his sizable chip stack. "Looks like you got lucky."

"Yes, I did," Jason said. "Last night!"

"Lucky you, lucky me." She grinned.

"How are you doing at the Mirage?"

"So far, so good. I'm playing tight right now to let the players thin out a little. I'll try to hang in there and start being more aggressive to accumulate chips later today or tomorrow as the blinds go up."

"What's the payout?"

"A million to the winner."

"Wow! Will I see you on TV?"

"Maybe, if I make the final table. What are you playing here, one, two hundred?"

"No, we switched to no-limit."

"Remember, no-limit is not so much about the cards as it is about the people. You've got to read 'em and not let them read you. Hey! I gotta run. Will I see you later?"

"I'm excited already." Jason gave her a sideways glance.

"I'll bet you are." Belle smiled and gazed below his belt.

Jason returned the smiled and then became somber.

"Belle, there's something I need to ask you."

"Yes?"

"The picture."

"You mean my fiancé?"

"Yes, I mean, you're not wearing a ring."

"It was five years ago, Jay. He died in a sky diving accident."

"I'm sorry."

"Thanks, but that's history. You have to play the cards you're dealt, and I've moved on," she said.

Jason nodded.

"Speaking of playing cards, I'm in a tournament. I'm out of here. Remember," she said, waving her finger from side to side as she turned to walk away, "No telling, Jay. No telling."

Jason watched as Belle left through the casino and was surprised to see many of the tourists staring at her. He had almost forgotten she was a celebrity in the poker world. His eyes were drawn to a lady sitting at an outer table in a nearby lounge who seemed to be particularly interested. She was wearing a wide brimmed Audry Hepburn hat, a fitted blue dress, and big dark Chanel sunglasses.

Chapter 33

Monday, January 14 (Moon in Aquarius) Ghosts of yesterday haunt the present. Opposing forces seek your favor. Remember, you cannot think with your heart.

Jason exited the men's room walking back toward the high limit room at the Bellagio thinking about Birmingham Bernie being on tilt. He tried not to be too obvious about noticing the presence of the lady in the broad brimmed hat. Nonchalantly, he strolled past the lounge where she was sitting. In no way was Jason expecting what happened next.

"Jason."

The sound of the voice stopped Jason dead in his tracks. He didn't have to look into the lounge to know who it was. He was shocked when he watched the tall lady in the blue dress stand and remove her dark glasses.

"Cassie?"

"Hello, Jay."

They hugged for a moment and memories began to flood Jason's mind.

"What a surprise. What are you doing here? Are you working undercover, or something?" Jason asked. He stepped back and scanned the hat and dress.

"I'm undercover, but I'm not working. I wanted to see you so I took a long week-end."

"How did you find me?"

"Jason, really. I am with the FBI, remember?"

"Yes, I do. I remember very well," Jason knew the Clayton-Ashley connection to the Hooverville office was the likely source of her information on his whereabouts.

"I wanted to talk to you, Jay, about a lot of things. Would you let an old partner buy you lunch?"

"Never," Jason said. He sensed a vulnerable tone to Cassie's voice he had not heard before. "I'll let the boys buy us lunch. I have a lot of their money stacked up on the table over there. I'll be right with you."

Jason cashed in his chips, enduring an "I knew you didn't have the balls to play no-limit with me" look from Birmingham Bernie.

"So you know Annabelle Duquemin?" Cassie asked while they settled into a booth in the back of Jasmine.

"Yes. Do you know her?"

"No, but I've seen her on TV. She's a pretty girl."

"She's also a pretty fair poker player."

The waiter came and took their drink orders and disappeared toward the kitchen. Cassie reached across the table and gripped both Jason's hands. She had another expression on her face which Jason had never seen, something akin to sadness.

"It's good to be with you, Jay. I've missed you."

"It's good to be with you, too," Jason said. He squeezed her hands. "I love being with a beautiful woman."

"So do I, Jay. So do I," Cassie said.

It took a few moments for Jason to comprehend what he had heard. He stared at her intently. She held his gaze.

"What do you mean? Do you mean . . ."

"Yes, Jay, It's true. That's one of the things I wanted you to know."

"Oh! Cassie, why didn't you tell me?" Jason found himself squeezing her hands even tighter in response to the blood-draining grip she had on him.

"I wanted to tell you, so many times."

"Cassie, I was your partner. Hell! I was in love with you. You could have told me anything."

"Two of the very reasons I couldn't say a word, Jay. The Bureau would bury me."

"The Bureau doesn't discriminate, Cassie, you know that."

"Maybe not, but the good ole boys who run it sure do. Well, anyway, we'll see what happens."

"Cassie, what you tell anyone else is your business. I'll never say a word. Don't you know what you tell me in Vegas, stays in Vegas? Besides, I'm no longer with the Bureau."

"That's another reason I wanted to talk to you. I feel badly about what happened and I'm so sorry for what I did. I never wanted to hurt you, and I never dreamed you would resign your job because of me. I didn't know you cared so much."

"Oh! Cassie, Cassie, Cassie." Jason knew Cassie had been aware of how crazy he was about her so it was logical for her to conclude her actions led to his resignation. "What a fine bucket of worms this has turned out to be."

"I'm so sorry, Jay."

"Let me guess. Attractive brunette, dark blue BMW convertible, speaks Arabic, right?"

"Yes, how did you know?"

"Cassie, really, I was with the FBI, remember?" Jason couldn't suppress a smile.

Cassie replied with a 'touché' expression shared only by spouses or partners.

"I'm confused here, Cassie. If you are what you say you are . . ."

"I am, Jay. I'm gay," Cassie said. She was more confident now.

"If that's the case, how could you be so intimate with me?"

"It's probably insane, but it made sense to me at the time, Jay." She still clung to his hands, searching for words. "I gave you my sex, but not my intimacy."

"Well, you sure had me fooled. And with sex like that, who cares about intimacy?"

"Exactly, and here's where I'm supposed to say 'all you guys are alike.'"

"So you're telling me you faked the whole thing, including all those orgasms."

"Maybe I did, and maybe I didn't."

Jason chuckled. He knew there was no way he could dislike this woman.

"But, why Cassie, why any of that?"

"I knew you liked me and enjoyed being with me."

Jason started to interrupt . . .

"Let me finish, Jay. I was, and am, grateful for what you've done for me professionally and personally. I've always had this overwhelming desire to please you. I know it was wrong, but I knew you weren't married and had no steady girl friend, so I thought some occasional sex wouldn't hurt anything. I knew the guys would talk, and I would rather them talk about us being a 'thing' than me being a lesbian."

"Well, thanks for the mercy fuck, Cassandra." Jason released her hands, suddenly agitated thinking the private time Cassie had spent with him had more to do with charity than with feelings or desire.

"Jason, please, I said I was sorry. And I came out here to beg you to come back to the Bureau; come back and be my partner."

"What? So you can avert the rumors? Are the guys beginning to talk? Why don't you just start screwing your new partner?

"Russo? I can't screw Russo. He's my boss! Besides, he's only working with me on this case until we catch the al Din's, or until you come back."

"I won't be coming back, Cassie."

"Russo thinks you will. I think he feels a little guilty for not listening to you the morning you left. By the way, Clayton told Ashley. She's crazy about you, you know."

"What did Clayton tell her?"

"He told her you were fine and where you were and what you were doing. She told Russo, so he figures Vegas will get old in a hurry, and you'll be back. He told me to tell you you're on personal leave and the job is yours whenever you return."

The puzzling signs of the morning rituals were beginning to make sense to Jason.

Chapter 34

Monday, January 14 (Moon in Aquarius) Confession is good for the soul. The truth enables understanding. Pisces and Scorpio weigh heavily.

"I said I won't be coming back, Cassie."

"O.K. here's the deal, Jay. Because I feel responsible for the situation here, if you'll come back, I'll transfer. Hell! I'll even quit. The Bureau certainly needs you now more than it needs me."

Jason was beginning to get a twinge of guilt himself. He realized all this time Cassie had thought she was the reason he left Washington and the Bureau. Should he tell her the real reason he quit his career and changed his lifestyle? He had never tried to hide the fact he enjoyed reading his horoscope, or for that matter, his interest in tarot. But he had never admitted to anyone the extent to which it controlled his life. What would Cassie think? Would she tell?

"Very noble of you, Cassie. I hate to tell you this, but you had nothing to do with me leaving the Bureau."

"Sure, thanks. I feel better already."

"No really." Jason paused for a moment, hesitant to speak the words he felt he had to share with Cassie. "Alright, here goes. What's said here stays here, right?"

"Sure."

"Cassie, I'm not really the man you think I am."

"Oh! My God! You're not going to tell me you're gay, are you?"

"No, nothing like that."

"Hey! You're a stallion. I remember your birthday party."

"Stop it! You'll never be able to convince me you're a lesbian if you keep reminding me of that night," Jason said. He stared at her. "When I was eleven years old... " he finally began.

Jason recounted to Cassie the events which happened on the day of his mother's death and her infatuation with horoscopes and the tarot deck. He told her how he grew up sharing his mother's love for those interests, as well as poker.

"What no one else knew, until now, is how my every decision is governed by my horoscope and the tarot. On the day I got the call from Russo to fly to St. Louis, my horoscope and the tarot card were the exact same ones which foretold the death of my mother; it was more than I could take. I knew I couldn't get on that plane. When Russo ignored my pleadings for a delay, he left me no choice but to resign. So, now you know."

"Well, your readings couldn't be totally correct," Cassie countered. "The plane didn't crash."

"Only because I wasn't on board. You should thank me for saving your life."

"Oh! Jay. I'm not one to try to tell you what to believe. I mean, I understand where you're coming from, but I'm not so sure. Do you use these readings in your poker games?"

"Yes."

"How's that working out?"

Jason remained silent.

"Well, Jay, while we're doing true confessions, there's something else I want you to know."

Cassie removed a tattered piece of paper from her purse.

Chapter 35

Monday, January 14 (Moon in Aquarius) Questions provide answers, only to proffer more questions. When possible, always give benefit of the doubt. Pisces entrusts.

The waiter refilled their glasses and delivered a large barbeque chicken pizza on a thin sourdough crust as Cassie handed Jason the letter. He unfolded it carefully.

My Dearest, Precious, Cassandra,

If you are reading this, it means your father and I have passed on. I hope the circumstances of our deaths . . .

Jason continued reading the letter, occasionally glancing up, seeing a dolorous expression on Cassie's face.

Golly returned to Dharma and married a merchant named al Din. Sadly, she died giving birth to her second son. That's the other thing I wanted tell you, dearest one. You are sharing blood with a couple of half-brothers somewhere on the planet.

So now you know, my darling. May God bless you for all your days, because indeed you were a blessing for us.

— Your Loving Mother

"Dear God in heaven, Cassie, tell me this isn't true!"

"It is, Jay. Is that not the cruelest of all ironies?"

"Are you absolutely sure about this? How long have you known?"

"I found out about three days before you left, and DNA confirmed it."

"I saw the DNA results."

"I had Jim run another test and I kept it private."

"Do the brothers know?"

"Yes."

"Does the Bureau know?"

"No."

"Cassie, you're withholding critical information and tampering with evidence."

"Don't lecture me, Jay. You didn't stay around long enough for me to tell you. After you left, I knew Russo would take me off the case if he found out."

"So, Cassie, what really happened in St. Louis? Did you help the brothers escape?"

"Absolutely not!"

Cassie told Jason the entire story about how she got the drop on Ali, and then Abdul jumped from the linen cart to get the drop on her, and about their escape in the linen truck.

"Abdul promised he wouldn't shoot me if I promised I wouldn't shoot Ali and we would all live to meet again another day. I pleaded with them to give themselves up, but they would hear none of it. Then I promised the next time I saw them, I would

...And they promised the next time they saw me
...e to hell. You know, typical family spats."

...ing at his pizza and shaking his head.

...ne, Cassie. Thanks for coming and telling me
...f this is at all sensible, but, strangely, it's
...sense. Any ideas about where the brothers

...the tail end of a very disturbing message a
...ended with something like 'you will be the
...s.'"

Chapter 36

Monday, January 14 (Moon in Aquarius) Seek direction rather than wander in the wilderness. Devine a plan and follow it to paradise.

Abdul and Ali were exhausted. The ordeal with the pre-martyring of Scarface in the Gulf, the endless trudging before sloshing across the Rio Grande, and the all-night drive across the badlands of Texas to distance themselves from the border, had taken its toll. The physical drain was understandable, but they had no experience with the unremitting mental fatigue from the responsibility of carrying the Halliburton. Abdul was suspicious of the technology of the infidels of the West. Could they somehow detect nuclear radiation? Could they track it? Was there a way to make it less detectable? Stressful. Very stressful.

Ali had both hands on the wheel of the silver Camry, fighting to stay awake. The brothers could not risk breaking a single law. Even a routine traffic stop by a local yokel could spell doom for their mission, although they were still unsure of their ultimate target. The drug trafficking along the southern border had created a climate which ensured a thorough search of all vehicles stopped by any law enforcement officer. Especially if the occupants of the vehicle spoke with an accent. And there would be no way to explain why they had in their possession several firearms and a large amount of cash, not to mention the nuclear device hidden in the trunk.

"Abdul, wake up. We're here."

"Huh? Where?" Abdul jerked his head, then yawned and stretched. He squinted at the brilliant sunrise beaming through his passenger window.

'We're here," Ali repeated.

"We're always here," Abdul said. He stared at Ali, showing his obvious annoyance.

"We just passed a big sign that said 'Welcome to San Antonio, Remember the Alamo.'" Ali waved his arms grandiosely and quickly grabbed the steering wheel again.

"Ali, what in Allah's name is the Alamo?"

"I have not a clue."

"Neither do I. So how can we remember it?"

"We can't. In fact, I've already forgotten it." Ali chuckled.

"Me, too." Abdul laughed louder, Ali joined in and they both laughed almost uncontrollably.

The giddiness finally subsided with Abdul and Ali wiping tears of laughter from their tired eyes.

"My brother," Abdul said. "We can't even think straight. We need some rest."

They were continuing northbound on I-37 approaching Exit 137, Hot Wells Boulevard.

"There's a Motel 6 at the next exit," Ali said. "And an IHOP, too."

"Perfect. We will eat and sleep and clear our minds."

After devouring two towering stacks of pancakes, the brothers slept the day away. Abdul was glad to be back in civilization where blending in was easier to do than on some isolated road or in some small town where the local deputy sheriff was looking to amuse himself and sweeten the courthouse coffers by fleecing out-of-towners who didn't follow the letter of their law. He had only been awake a few minutes when he began stirring, looking for a phone book. He found it in the drawer of the nightstand, underneath the telephone. It contained all the information he needed. He tore out the page that was a detailed map of San Antonio.

"Ali, I'll be back in an hour or two. You stay and guard our "little gift. It's under the bed."

"Where are you going?" He asked with a groan.

"To the Collins Garden Library, a few exits away off of I-10."

Ali raised his head. "I'm starving."

"I'll bring you some food. What would you like?"

"Anything but Mexican," Ali said.

"Don't worry, I hate Mexican food." Abdul thought for a moment. He said, "In fact, I hate Mexicans too. Just another bunch of infidels."

"Surprise me brother, just make it good."

"You can count on it," Abdul said. Looking at Ali, he was unable to suppress a grin. He grabbed a light jacket, stuck his pistol in the pocket, and was out the door.

The Collins Garden Library was easy to find. It was grandfathered into a middle-class neighborhood that had been bisected by the construction of the interstate many years ago, condemning the surrounding area to decades of decline. Yet, there was still a feel of vibrancy to the area. Kids played in the streets and neighbors visited from porch to porch and over back yard fences. And the Collins Garden Library had stood the test of time, and was functionally modern for an old public facility.

Abdul was sporting a new vintage Juan Valdez mustache, dressed in jeans and a plaid shirt. This chameleon look created the best and worst of situations. He blended in perfectly as a Latino, but could not interact as a Latino because he spoke no Spanish. As he approached the entrance, he was surprised to learn from the decal on a glass panel near the front door that the library closed at six. Abdul quickened his step after glancing at his watch and noticing he had only forty-five minutes to complete his task. He never liked to be in a public facility near opening or closing time because there were usually fewer people around; hence it was easier to be noticed. Or worse, remembered. His apprehensions were quickly assuaged once he entered and noted the library was still bustling.

Abdul found the computers against the far wall past the newspapers and periodicals. On the partition separating the section there was a sign, hand-written with black magic marker on a sheet of typing paper. It said, TO USE COMPUTERS SEE ATTENDANT. Abdul had a sudden pang of biliousness. Still, he was on a mission, and he desperately needed to find out exactly what that mission was. He cautiously sauntered to the Help Desk.

"Cómo puedo ayudar usted hoy, Señor?"

Abdul was staring into the dark brown eyes of a Senorita with the brightest smile this side of Brownsville. She reminded him of Ali's wife back in Dharma, someone he was sure he would never see again. Bright Smile stared back at him, waiting for his response.

"English please," Abdul said. "I try to learn English."

"And you are doing very well. Good for you." Bright Smile pointed a finger at him enthusiastically. "How may I help you, Sir?"

"I need to use computer, please."

"Oh, sure. Just let me see your driver's license."

"Driver's license?"

"Yes, the whole world has gone bonkers since nine-eleven."

Abdul chuckled, but was feeling more anxious with each passing moment. As he handed her his license, a huge uniformed man wearing pointy-toed snake-skin boots with a long-barreled pearl-handled pistol strapped to his waist entered the room. He tipped his white ten-gallon hat to Bright Smile as he clomped by. She beamed back at him.

"Howdy, Cal." She gave a half-wave, half-salute to the man with her hand that was holding Abdul's license. Then to Abdul she said, "There would be a lot less trouble in this world if everyone had the Texas Rangers around."

Abdul nodded. Bright Smile glanced at the license.

"Mr. Doukas … Constantine Doukas, from Tarpon Springs, Florida. That's a Greek name, right?" She entered his name on a logsheet.

"Yes." Abdul noticed the big man with the big gun and the big hat had gone straight for the periodicals and was reading a newspaper.

"What brings you to Texas, Mr. Doukas?"

"Vacation."

"Great. Welcome to Texas. Here's your password for computer #3." She handed him an index card with a number on it. "Enjoy your stay, and you should see the Alamo, if you can."

"Thank you." Abdul nodded. The Alamo. These people are crazy for this Alamo thing. Is that the home of the rental car company? He wondered.

On the way back to the computer section Abdul was comforted to notice that the Ranger was completely engrossed in his newspaper, and Bright Smile was already busying herself with other customers. He quickly settled into the chair at computer #3, inserted the password, activated Internet Explorer and found the wedding website for the couple in Kabul. A couple of clicks later, he saw it: *We thank our brothers for the fabulous honeymoon trip to Las Vegas, Nevada, USA; the Hoover Dam under a full moon was very special.* He fought to contain his excitement. Now Abdul knew his destiny. He clicked on the comment section of the website and posted: *We thank the Groom for the special favor gift. It will be put to good use on the next special occasion.* The Director was notified that he had the special gift and would carry out the mission.

Abdul did a quick internet search for moon phases and learned that the next full moon was Monday, January 28, 2002. Just two short weeks. The virgins await. Praise be to Allah. On this day we, my brother and I, will be the greatest of all martyrs.

In his excitement, Abdul almost forgot one other task he had to do while he had access to a computer. He typed "dental supplies San Antonio" in the search engine. In a moment, he had exactly the information he needed. He wrote the nearby address on Flores Street just off I-10 on the index card and logged off the computer.

Abdul quietly exited the library without catching the eye of the Ranger or Bright Smile. He felt overwhelmed with exuberance. He looked forward to giving the good news to Ali, along with some comfort food. Something filling and Americana.

Abdul decided to take back roads for his return to the Motel 6. The scenic route. After meandering the silver Toyota south and eastward for several miles, he saw a sign he had been looking for. ACE HARDWARE. He parked on the street in front of the store which was about to close. Within two minutes he was back in the car. Abdul placed the crowbar he had purchased under the passenger seat and pulled back into the traffic.

Abdul continued working his way southeastward for the longest time. A chilly mist peppered the windshield. He was beginning to fear he was lost when he finally came upon a street which was on his phone-book map. He turned east on Steves Avenue. Abdul noticed the surroundings on this side of the freeway changed with every passing block. Less affluent. It was residential with some small industrial thrown in here and there. But there were definitely no neighbors visiting over the back fence or kids playing in the street in this neighborhood. He stopped at the first convenience store he saw and bought a couple of six packs of beer. A little surprise for Ali. Abdul scanned his surroundings as he streamed with the traffic, continuing down Steves Avenue. He caught a red light crossing Roosevelt Street and came to a stop in the center lane behind a pickup truck with half a dozen workers hunkered down in the back trying to stay warm.

The men in the truck were whistling and cat-calling to a young woman standing on the curb across the intersection to the left.

Abdul watched her as she preened and posed, and seemed to be having fun as she encouraged the ogling workers. Behind her he saw a busy parking lot and a large orange colored building. WHATABURGER. Open 24 hours with a drive-thru. Perfect.

After checking for traffic to his left, Abdul steered the silver Toyota into the left turn lane. The woman on the curb now directed her attention in his direction. She smiled. He returned the smile as the turn arrow illuminated green and he made the left turn onto Roosevelt. She waved. Abdul waved. He drove passed her and turned on his right turn signal to enter the drive-thru lane of the burger joint. The hunger in his stomach had suddenly switched to his loins. How could she not be freezing, being so scantily dressed? He wondered.

Abdul brought the silver Toyota to a stop in the drive-thru lane behind a couple of cars waiting for their turn to place an order. He increased the intensity of the windshield wipers as the raindrops grew larger and the wind began to howl. He glanced back at the woman. She was still looking at him.

Abdul's mind flashed back to that September night in Mt. Vernon. The growing firmness inside his jeans brought a smile to his face as he remembered the girl who said her name was Sandy. He fantasized, as often he did, about her breasts and every glorious orifice of her body that he and his brother sullied that night. Whatever happened to her? Did she live, or die? Abdul scanned the news accounts for days after nine-eleven, but could never ascertain her fate. Not that Abdul cared, but still he wondered. As infidels go, she wasn't too bad.

Tap, tap, tap.

Abdul was startled back into the moment by the knocking on the passenger side window. He instinctively checked for the pressure of the pistol in his jacket pocket as he appraised the woman staring at him. She was no longer smiling, but had more of a look of despair. Her long black hair was sopping and heavy mascara dribbled from her melancholy eyes. Abdul lowered the passenger side window.

"Would you please buy me a cup of coffee?" The woman's alto voice was faint, and intoned desperation. The bitter rain pelted her porcelain skin.

Abdul was taken aback by the woman staring into his window. She spoke perfect English, without a hint of an accent. She just wanted coffee? Was she just a beggar, not a seller? Her attire, or lack thereof, shrouded a pretty face. She was beautiful, in fact. And she was cold.

Abdul reached over and opened the door for her. "Come get out of the rain," he said. The shivering woman slid into the car.

"Thank you," she said. "You're very kind."

Abdul inched the car forward toward the ordering station.

"Coffee?" he asked.

"Yes please."

"Are you hungry?"

"Very."

"What would you like?"

"Anything."

Abdul lowered his window and ordered three #2 WHATAMEALS: double hamburgers with fries, and a large cup of coffee.

The woman removed the top from the steaming cup and cradled it near her lips. Abdul gently made the left turn back onto Roosevelt, caught the green light and headed southeast on

Steves Avenue. He watched her savor a prolonged sip. Their eyes met.

"What's your name?" Abdul asked.

"Honey. What's yours?"

"John. Are you a working girl?"

"Are you a cop?"

"No."

"Then yes I am, *John*."

A wry smile vivified her face. Abdul wondered what was amusing her.

"What's so funny, Honey?"

"You are John. You are a funny John." She giggled. Her cheeks were beginning to show some color as she warmed to the hot coffee.

Abdul chuckled, even though he had no idea what was so humorous.

"How much?" Abdul asked.

"It depends. You want hand, mouth, or everything?"

"Everything."

"Yeah, I thought you were an everything type guy when you ordered the WHATAMEAL."

Abdul was laughing out loud, and it felt good. He now knew his destiny. He was blessed with a chance to redeem himself in the eyes of the Director, after his failure to accomplish his mission on nine-eleven. The aroma of the burgers filled his senses. And the girl in the car with him was pretty and pleasant. "How much for the WHATAGIRL?" He asked.

"Two hundred."

"How much for a couple hours at the motel for my brother and me?"

Honey became contemplative. She gazed at Abdul, then at the bag of burgers. She took another sip from the steaming cup and returned her glare to Abdul. "Five hundred," she said.

"How about a thousand and we forget about this night; it never happened."

"It's a deal, John. Money talks and I don't. In fact, it's already forgotten. This night never happened."

"Very good, Honey. Very good." Abdul felt the pressure of the pistol in his jacket pocket and quickened his pace toward the Motel Six.

CHAPTER 37

Tuesday, January 15 (Moon in Aquarius) You are the modern day Trojan horse. A great victory can be yours if you are true to your heart and follow a plan.

Hot air from the heat setting of the reverse cycle wall unit stifled the small room on the ground floor of the Motel 6. The thin walls and the seventies-vintage jalousie windows barely dampened the incessant roar of traffic rushing by on I-37 still slick with rain. Empty beer cans and WHATABURGER food wrappers were scattered about. Abdul was covered with sweat and smelling of sex, sleeping naked on one of the double beds. He kicked his legs, as if trying to remove the covers, which were long ago on the floor. He awakened with a flinch, and lay motionless for a few moments trying to recall where he was. Then he remembered ... Honey. He looked around. Where was she? She's gone!

"Ali, wake up."

Ali groaned and raised his head slightly, looking around. "What time is it?" he asked.

Abdul turned on the light and glanced at the digital clock on the night stand. "It's 3:30. Get up. Where's the girl?"

Abdul was frantically searching around the room, taking inventory. He looked under the bed. The Halliburton was still there. He turned the heater off and parted the curtains slightly and looked outside. The silver Toyota was still there where he had parked it. The fanny pack was sitting on the dresser where he had left it. His money and everything else was still there.

Ali didn't appear to be concerned. "She was with you. It was your turn and you were pounding her again. After all the beer and the burgers and that incredible infidel bitch, I guess I just fell asleep."

Abdul checked the bathroom, even behind the shower curtain.

"She was quite a bitch, wasn't she?" Abdul sat on the bed and smiled. He remembered how she had pleasured him for the longest time in every way imaginable, then softly cuddled him until he fell asleep; certainly not your usual infidel bitch. Abdul felt guilty for letting his guard down, but it appeared no harm had been done.

"She just left," Abdul said. "She took only the money I gave her and left."

"So you found the only honest whore in San Antonio. Turn off the light. Go back to bed." Ali pulled the sheet up over his head.

"We must leave now, Ali. Get up and get in the shower." Abdul snatched the sheet that covered Ali and threw it at him. "I'll explain later. Now, move."

The brothers dressed quickly and loaded the silver Toyota. Abdul carefully lifted the Halliburton into the trunk. He handed the keys to Ali and climbed into the passenger seat.

"Go north on I-37," Abdul said. As Ali steered the car out of the parking lot, Abdul checked to make sure the revolver in his right pocket was loaded. He reached under the seat and felt the crowbar he had bought the night before.

Ali joined the interstate northbound and accelerated to the speed limit. "You want to tell me what's going on here?" he asked.

"My brother, praise be to Allah, we have our target."

Ali said nothing but stared straight ahead and nodded stoically.

"It's Hoover Dam, near Las Vegas."

"When do we strike? Are we going there now, at four o'clock in the morning?" Ali asked.

"Relax, my brother. We strike when the moon is full. In thirteen days, we will become the greatest of all martyrs." Abdul emphasized his words with a celebratory fist clinch.

"Praise be to Allah," Ali said. The enthusiasm of his words did not seem to match the gravitas of Abdul's announcement. "So where are we going now?"

"Go westbound on I-10."

Ali nodded.

"Do you remember back in Afghanistan when our Pakistani friend was talking to us about nuclear devices?"

Ali nodded. He steered the Toyota to join I-10 westbound.

"And how they always emit some level of radiation?"

"Yes, yes," Ali said. The tone of his voice directed Abdul to get to the point.

"I was thinking we should wrap our little gift package in a lead shield and that might reduce the radiation leakage. When I was on the internet I found this place that should have something that might just work for us. It's a dental supply store about ten minutes from here, very near I-10."

"Look, Abdul, if we get sick, we get sick. I don't think the virgins are going to mind."

"It's not for us, you camel-brain." Abdul grinned, thinking that it had been a long time since he had used his favorite sibling zinger on his brother. "It's to try to avoid being picked up by radiation detectors the infidels may have placed along the highway."

"Do you really think the infidels are up to speed on this?" Ali asked. "The Director has them chasing their tails in Tora Bora. They are destroying caves that haven't been occupied for centuries."

"Yes, our glorious brothers really stirred up the hornet's nest on 11 September. We failed them on that day, Ali. We must not fail them now. Turn right at the next exit."

Ali exited the interstate. "There are no stores open at this hour," he said.

Abdul reached under his seat and raised the crowbar into the air. "The store will be open soon, my brother. Take a left on McCulough, then a right on Flores."

Ali stared at his brother in disbelief, yet followed his directions. He made the right turn on Flores and followed it for a few minutes.

"There," Abdul said. "On the right." He pointed to a large one story building on the corner across the street. The cinderblock structure was painted an opaque gray and receded timidly into the foggy early morning mist. The walls of the building appeared to extend the length of the entire small block in each direction, with head-in parking spaces also extending the length of the block. A couple of empty cars were parked along the building in each direction. The only visible entrance to the facility was a single panel glass door facing Flores Street.

"Park down there," Abdul said. "Back in between those two cars so we can be ready to get out of here." He grabbed the crowbar, retrieved a flashlight from the glove compartment and quietly stepped out of the car. He watched. He listened. Nothing moving anywhere.

Abdul approached the glass door and noticed it was secured by a keyed entry single deadbolt lock. The deadbolt, however, tumbled into a metal door jam, which was protected by a metal shield. He tried to pry the door with the crowbar, but it would not budge. Abdul beamed his light inside. He saw a medium sized room, with a service counter. There were no items for sale visible in the room, so Abdul knew this was definitely a wholesale operation. A cash register sat in the middle of the counter with a single door behind it. He looked at the door. He looked inside. He glanced down the street at Ali. No time to be neat and tidy, Abdul thought. He tightened his grip on the crowbar. With a single blow, he smashed the glass door into a thousand pieces.

An earsplitting noise pierced the stillness of the night. Abdul moved swiftly, although he was sure he had at least five minutes before anyone would respond to an alarm in this part of town, if they would respond at all. Plenty of time. He dashed inside and around the counter past the cash register and started to pass through the door into the back room. He looked back at the cash register and had a sudden thought.

Abdul had no interest in money from the cash register. He was also certain it would contain no money when the store was closed. It occurred to him if the cash register was pilfered, the authorities would think it was just another routine smash and grab break-in for petty cash. So, he crudely pried the cash drawer open with the crowbar. To his surprise, he was looking at a few small bills. He stuffed them into his pocket and hurried through the door into the warehouse.

It was a mammoth enclosure with boxes stacked all the way to the ceiling on endless shelving bins. Now Abdul was concerned. How could anyone find anything among these caverns of cartons? He picked an aisle and scampered towards the back of the building. About half-way back, the bins of shelves ended and there were rows of dental equipment: chairs, lights, cabinets, x-ray machines, porcelain spit-basins, and anything else that wouldn't fit in a box.

Abdul felt pressure mounting from his mental clock with each passing second. The perpetual pulsating shrill of the alarm was extremely disconcerting. Maybe this wasn't such a good idea after all. He ran to the left wall and then to the rear of the warehouse and he saw them. Against the back wall on a long row of hangers was every kind of x-ray radiation apron you could imagine.

Abdul surveyed the entire row of lead aprons and chose one from the section of the largest aprons, the ones hanging closest to the floor. It was much heavier than had thought it would be. With that in mind, he snatched two more from their hangers, all that he thought he could safely carry, and folded them over his left arm with the other apron.

Abdul felt like he had been inside the building forever. The screeching alarm had given him a brutal headache. He hobbled awkwardly towards the front of the building. He opened the door between the warehouse and the office.

"Freeze! Police!"

Abdul stood motionless in the doorway to the office. He was looking directly into the brilliant beam of a flashlight held by a young, boyish looking police officer who was standing in a pile of glass from the smashed front door. In the officer's other hand was a pistol pointed directly at Abdul. The exasperating alarm continued to wail.

"Hands in the air. Now!" The officer extended his pistol menacingly towards Abdul. His hand was shaking.

Abdul remained perfectly tranquil, but his mind was racing. What had he done? Would it end like this? Where was Ali? Did he flee with the bomb? Would they be a failure again like they were on 11 September?

Abdul slowly extended his right hand to show the officer he was holding only a flashlight. He released the flashlight and it dropped to the floor with a thud. The officer's light diverted downward momentarily. Abdul went for the revolver in his right jacket pocket. Before his hand reached the gun, he saw the muzzle flash from the officer's gun. He felt the impact of the bullet. Another flash, and the thud of another bullet. Without thinking, Abdul pulled his revolver and fired. The officer went down with a yell. Abdul realized he was saved by the lead aprons he was carrying, which stopped both bullets from the officer's gun.

Abdul walked to the pile of glass where the semi-conscious young officer lay writhing in pain. He placed his revolver tight against the officer's temple and pulled the trigger. He lugged the lead aprons outside past the police cruiser with the blue flashing lights and looked around for Ali.

CHAPTER 38

Tuesday, January 15 (Moon in Aquarius) The wise old owl watches and listens, but speaks not. Be that owl. Every turn of the river gives a new and different perspective. Local flavor could be appealing.

The bright desert sun warmed Jason while he strolled down the strip towards the Mirage. When he'd been inside in the air-conditioning for a long period of time the rays of the sun was therapeutic, even during winter. Jason likened this experience to being 'baked Alaska;' warm and toasty on the outside, yet chilled to the core on the inside.

Cassie's revelations were more than Jason could fathom in one afternoon. He was especially cognizant of the fact he could not be 'fathoming' and trying to play poker at the same time. Especially no limit poker. One thing her visit confirmed was he had made the right decision in leaving the Bureau. He was glad he would not be around when the particulars of Cassie's family history and her sexual orientation became public. He knew he would be the butt of endless jokes, being shot out of the saddle by, of all things, another woman. This is a good time, he thought when he entered the Mirage Casino, to visit Belle and watch a professional at work.

It was obviously not business as usual in the poker room. The entire area was roped off from the public with the feature table and the TV lights taking up most of the high limit section. Belle was sitting at position three between Fresno Fats, a used car dealer wearing mirrored sunglasses, and Perry the Pounder, a former wrestler turned poker pro from New Jersey.

Belle acknowledged Jason with a smile and a slight nod when he edged his way into the bleacher seating viewing area, which reminded Jason of the "peanut gallery" from the old "Howdy Doody" show. His mother had shown him tapes of some of the early kid shows and 'peanut gallery' was one of her favorite terms. He had thought of his mother often since coming to Vegas, a place she never was able to visit. He knew she would have loved the life out here, with poker games going twenty-four hours a day.

Belle had her game face on. Occasionally, when she thought someone was trying to 'read' her, she would flash the same quick, ingratiating smile.

Judging by the stack of chips in front of her, Belle was well into the chip accumulation stage of the tournament. This is where many of the amateurs go broke playing too tight trying to 'cash' as the blinds and antes increase. Their flawed thinking is to hibernate and wait for other players to knock themselves out. Unfortunately, they become easy pickings for the old pros, like Belle, who steal their blinds and bluff them out of most hands.

... no-limit is not so much about the cards as it is about the people. You've got to read 'em and not let them read you ...

Belle's words of wisdom resounded in Jason's mind while he sat with the other spectators. He had never really watched a live poker game in which he wasn't playing.

"Remember, no telling, Jay, no telling."

Nothing happened around the table Belle didn't see. Indeed, she was no less observant in the hands in which she folded.

Jason studied the players carefully to see if he could catch any tells, concentrating on Fats and the Pounder.

Fresno Fats won two sizable pots in a row and appeared to be the chip leader. He was a very aggressive player and won both pots with a large raise after the river card.

In the first hand, the victim was a young surfer dude, an internet qualifier in position seven. Fats nonchalantly pushed his sunglasses up on his nose and made a bet of two hundred thousand chips after the river card hit the table. Belle meekly mucked her cards. What did she know? The kid called him with aces and sevens, only to find out Fats had made a full house on the river.

The very next hand Fats had been calling the housewife in position six after every bet until the river. Having caught no help on the last card, the housewife checked. Fats sat there for a moment shuffling the chips in his right hand and made a bet once again of two hundred thousand, but Jason noticed this time he didn't touch his glasses. Was that a tell? The housewife folded a pair of kings, only to see Fats take the pot with a jack high and subsequently turn over his "rags" hand, celebrating his bluff.

After a couple of no flop hands, the action was on Belle. The flop was queen, jack, and nine with two spades. Belle raised with a bet twice the size of the big blind. Perry the Pounder called, as did Fats. The turn was the deuce of diamonds, no help. Belle bet again, only to be called again by Fats and The Pounder. The river card was the ace of spades, a very troubling card for Belle because it could have given one of them a straight or a spade flush. Belle checked, and The Pounder quickly followed suit. Belle watched Fats while he shuffled his chips and bet two hundred thousand, without pushing his sunglasses up on his nose.

"Raise," Belle said. After a moment of concentration, she stacked her chips in front of her. "All in." She pushed the chips forward and stared down at the table.

The Pounder folded, sliding his cards forward. Fresno Fats was not so nice, slamming his cards down on the muck pile so hard they bounced and flipped over, revealing the nine of diamonds and the king of spades. He had a middle pair, but missed his straight and his flush. Belle had picked up on that, and won the hand with her 'all in' bet. She didn't have to show she hadn't helped the pair of aces she held after the flop.

Jason had a real feeling of accomplishment. He was beginning, with Belle's help, to get a read on players at the poker table. It all boiled down to telling the difference between truth and lies. Jason was able to do this easily with Fresno Fats. Maybe his FBI training was a help to him after all.

There was another thing Jason noticed as he sat there watching this Texas Hold 'em tournament. He noticed something about Belle.

Chapter 39

Wednesday, January 16 (Moon in Aquarius to Pisces 9:01 a.m.) Limitations are boundaries you place on yourself. Big fish are found in deep waters. Live by the lessons you have learned.

Jason awakened in the bedroom of his ninth floor condo to dead silence and complete darkness, thanks to the thick blackout curtains. The numbers on the clock radio on the dresser said one thirty-five p.m. He flipped his pillow over to the cool side and again closed his eyes, showing little interest in meeting the day. Whatever happened, it couldn't be better than the night before.

Belle had finished third in the tournament, getting trip aces busted by The Pounder who had a pair of kings and swam the river to make a gut shot straight. Belle wasn't devastated about not winning because she got her money in with the best hand. The Pounder hit a two outer to beat her on the river. There had been only two cards in the entire deck which would give him the winning hand and he had caught one of them. As they say in the game, "that's poker."

When Belle collected her three-hundred and twenty-five thousand dollars, she was ready for a party, and Jason was the only invitee. They took a limo to Ruth's Chris Steak House where they ate the greater part of a cow and consumed large amounts of expensive adult beverages.

During dinner they compared notes on the players at her table and Belle was impressed at how Jason was spot on with the tells he had observed. She encouraged him by remarking that with the keen instincts from his former profession, he might be closer to prime time poker than he imagined.

When the limo returned to the Mirage at three in the morning, Belle instructed the driver to wait to take Jason home. She had taken a penthouse suite for the evening.

"Thanks for a great evening," Jason said. He kissed her softly at the door to her suite.

"It hasn't been a great evening, yet," Belle said. She placed her arms around his neck and kissed him long and passionately. She maneuvered him inside and kicked the door closed behind her.

"What about the limo driver?" Jason asked. He breathed deeply as Belle ripped off her clothes, and his.

"No, he doesn't get any," she said.

Jason lay half awake in his bed. He laughed out loud thinking about what she had said. He reverted to a contented smile when he recalled how she took control of him and used him for her total pleasure for almost an hour before collapsing on top of him.

"Now that's a great evening," she had whispered.

Jason finally rolled out of bed, plugged in the coffee pot. He collected the morning paper from outside the front door and opened it directly to the page with the horoscope.

Libra. September 23–October 22. Riches await those who are passionate in their pursuit. Be not meek.

He read it again, knowing he was going to play in a no limit game in the afternoon. He performed three shuffles and a cut on the tarot deck, and flipped over the top card.

The Five of Wands appeared, a card of gain and opulence. The signs could not be clearer; he should play no-limit, and if he was very aggressive, riches would be his.

"Good afternoon, Mr. Lancer," Fred said when Jason approached the poker room of the Bellagio.

"Hi, Fred. What do you have going up top?" Jason asked, nodding towards the high limit area.

"We have a sixty, one-twenty, and a no limit, with a ten grand buy in."

"Let me swim with the big fish," Jason said. He handed Fred a stack of hundreds with the bank wrapper still intact.

When Jason settled in at the table, he recognized four of the players as local pros and assumed the others were whales. Maybe this would be a profitable afternoon.

After mucking a few hands, he noticed Belle walking in carrying a couple of shopping bags and wearing a new designer warm-up suit. It appeared she was treating herself after cashing so well at her tournament. She smiled at him from the rail and pirouetted, modeling her new purchase. Jason returned the smile, giving her a thumbs-up. Belle settled in a chair where she could watch the rerun of a football game and the action at his table.

While the game progressed, Jason recalled the readings from earlier in the day: *Riches await those who are passionate in their pursuit. Be not meek. The Five of Wands, a card of gain and opulence*. He knew that in order to fulfill the prophesies, he would have to play more aggressively.

The action was on Jason as he looked down to see ace, four, off suit. No time like the present to mount a charge.

"Raise," he said. "Five-hundred."

Everyone folded except the big blind, an airline pilot from Atlanta, who carefully measured out his chips for a call.

During the flop as the ace, queen, seven, rainbow hit the table, Jason watched the eyes of the pilot and saw him glance down at his stack of chips. Even though this usually indicated a strong hand, Jason felt he had to be forceful.

"One-thousand," Jason said. He pushed forward a stack of ten chips.

"Call," the pilot said, measuring chips.

Jason bet another thousand on the turn and then two thousand on the river, only to be called by the pilot. Jason flipped his cards showing his aces which were no good against the pilot's winning aces and queens.

Jason glanced at Belle who gave him one of those 'what were you thinking' shrugs.

While trying to comprehend what had happened, Jason mucked his hand for a few minutes until he found himself staring at 'big slick' suited, the ace, king, of clubs. He raised a thousand. After everyone else folded, one of the whales called, splashing the pot with ten chips. The flop was jack, ten of clubs, and the two of diamonds.

"Two thousand," Jason said.

The whale tossed twenty chips into the pot.

The turn card was the ace of hearts, giving Jason a pair of aces, even if he didn't make his straight or flush. And this time he wasn't playing ace, rag, because he had the king as a kicker. The whale would have to worry about the ace hitting on the turn because Jason had been betting strong at every opportunity. The whale was staring around the room showing no interest at all, almost like he was watching for a pizza delivery, or something. *Be not meek*. Now's the time!

"All in," Jason said. He pushed all his chips forward.

"Call," said the whale.

Chapter 40

Wednesday, January 16 (Moon in Aquarius to Pisces 9:01 a.m.)
It's not whether or not you are knocked down that's important.
It's whether or not you get up. The longer you look at a picture,
the more you see.

Jason was stunned. He suddenly felt as if he had taken another
sucker punch in the gut. The river card was the deuce of spades,
giving the whale a full house, tens over deuces, and all of
Jason's chips representing ten-thousand of his dollars. When
Jason left the table he looked over at Belle with
embarrassment, wishing she had not been there to witness his
humiliation.

Jason approached the rail where she was sitting.

"What happened?" she asked.

"You saw what happened."

"I know. I'm sorry," she said. She continued to commiserate as
she took his hands in hers and squeezed them tightly. "It'll be
alright."

"I'm not so sure," Jason said.

"Are you going to reload?"

"No, not until I recover from this episode of terminal tilt."

Belle wanted to change the subject.

"Oh! By the way, Jay, I came by to thank you for the flowers. They are beautiful!"

"Oh! Good. I'm glad you got them."

After returning home in the early morning, Jason had gone online and ordered a dozen red roses to be sent to Belle's room at the Mirage. The card, which was clipped to a playing card, the queen of diamonds, read "Congratulations on your tournament, and thanks for a really, really, great evening. Love, Jay."

"They were there when I woke up. And the card was so nice. I mean, 'Love, Jay.' That's so sweet."

"I wanted you to know I really care about you. You know, you as a person, not just your …"

"My passion poker?" Belle asked.

Jason managed a smile.

"Yea, that, too. Especially that, too. You let me go all in and I always win."

"I care about you, too, Jay. I really do," Belle said.

"So, when's your next tournament?"

"Actually, I'm flying out tonight on the redeye to Atlanta, and then on to Aruba. The following week I'm back here for the big one at the Rio."

"Tough life."

"Why don't you come with me?"

"Thanks, but I need to hang around here and cool my jets until I can figure out some things."

"While your jets are cooling, why don't you hustle over to the Rio and enter the thousand dollar satellite for the Main Event the next week?"

"I'm obviously not ready for prime time."

"Who is? One thing about it, unlike a cash game, you can only lose your entry fee. Even though there'll be hundreds entered, if you finish in the top ten, you get an automatic entry into the big one."

Jason remained silent, pondering.

"Give it some thought," Belle said. "Oh, by the way, Jay, could I ask you to do me a huge favor?"

Chapter 41

Wednesday, January 16 (Moon in Aquarius to Pisces 9:01 a.m.) A full stomach goes a long way toward contentment. If you can see the trees, you are looking at the forest. Again, Scorpio has an impact.

The aroma of Chinese food flooded Pearl's interior as Jason steered the white Escalade up Kyle Canyon Road. No need for the navigation system on this trip because he remembered the way precisely. Belle had asked Jason to give her a ride to the airport because she was going to be gone a week and wanted to leave her car parked at home. Jason, of course, agreed and asked to take her to dinner on the way. Belle declined, claiming she had yet to pack and didn't think there would be enough time.

"What if I bring Chinese?" Jason had asked.

"Sounds wonderful," Belle had said. "See you at eight."

Jason went for a five mile run to clear the cobwebs from the afternoon's no-limit catastrophe. At least the sick feeling and the guilt of losing the ten grand was beginning to subside when he eased into the driveway past the mailbox with the two queens. The feeling was replaced by one of emptiness at the thought of Belle being gone for a week.

"Hi! Come on out back!" Belle yelled through the open sliding glass door. "I have a table set on the deck."

Jason was not surprised, knowing she loved to dine outside with that spectacular view.

"Where's the Queen of Hearts?" Jason asked as he looked about. He noticed the picture was gone from the table.

"Oh, Duchess is already at the neighbor's house. They have a teenage daughter who loves her, and vice-versa. She watches her when I have to be away."

Jason pulled out Belle's chair. The table was elegant with white tablecloth and napkins and real silver. The tall globe of the hurricane lantern buffered its glowing flame against the stiffening breeze which was not uncommon on the mountain.

"Thank you," Belle said. She looked back over her shoulder at Jason.

"You're welcome. And I want you to know you look ravishingly beautiful tonight."

"Thank you again."

They chatted about nothing in particular as they attacked the Chinese sampler which included everything from Moo Goo Gai Pan to Fortune Cookies. When they were finishing the meal and the chit-chat subsided, Belle put her silverware down and sipped her peach flavored Snapple and stared at Jason.

"So, Jay, what really happened at the table today?"

"I'm not sure I know".

"Don't tell me you didn't have a read on the pilot. I mean, he measured his chips like his hand was so strong he wanted to know in advance exactly how much money he was going to make. After the flop, when he glanced down and checked his stack of chips, you had to know he was strong."

"I know, I know," Jason said. He didn't know what else to say.

"Then when the whale was acting weak, splashing the pot and looking around the room like he didn't think his hand was worth playing, you had to know he had something big."

"I did."

"Then why would you go all in?"

"I thought I could move him off the hand, I guess."

"Jay! He was pot committed, and really all you could beat was a bluff. What were you thinking?"

Jason knew he was in denial. He dreaded the day when he would have to face the truth, but it looked like that time had come. What choice did he have? Without an explanation, the one person he had really come to admire would think he had a loose screw. What's worse, he feared if did tell her the truth, she would think the exact same thing. Jason glanced at his watch trying to determine if he had time for an elucidation.

"Belle, can I tell you something?" Jason asked.

"Anything, my sweet. You can tell me anything."

Jason no longer felt threatened. For the second time in as many days, he recounted the tale that until yesterday he had never told: "When I was eleven-years-old . . ."

Jason started at the beginning and revealed everything as Belle sat listening attentively. Finally he reached the part about the no limit game earlier in the day.

"So I knew after my horoscope and tarot reading this morning, today was the day when I must be very aggressive. And so I was. I saw the tells, as you did. But I didn't have the balls to act contrary to the horoscope and the tarot. I'm ashamed to admit how much control the readings have over my daily life, but I don't know how I could face the day without them."

When he finished, Belle remained silent and still for the longest time.

"Wow," she finally said. "My poor, poor, Jason."

"I don't want your pity."

"You're not getting pity, Jay, you're getting understanding. I understand how you got here. I understand how much you loved your sweet mother and the impact she had on your life."

Tears welled in Jason's eyes and ran down his cheeks. Belle gently brushed them away with her thumb but continued to talk.

"I understand the dilemma you faced with the FBI and why you resigned. I understand the love for poker you shared with your mother and how that led you to come out here. And finally, I understand exactly why you played like the mother of all donkeys today."

"The memory of my mother is still so vivid," Jason whispered. "I don't know how I can change."

"Oh! Stop it, Jason," Belle said. She kissed him firmly on the lips. "I fall for this sensitive man act every time."

"I know I have to get a grip here, but I don't know where to start."

"I know where to start, Hon, I can help you. Here's what you do ..."

Chapter 42

Thursday, January 17 (Moon in Pisces) When a storm approaches, take shelter. Yesterday's leftovers often make the best soup. Don't be an ostrich; when you take your head out of the hole, the problems are still there.

Jason entered the Pepper Farm restaurant and nodded to the hostess whose breasts were exposed like she should have been dancing on a pole. She appeared uncomfortable, having her push-up bra cinched so tight her nipples were pointing at the ceiling. He took a seat nearby at the counter and ordered a cup of coffee, looking around the restaurant to see if Clayton had arrived. Last evening after dropping Belle at the airport he had returned home to find a note under his door. It read: *Why don't you get a phone? Meet me at the Pepper Farm tomorrow at 9 a.m. Love, Clayton.* Jason smiled as he stared at the note. He realized that, other than Clayton, he really didn't have any close male friends. What a character.

"Hi, Sweetie!" The hostess shrilled from behind Jason while he took a sip of his coffee.

"Hi, Sugar Booger!"

Jason didn't have to turn around to know Clayton was in the house.

"Would you like to sit here at the counter, Honey Bunny, so you can be real close to me?" The hostess took in a deep breath and put some air under those push-ups.

"No, Darlin', I need a booth today," Clayton said. He stared openly at her finest features. "I'm meeting someone." He scanned around the room. "In fact, I think I see the suspect now." Clayton pointed to Jason who was sitting there with a smile, taking it all in. The hostess walked away after seating them in a booth by the window with a view of the strip.

"I mean, really, Clayton, do you screw them all?" Jason asked.

"No, sometimes even the more prim and proper ones like a little oral gratification. You know as in 'eatin' ain't cheatin,'" Clayton said.

"I don't know how you do it."

"Actually, don't tell anyone 'cause I don't wanna ruin my reputation." He glanced around as if to see if someone was listening. "But I don't do it anymore."

"I'm not a priest and this is not a confessional, Clayton. You don't have to lie to me."

"No shit, Sherlock, I've found true love." He leaned closer to Jason. "I'm dating a widow woman."

"Don't tell me you're screwing the owner of your company," Jason said.

"Don't say it like that, Jay-Jay. You make it sound so cheap. I love that woman. Besides, who are you to talk? At least I never screwed my own partner."

"And who do you think around here did?" Jason asked.

"I thought that might hit a nerve. Couldn't blame you though. She's a knockout, especially in that tight fitting blue dress."

"I knew it was you who ratted me out. Thanks, old buddy."

"I only told her where to find you, not where you were living. Look, Jay, I don't know what went down back there at the Bureau, but it couldn't have been too bad. They want you back."

"It's not going to happen. Besides how do you know all this?"

"Well, Ashley has mentioned it a couple of times. Then Cassie called me last night with some interesting developments. You wanna hear?"

"No."

"Good. Now, you didn't get any of this from me. Here it is in a nutshell. The CIA, in their new 'spirit of cooperation' told the Bureau a source in Uzbekistan reported one of the former Soviet generals sold a stray suitcase nuke to an extremist called Scar Face, then spilled the beans to our boy, for a price. Scar Face was spotted in Havana last Friday, so they think that one is headed for the states. Then your old college pal from the agency called for you. When you weren't there, he eventually talked to Cassie. Parts of a call from the Director were intercepted instructing the perp brothers you were chasing to receive the gift from Scar Face, kill him, and then deliver the gift, making them the greatest of all martyrs. The brothers were spotted near McAllen, Texas last Sunday evening driving a silver Toyota with Texas plates, believed to be headed for L.A. A local cop spotted them, but he said it was the next day before he realized who they were and filed a report. Finally, last Tuesday, just two days ago, a young cop in San Antonio was killed at a smash-and-grab of a dental supply store with the same gun that shot your tires out in front of the Delta terminal at Reagan Airport on nine-eleven. What do you think?"

"I think the Bureau has its hands full. And I'm not going to be taking any trips to LA anytime soon."

Chapter 43

Friday, January 18 (Moon in Pisces to Aires 9:34 p.m.) Skepticism can be healthy. Trust everyone, but always cut the cards. The road map is there to simplify the journey.

The poker room at the Rio was a bustling sea of humanity, and Jason felt like a very small fish swimming amongst the sharks and barracuda. He couldn't remember being this nervous since the first day of training at Quantico. Unlike other sports or competition, poker tournaments require no personal skill for participation, only the ability to muster the required entry fee, which in this case was one-thousand dollars. Hopefully, Jason thought, many of these two to three hundred hopefuls would have more money than ability.

This particular tournament was a qualifying event for the World Series of Poker Main Event being held at this very same venue the following week. There would be ten equal winners; each of ten players to reach the final table would receive ten-thousand dollars and an entry into the main event, which was also worth ten-thousand dollars. Jason had taken Belle's advice and ventured the grand to get some experience in no-limit Texas Hold 'em tournament play, and also have a chance to get into the main event on the cheap.

Jason had thought a lot about what Belle had said on the night she left for Aruba. Since he was eleven-years-old no one had talked to him this frankly. He realized for her to be so honest and lay it on the line in the manner in which she did, she must really be fond of him.

"I don't want you to think I'm disrespecting your mother," Belle had told him, "but there is a time and place for the readings of the stars and the cards. That time and place would never be in the poker room. When you're playing poker, you must be totally in the moment. If you are harboring preconceived biases about how to approach a particular game, or even any particular hand, you are inviting disaster. Of course, you must have a strategy. Everyone does. What it really comes to, my sweet, in poker and in life, is the ability to read people. You must be able to detect tells from others, yet not give them yourself. Then you must act on your intuition, which in reality is only a subconscious assessment of tells. Am I making any sense at all, Jay?"

"Yes, you are," Jason had said.

"Then do me a favor. Put away the tarot deck and forget about your horoscope for a while and react to whatever you perceive happening at the moment, not what some soothsayer has written or the chance flop of some medieval mystic on a card. What do you think?"

"I don't know. Let me flip a tarot card," he said. He made a move to his pocket as if he really had a deck with him.

"Jason!" Belle shouted.

"Alright, alright, I'll do it."

"Then hustle over to the Rio and pony up for that satellite. I'll see you the following week in the big one."

"Oh! Right. Absolutely."

"Stranger things have happened. Remember, tournaments are totally different from cash games."

"Let's hope so," Jason said. He was still reeling from dumping the ten grand.

"There are three stages to a tournament," Belle continued. "In the first stage you play conservatively while the donkeys eliminate each other. Be careful not to risk all your chips early in the tournament against anyone who can put you all in, even if you have aces. In the middle stage, when the antes and blinds increase, shift gears into selective aggression to build chips. Then in the final stage, you go for the win, using your chip stack to bully the others."

Jason settled into position three at his assigned table in the middle of the expansive room. He had no game plan for the day. Thus far, he had taken Belle's advice and avoided his horoscope and the tarot deck.

"Shuffle up and deal." A lady's voice boomed over the PA system, and the cards started flying from the dealer's hand. Jason concentrated on the players at his table, none of whom he had ever seen before. It was difficult for him to stay focused because of the continual stream of terrible cards coming his way. He caught a Doyle Brunson and a Dolly Parton hand, back to back. The hole cards of a ten and a two are called the Doyle Brunson because the legendary champion won two tournaments with that very same hand. The Dolly Parton hand of a nine and a five was named for the movie.

While Jason tried to settle in for the grind, it was hard for him to clear the remnants of Clayton's visit from his mind. He knew Cassie had called Clayton because Jason had never bothered to get a phone. Still a good decision, he thought. He understood

Cassie's angst over the brothers, especially after finding out she was their sibling. Jason still felt guilt over being unable to personally take down the brothers in DC or in Florida and bailing out on the trip to St. Louis. Although the fact they were still on the loose troubled him, the situation was certainly out of his control.

After mucking hands for what seemed like hours, Jason, on the button, looked down to find the king of spades and the king of hearts. Finally, he was about to play a hand.

To Jason's left, under the gun, was a truck driver from Teterboro, New Jersey. The way he dressed, the flamboyant hat with the flashing "I Love Vegas" sign along with the fish-net New York Giants tee shirt was certainly different. But combined with his brash-talking, trash-talking personality only meant one thing to Jason. This guy was a donkey: a novice, with very few poker playing skills.

"Call," said the donkey. He limped into the pot.

Everyone folded around to Jason.

"Raise," he said. Jason pushed chips equal to three times the big blind into the pot.

"Call." The smooth call from the donkey didn't really surprise Jason.

The flop was ten, jack, queen, of diamonds. Jason now had an open-ended a straight draw, along with his two kings.

"All in," the donkey said.

Chapter 44

Sunday, January 27 (Moon in Cancer) All snakes will bite, and some are poisonous. Be vigilant. With great beauty often comes the greatest threat.

The visitor's parking lot on the west side of Black Canyon, the Nevada side, was almost full. Weekend tourists were coming in to visit the mammoth landmark built in the 1930s and named for President Herbert Hoover, the nation's leading conservationist at the time. Once considered one of the seven wonders of the world, Hoover Dam, east of the city of Boulder, Nevada, and about thirty miles from Las Vegas, remains the largest concrete structure in the Western hemisphere.

At the north end of the parking lot two men looked down at a small employee parking lot below. They watched while vehicles approached the guard gate, slowed for a moment while the drivers flashed ID's at the watchman, and continued into the lot. The employees proceeded to the cheese grater entry gate and were allowed automatic entry after successful scans of the thumb and a swipe of their ID card. The men watched this process for awhile. Several employees entered the area, some driving their own cars, and others driving white vans with tiny letters written on the doors: *U.S. Gov't, Bureau of Reclamation.*

Eventually one of the men looked at his watch and nodded to the other. They exited their car and started walking toward the visitor's entrance after making sure they had properly locked the silver Toyota Camry.

After re-entering the country from Mexico, the brothers had made it as far as San Antonio before finding a public library they could use for internet access. Once again they visited the Kabul wedding website and found their final assignment in the following posting: *We thank our brothers for the fabulous honeymoon trip to Las Vegas, Nevada, USA; the Hoover Dam under a full moon was very special.* They had the target and the time; Hoover Dam and the next full moon. San Antonio was also where they obtained the lead apron shields for the Halliburton. The narrow escape may have been worth it. So far, so good.

"The last tour of the day will begin in ten minutes," blared the voice over the PA. "Purchase your tickets and assemble at the elevators beyond the security checkpoint."

Abdul and Ali paid the ten dollars each for their tickets and rode the escalator down a level and breezed through the security checkpoint. Even though security here was not as stringent as the airport security, it would not be possible to slip a Halliburton past this checkpoint.

"Welcome to Hoover Dam," the perky guide said to the group of nearly three dozen gathered at the elevators. "My name is Josephine and I'll be your guide today. This structure, once the largest dam in the world, currently supplies water for over twenty-five million people and electricity for more than one-hundred and thirty-five million people in over one-hundred cities in Arizona, Nevada, and California."

Abdul had wondered why the Director would pick this dam as a target. Now he understood perfectly. A nuclear detonation here would not only kill and contaminate residents near the licentious city of Las Vegas, but it would also deprive millions of others of electricity and water. It would turn the Imperial Valley farmland of California into a dust bowl. Brilliant! How could the wisdom of the man who masterminded the collapsing of the buildings ever be questioned?

After descending over five-hundred feet in the large elevator, the brothers followed the cluster of tourists through a long, damp tunnel. A constant vibrating hum grew louder and louder until they reached a large opening which housed the seventeen generators. Abdul noticed several workers around wearing green coverall uniforms. Josephine was almost yelling to the group while she led them down to a location between the ninth and tenth generators.

"Straddle this line," she shouted, "and you will have one foot in Nevada and the other in Arizona."

Abdul signaled to Ali. They had found the location which would be ground zero: between the ninth and tenth turbines, in the middle of the river, on the border between Nevada and Arizona. On this spot they would become the greatest of all martyrs.

After the tour the brothers lingered in their car gazing down at the employee parking lot.

"Just look at that gigantic dam," Abdul said. "And all the water in that vast lake up there, and the emptiness of valley below." He smiled and gestured broadly up to the lake and down to the valley, trying to get a response from his always pensive brother. "Tomorrow, all that water up there will be down there," he said, repeating the grand gesture.

Ali finally acknowledged his brother with a nod and a meek smile.

Soon they saw a medium sized young man with black hair wearing a green worker's jump suit exit the gate. He climbed into a white van, and drove away. The silver Toyota Camry followed.

CHAPTER 45

Sunday, January 27 (Moon in Cancer) The chase can be more rewarding than the kill. Be careful. The hunter sometimes becomes the prey.

"Why this man, my brother? Of all the workers leaving the dam, why did you suddenly choose to follow the one driving a government van?" Ali asked.

Abdul said nothing, trying not to be too judgmental about the tone of his brother's voice. He knew the pressure of the rapidly approaching virgins was once again taking its toll on Ali. And as of late, he talked more and more about his wife in Dharma. Abdul was pleased that irrespective of his brother's lack of enthusiasm, there was no reason to question his commitment. He watched the white van turn westbound onto Nevada 172. After a few cars passed by, he steered the silver Toyota in trail and paced himself with the traffic. No one spoke for several minutes.

"If you have a plan, I have a right to know," Ali said. "It's my last day, too."

After a prolonged glance at Ali, Abdul returned his attention to the road and the white van ahead. He spoke in a soft tone and a measured pace. "I picked this man first of all because he was wearing green coveralls, like the workers down by the turbines. I also picked this man because he happens to be about our size; meaning we could wear his clothes without looking ridiculous, like you did wearing that linen truck driver's uniform back in St. Louis."

Ali gave a half-chuckle, but a genuine smile for the first time in days.

The white van joined US-93 towards Las Vegas. Abdul veered to the left to follow, keeping a safe distance back.

"And lastly," Abdul continued, "I picked him because he was a younger man and very nice looking. That means chances are he has a young, nice looking wife or girl-friend. Are you beginning to catch on to the plan now?"

"I am, and I like it. Maybe she'll be like the girl in San Antonio."

"Maybe she will, my brother. Maybe she will."

"Do you think our San Antonio Honey talked to the police?" Ali asked.

"Not a chance. You know what she told me? 'Money talks and I don't.'"

"Maybe we should have put her out of her misery, like we did the bitch in Washington. What did she say her name was? Sandy?"

"Do you think she died?"

"Probably. The last time I screwed her just before daylight, she never moved. It was like screwing a corpse."

"So, Ali, what you're telling me here is that you have personal experience at screwing a corpse?"

Ali laughed. "No, not really, unless you could count one of those pining burka babes you left in Dharma when you joined the cause."

"You bopped one of my burka babes? You're bad, my brother. You're bad." Abdul was happy to see Ali lighten up and laugh. They needed to have a clear mind for their last twenty-four hours.

They passed a couple of exits to Boulder City. Abdul noticed the white van had picked up the pace and was now cruising ten miles-per-hour over the speed limit. He pressured the accelerator to maintain visual contact, keeping a close eye out for cop cars.

US-93 became US-95, otherwise known as the Great Basin Highway, or Veteran's Memorial Highway, depending on what sign you believed. Abdul didn't care which road he was on. All he needed to do was follow the white van. Once again he knew, as he did on 10 September, that after tomorrow, there would be no tomorrow. No need to worry about future consequences of their actions of their last day prior to the virgins and paradise. He would not vex his always pensive brother with the minutiae of his plans. He would take care of their basic needs until tomorrow: food, drink, lodging, and of course a good woman. And Ali would be grateful.

The minutes and the miles clicked by the desolate desert landscape, with River Mountain looming to the north. The brothers remained silent, but resolute, as the silver Toyota weaved through the Sunday drivers while keeping a comfortable interval between them and the white van. Soon after the road changed to I-515 approaching Henderson, Abdul saw the right blinker illuminate on the van. He knew they must be getting close. They took the exit to the right onto South Boulder Highway and entered the town of Henderson.

"This is good," Abdul said. "I was afraid he might take us all the way back to Las Vegas."

Abdul nodded.

A few minutes later the van exited onto North Major Ave.

"Here we go," Abdul said.

The white van took the exit and turned right immediately into the Boulder Marketplace parking lot and stopped at the door of a Pizza Hut.

"There he is," Ali said. Abdul steered the silver Toyota past the van and into the parking lot of the grocery store next door. "What now?" Ali asked.

"Wait here. I'll go in and see if I can find out what he's doing." Abdul left the keys in the car and opened the door to get out.

"I like pizza, you know," Ali said.

"I know you do, my brother." Abdul casually strolled across the parking lot. He noticed the white van was parked in a space reserved for carry-out customers. He pulled his Texas Rangers baseball cap down to his eyes and entered the Pizza Hut.

The restaurant was busy with customers seated at most of the tables and booths. The mouthwatering aroma from the hot ovens engulfed the room. There was a full buffet in the center of the eatery, with every kind of pizza, salads, and even a chicken corn chowder soup along with a vat of chili. The man in the green coveralls was next in line at the counter.

"One for dinner?" A man In his early thirties with a pencil-thin mustache and black butched hair wearing gray Dockers and a white short-sleeve Pizza Hut shirt offered a menu to the man in the green coveralls.

"Could I get a pizza to go, please?"

"What would you like?"

"How about a Supreme with no mushrooms?"

Abdul was eavesdropping behind the man with the coveralls. He looked up at the menu and knew immediately the Supreme would not work for him and his brother. Among all the ingredients and the kitchen sink, was pork. No squalid swine would they consume today.

"Sure, that'll be about twenty minutes. Name please?"

"Jones. Bill Jones." He handed the man a twenty, collected his change, and glanced at his watch. "I'll be back shortly," he said. Bill Jones turned and walked out the front door.

Abdul pivoted to stay directly behind the green coveralls as he turned for the door and was confident the man never realized he was there. He looked to be much younger up close than Abdul originally thought. He had a scruff that hadn't seen a razor in a few days and a tousled head of blond hair that needed combing. Or, maybe not. An ID card was alligator clipped to the pocket of his coveralls.

"Dining in or taking out?" the man with the pencil-thin mustache asked.

"Taking out," Abdul said. He studied the menu posted over the counter. "How long for two large Chicken Supreme pizzas?"

"I have two Chicken Supers for the buffet coming out of the oven now. Could I box those for you?"

"Yes, please." Abdul was relieved because he knew he couldn't wait twenty minutes and continue his journey with Mr. Jones. He quickly paid the man and hurried back to the silver Toyota with the two pizzas.

Abdul slid into the driver's seat and carefully placed the pizzas on the back seat.

"Hmmm, smells good," Ali said. He looked back at the boxes and licked his lips.

"Where did he go?"

"In there." Ali nodded at the grocery store across the parking lot.

"We'll be here for a few minutes. He's waiting for a pizza to go." Abdul surveyed the crowded parking lot. "This is where we will leave the Toyota tomorrow," he said.

Ali nodded, then asked, "Where's the beer?" He rubbed his hands together as if he was ready to get the party started.

"Why don't you run into the grocery store and grab us a couple of six packs?"

Ali opened the door and started to get out, then abruptly changed his mind and pulled the door closed. "My, my. Just look at that," he said. "My brother, do you know how to pick 'em, or what?"

Bill Jones walked out of the grocery store with a case of Coors on his shoulder. He placed it on the front seat of the white van and walked back into the Pizza Hut.

"Perfect." Abdul smiled. He knew his plans were falling into place.

The brothers had already raided one of the pizza boxes from the back seat before Bill Jones departed the Pizza Hut and headed north on North Major Avenue.

"Follow that van," Ali said. "He has the beer."

Abdul chuckled to himself at Ali's dry humor, even in the midst of the most important day of their lives. Until tomorrow. He was also thirsty. Did the slice of pizza leave his mouth dry, or was it just the angst of anticipation?

Bill Jones whistled happily as he bounced along in his van on North Major Avenue, less than a mile from his newly acquired home on Elm Street in Henderson. And his new bride. The sun had disappeared behind the mountains to the west and he had completed his work week at the dam. He didn't mind working Saturdays and Sundays because that would give him Mondays and Tuesdays off. You had to start somewhere and the new guys were the ones to catch the weekend duty. Bill Jones, recent graduate of the Colorado School of Mines as a chemical engineer, was grateful to have a job. Especially a career job in the lab at the dam, which included the use of a vehicle. He could adequately provide for his All-Conference tennis player, Miss Freshman, and Homecoming Queen wife, Ginny. And, flash flash, bulletin bulletin: there was a little one on the way. Ginny Jones had missed her period a couple of weeks ago and took a home pregnancy test. She dipped the strip and saw the blip. Bill Jones was going to be a daddy.

Bill Jones steered the white van left on Burkholder Boulevard, then right on Center Street, and another right on Elm and into his driveway a few houses down on the right. He pressed the remote to open the garage door and stepped out of the van. There she was, walking towards him wearing fleece warm-up pants and a loose fitting sweat shirt that said, "Oredigger Athletics." Ginny Jones was a tall, willowy, sun-streaked blond, oozing grace and confidence. She gave him a long, wet, sloppy kiss on the mouth.

"Hi Baby's Daddy," she said. "Welcome home."

"Wow, it's nice to be home." He whispered in her ear, taking a moment to catch his breath. "Are you sure you're really pregnant? I think we should go inside and eliminate any doubts."

 "I think maybe we should," Ginny said. She repeated the fantasy kiss and added full lower body pressure, which drove Bill crazy. "But we should wait 'til after dinner; gotta make sure you keep your strength up."

"Then let's cut straight to the main course, so we can get to the dessert."

"I would like that. Get the pizza from the van; I'll run set the table." Ginny frisked back through the garage and up the concrete steps into the house.

Bill Jones removed the pizza and the beer from the van and started walking through the garage past their green 1995 Nissan Sentra.

"Excuse me, Sir." The voice startled Bill Jones. He wasn't aware that anyone was nearby. "Could you help me, please?" A medium-sized man speaking with an accent and wearing jeans and a Texas Rangers baseball cap hurried towards Bill Jones. He was holding out a piece of paper in his left hand.

Bill Jones glanced at the door to the house, and back at the stranger. He noticed a silver Toyota parked behind his van with another person sitting in the passenger seat. He placed the pizza and the beer on the trunk of the Sentra. "How can I help you?" he asked.

"Could you please direct me to this address?" The stranger held out the piece of paper.

Bill Jones leaned forward and reached out to take the paper from the left hand of the stranger. He never saw it coming but heard a loud, ringing crunch and saw a flash of light. And the lights went out.

Abdul tried to grab Bill Jones after connecting with a palm thrust from his right hand directly to his chin, but he was unable to prevent him from bouncing off the Sentra and hitting the floor with a thud.

"Bill, are you okay?" The voice from inside the house showed a degree of concern. "Bill, you dropped the beer, didn't you?" The voice, now with a jocular tone, was getting closer. Abdul stepped over Bill Jones and bounded three quick steps to hide behind the door to the house when it opened.

"Bill … " The door opened. "Bill!" Ginny Jones started down the steps to her husband lying on the garage floor. Abdul grabbed her from behind with a rear naked choke hold. She tried to scream, but could only manage a rasping squeak before falling limp. He dragged her through the garage door and into the kitchen, across the living room and into the master bedroom. Abdul knew when he released the choke pressure she would regain consciousness, or at least he hoped she would. He sympathized with how Ali felt about having a relationship with a corpse.

Abdul reached into his jacket pocket for duct tape and flex cuffs, tools of the trade brought along for the occasion. He taped the young women's mouth to keep her quiet, and bound her to the rough-hewn headboard of the king-size bed. Through the door he could see Ali dragging Bill Jones through the living room.

"Bring him in here and cuff him to the foot of the bed," Abdul said. "Then put the Toyota in the garage beside that green car and close the garage door."

Abdul taped the mouth and bound the feet of Bill Jones. He heard the car door close and the garage door coming down. Ali walked back into the house carrying the pizza boxes and the case of Coors and placed them on a small dining table in the breakfast nook between the kitchen and the living room. Abdul looked at Ali and exhaled loudly with relief. "Welcome home, my brother," he said. "Now we prepare for paradise." He hugged Ali and kissed his stubbled cheek. He was surprised that Ali returned the embrace.

Abdul did a quick check of the rest of the house to make sure all the window blinds were closed and there were no surprises. The master bedroom had a large bath and an ordinary walk-in closet. Most of the closet held women's clothes, but on the right wall there was a small section of men's attire. Above the men's clothes on a shelf, he noticed a small caliber hand gun. Hanging in the very front, Abdul found what he was looking for: two clean sets of green coveralls. There were two other bedrooms joined by a Jack-and-Jill bath. One bedroom had an unmade double bed with an old metal frame. The other bedroom had no furniture at all and was strewn with boxes of clothes and household goods seemingly waiting to be unpacked.

Ali tossed a beer to Abdul and opened one for himself. He took a deep swallow and stashed the remainder of the case on the bottom shelf of the sparsely stocked refrigerator. The brothers sat at the small table and attacked the Chicken Supreme like a couple of starving lions on a fresh kill.

When they were finishing the pizza and their third beer, the brothers began hearing noises from the bedroom. Abdul expected to hear from them sooner, but now he knew at least one of them was conscious. He found a pair of scissors in a drawer in the kitchen and motioned for Ali to follow him into the bedroom.

Bill Jones was thrashing about at the foot of the bed, fighting against his restraints like a wild stallion. He was imparting a desperate humming, screeching sound, muffled by the double duct tape on his mouth. Ginny Jones was awake, leaning back against the headboard, regarding the determined struggles of her husband. The calmness of her stoic posture was betrayed by the frenzied look in her eyes.

"What do we do with him?" Ali asked. "You want me to finish him?"

"No, no. We need him for later." Abdul smiled. "At least part of him."

Ali laughed.

"Take him to the other bedroom and double cuff him to the metal bedframe," Abdul said. "That should keep him out of trouble for a while."

Ali horse-collared Bill Jones and dragged him out of the room amidst a crescendo of humming and screeching.

Abdul went to work on Ginny Jones. He cinched additional flex cuffs to her legs and arms. Ropes were tied to the cuffs of each arm and leg and connected to the four corners of the colossal Ponderosa Pine bed frame. Abdul methodically tightened the ropes. He paid no attention to the violent contorting of the young bride as he spread-eagled her face up across the center of the bed, reminiscent of Sandra Thompson at the Mount Vernon Holiday Inn. Taking the scissors and beginning just below her chin, Abdul cut the sweat shirt from her braless chest, exposing pink nipples on bountiful breasts. He continued downward, scissoring away at her warm-ups and panties. Methodically, he hacked with the scissors until the disrobing was complete. Ginny Jones lay naked, tethered to the bed.

Chapter 46

Sunday, January 27 (Moon in Cancer) Family matters return to the forefront and must be confronted. Libra remains reticent.

The quiet of the Crystal City flat was disconcerting to Cassie, even though her goal was just that — to have a quiet day. There was no denying the pressure of the futile search for the elusive brothers was weighing heavily on her psyche. And she missed working with Jason Lancer, regardless of how screwed up he was with horoscopes, tarot cards and poker. Who doesn't have a closet full of skeletons or surreptitious crosses to bear? Cassie certainly did. More than her share.

The Las Vegas trip to visit Jason proved to be personally therapeutic for Cassie. Even if she couldn't find the courage to tell Russo about the al Din's being her siblings, there was peace of mind in full disclosure to her old partner. She couldn't decide what, if any, effect it had on Jason. He was somewhere between understanding and indifferent. Why would he not return to the Bureau and be her partner? Was she really not the reason he abruptly ditched his career for what seemed like a life of certain insecurity? Lingering doubts, still lingering.

Cassie had begun her day by sleeping until almost noon. Russo had insisted she take the day off to recharge her batteries for the continuing pursuit of the deadly hijackers. She climbed into her most comfortable warm-up and ambled down to Starbucks for a large cup of coffee and a maple oat pecan scone. When that was gone, she refilled her cup and ordered a chocolate old-fashioned doughnut for dessert. Cassie had never had a weight problem. In fact, in the last few months she had lost a few pounds, if that was possible, from her long and lean frame. Thinking ahead, she ordered a roasted tomato and mozzarella Panini to munch on at halftime of the football game. She enjoyed the sandwich very much, despite rookie quarterback sensation Tom Brady having to leave the game with a leg injury late in the second quarter. Veteran Drew Bledsoe stepped up to lead Cassie's Patriots to a victory over the Steelers, and on to the Super Bowl. At least something was right with the world.

After the game, Cassie ran down to the "Y" for a game of pick-up basketball with the boys. It had been a while. They all wanted her on their team because she could handle the ball better than most of them and could still hit the quick jumper. It felt good to run and bump and jump and shoot. Unwinding. Recharging.

Back at the flat, she reveled in a timeless pulsating shower. Even though it was only around eight o'clock in the evening, Cassie slipped into a flannel nighty, turned off the lights, and nestled into bed. It had been a good day. Still there was the haunting silence, spoiled only by the faint sound of airliners taking off to the north from Reagan National. The cadence of the departing jets and the dull hum of the heater fan hastened the approach of deep slumber. Then there was another noise. It took Cassie a few moments to realize her cell phone was ringing. She finally found it on the nightstand and unplugged it from the charger.

"Hello."

"Reilly, it's Russo. Were you already asleep?"

"You told me to get some rest and unwind."

"I guess I did. I'm sorry to call you, but we have a situation out in Vegas."

Cassie said nothing, but immediately thought of Jason and wondered if he was involved in the situation. Or, did the brothers appear?

"Reilly, are you there?" Russo began to sound impatient.

"Yes, I'm here. What's happening?"

"As you know, because of recent events, we've been closely monitoring our radioactive detection sites around the country, especially Los Angeles. Nothing. I mean zippo. Then I happened to see a report from our Vegas office about a series of alerts around the city which they dismissed as false returns."

"How did they know they were false?"

"They said they received several alerts from south and east of the city. So many, that it seemed unlikely for that much nuclear material to be moving into the city. They also said the Gamma-ray spectrums on the returns were insufficient to identify the specific isotopes that might be responsible for the warnings."

"I think I understand now why they hit the dental supply store in San Antonio. The final inventory from that break-in showed missing lead aprons, right?"

"Right on."

"Did it ever occur to the Vegas office it might be a single device in one vehicle traveling around the area at various times and places? And the device might be shielded to mute the sharpness of the spectrum?" Cassie asked.

"No, but it immediately occurred to you. That's what I like about you, Reilly. You're always a step ahead of the conventional thinkers. You're good."

Here we go, Cassie thought. Here comes the kicker. But she had to ask anyway. "So what now?"

"I'm not exactly sure, but I think at least you need to get out there. And if there's any authentication to these warnings, I'll take the G-5 and be out there immediately. There'll be a car downstairs to pick you up in twenty minutes to take you to Dulles for a ten p.m. flight. Call me when you get there. Be safe, Reilly."

"Thanks, I guess," she said, "but there's something I've been wanting to tell you … " The line was already dead.

CHAPTER 47

Monday, January 28 (Moon in Cancer to Leo 3:29 a.m.) Destiny is defined in a single moment. Tomorrow is not promised to the timid. Scorpio has an impact.

"Ali … Ali … " Abdul groggily looked around. Where was Ali?

Abdul awakened naked, lying face down on top of Ginny Jones feeling pain from every muscle in his body and the worst headache of his life. Nevertheless, he was completely aroused. He wasn't sure if it was because he had a full bladder or the lust for the woman under him. Oh! Well. Why waste a perfectly good erection, he thought. He lunged forcefully into her again and began pounding. Suddenly, he realized she was stone cold.

The events of the night before were fleeting snapshots in Abdul's mind. The brothers prepared for the virgins by shaving and exfoliating every hair from their body, except what was on their head. Throughout the night they had their way with Ginny Jones. Savagely, brutally, unrestrained. Bound as she was, the young bride resisted valiantly. These efforts only intensified the excitement and gratification for Abdul.

During the late hours after most of the beer was gone, while he was occupied in the bedroom, Abdul remembered hearing his brother talking in muffled tones on the phone in the kitchen. He knew Ali was once again pledging his eternal devotion to his wife in Dharma and imploring Allah to watch over her and their young son. As on 10 September, Abdul forgave his brothers' breach of security.

Abdul stopped the pounding and lay very still on top of Ginny Jones. He realized she was dead. And he vaguely remembered what happened. Ali had finally gone into the other bedroom to get some sleep. As daylight was filtering past the blinds into the master bedroom, Abdul lay completely drained on the girl. He only wanted sleep, but she continued to struggle. He silenced her by pinching her carotid arteries against her windpipe. She went to sleep. Forever.

It suddenly seemed comical to Abdul. Here he was, fornicating with a corpse. Where was Ali? Was he still asleep? If his brother saw this, he would hold it over Abdul until his dying day. But, then again, that would be today. Still another reason not to waste a perfectly good erection. So Abdul pounded away until he was finished with the lifeless Ginny Jones.

Abdul slipped on his pants and shirt, looking around to make sure Ali hadn't been watching him. It was considerably after noon. Time passes quickly when you're down to your last day.

"Ali… Ali…" Abdul heard sounds and walked to the other bedroom. Ali was snoring loudly on the bare mattress. Where was the man? Where was Jones?

"Ali, wake up. Where's Bill Jones?" Abdul kicked the mattress violently several times.

Ali slowly sat up with a groan, holding his head.

"Where's Jones," Abdul asked again. He was now beginning to wonder if the man had escaped.

"I put him in the trunk of the Toyota,"

Abdul stared at him with a puzzled expression.

"He was thrashing around shaking the bed so much I couldn't sleep, so I dragged him into the garage and put him in the trunk."

"With the Halliburton?"

"Yes," Ali said. He appeared contrite, staring at the floor. "And Abdul, I think I may have hurt him."

"You hurt him?" Abdul asked. He was becoming irritated with his brother but resisted the urge to call him "camel brain" on their last day.

"I was dragging him by his feet and he may have hit his head on the door jam and the steps as we went into the garage. Anyway, when I put him in the trunk, he wasn't moving."

Abdul hurried to the garage. Ali pulled on his pants and followed. Abdul opened the trunk of the Toyota to find Bill Jones crammed head down on top of the lead aprons covering the Halliburton. His pallid face rested in a pool of congealed blood. Bill Jones wasn't hurt. He was dead.

"Ali, you… you…" Abdul resisted the name-calling urge again. His mind raced. Had Ali killed their chances for ultimate martyrdom? Maybe not. Abdul was thinking.

"Ali, go into the kitchen and find a small plastic bag," Abdul said.

Ali went into the house. Abdul moved Bill Jones' body aside in the trunk and pulled the Halliburton from underneath the lead aprons and placed it in the back seat. He saw a well-stocked work bench at the back of the garage with dozens of tools hanging from a pegboard on the wall, including an electric circular saw and an extension cord. Perfect.

Ali returned from the kitchen with the plastic bag. Abdul turned Bill Jones' body over in the trunk and unclipped his ID card from his green overalls and slipped it into his pocket. With the saw in his right hand he grabbed the end of Bill Jones' right thumb with his left hand and held it steady. Ziiinng. He handed the thumb to Ali to be placed it in the plastic bag. Abdul had sawed it off just above the second knuckle where it joined the hand.

"It will still get us in the gate tonight," Abdul said. "A thumbprint is good until it rots."

Ali gave a look of disgust and zipped the thumb into the bag and gave it to his brother.

"Is it time to go?" Ali asked.

"The virgins await patiently, my brother. We have plenty of time. We'll take a long hot shower and put on the green coveralls hanging in the closet. Although I'm sure you won't need it, I want you to take the pistol from the closet with you. We'll leave Jones in the trunk and drop the Toyota at the shopping center."

Ali nodded.

"No one will give any of this a second thought in the aftermath of what's about to happen." Abdul waved his hand in a grand gesture. "The die is cast, my brother. There's no stopping us now. We'll be the greatest of all martyrs. We leave at five."

Chapter 48

Monday, January 28 (Moon in Cancer to Leo 3:29 a.m.) Remain ever vigilant for opportunities to excel. Surprises await. Aires and Cancer involved.

Special Agent Cassandra Reilly arrived late in the morning at the Bureau's Las Vegas office on West Lake Mead Boulevard. She sat at a small cubicle normally used by out-of-town agents, looking over the latest radiation monitoring reports. Even though she managed to get upgraded to first class and slept most of the way on the late-night flight from Washington, she couldn't really consider that rest. Albeit she slept late this morning, she was still lagging.

She was thinking about Jason and how she could get a message to him through Clayton. Maybe they could have dinner. Cassie's cell phone rang, and she answered.

"Cassie, it's Russo. You made it."

"Yes, I'm here, but it cost you an upgrade."

"No problem. What are the Vegas guys saying about the readings?"

"They don't seem to seem to be concerned," Cassie said. "They're convinced they are false. By the way, I'm looking at another two alerts I received a few minutes ago that came in from east of town late yesterday afternoon."

"That's what I wanted to talk to you about, Reilly. I don't like the smell of this. I'm going to hop on the Gulfstream and I'll be out there tonight. In the meantime, I want you to round up some test equipment and check those sensors for accuracy, especially those at Boulder City. I'll call you when I get there. Good luck, Reilly." The line went dead.

Cassie called her liaison, the local agent assigned to assist her. She told him what she needed regarding Russo's request.

"Sure, we have a great techie," he said. "Just sit tight and I'll send Shriver by to see you."

Cassie focused her attention on the monitor reports to determine specifically the location of yesterday's alerts. The sensor was installed on US 93 where it crossed over Veterans Memorial Drive, east of Boulder City. Cassie circled the intersection on her map. A tall redheaded lady in a blue jumpsuit tapped on the door of the cubicle. Cassie looked up.

"Hi, I'm Pam Shriver," she said.

Cassie stood and smiled, knowing she couldn't resist it. "And I'm Mary Joe Fernandez," she said.

"That's strange, last week I ran into Chris Evert," the redhead said. They both laughed.

"I'm sorry. I know you must get tired of hearing jokes about your famous name... I'm Cassandra Reilly. Call me Cassie."

Pam Shriver extended a firm handshake. "No worries, I like the name. Great tennis player and a great lady. What can I do for you, Cassie?"

Cassie explained what Russo wanted her to do.

"I can't do the tests for you myself because I'm tied up with some wiretaps on a couple of our finest citizens. How about I get you the kits you need and you can do the tests?"

"That would be terrific. Thank you, Pam."

"You're welcome. I'll have the kits here for you by four this afternoon."

Cassie watched the redhead walk away from her cubicle and out the door. Pretty woman, she thought.

It was a quarter past four in the afternoon when Cassie slid into her Crown Vic loaner in the Bureau's parking lot. She had the test kits and was eager to find out one way or the other about the validity of the radiation reports. Traffic was already beginning to build, slowing Cassie's progress out of town and towards I-515 to the east. She wanted to get this done and get back to the airport by the time Russo's jet landed around six-thirty.

The farther Cassie traveled on I-515 eastward the more the traffic thinned out. She pressured the Crown Vic to speed limit plus twenty as she passed Henderson towards Boulder City. She was approaching Mission Hills when her cell phone rang.

"Reilly."

"Hi, this Tony."

"Tony? Tony? You must have the wrong number." Cassie couldn't remember anyone named Tony.

"No, I have the right number. I'm Jason's friend."

"Oh! I recognize your voice now." Cassie remembered talking to Jason's spook friend with the Southern accent a week or so ago. "I didn't know your name was Tony."

"It may not be Tony," he said with a laugh. "Look, I know you guys are busy, but you need this information. We got another VORS hit on your boy Ali al Din."

"Really? When" Cassie instantaneously slowed the Crown Vic and guided it to the shoulder of the road.

"Last night. He called his wife in Dharma. What really concerns me is the last time he called her was the night before nine-eleven."

Cassie's mind was spinning. So that's how Jason knew they were in the Mount Vernon Holiday Inn, she thought. "Oh! Dear God. This is trouble. Did he make the call from Los Angeles?"

"No, he made the call from Elm Street in Henderson, Nevada. I have the exact address for you right here." He gave her the address. "What's your location?"

"Oh! My! God! Thanks for the info, Tony. I gotta run!"

Cassie peppered away at the GPS on the dashboard computer unit of the Crown Vic inserting the address on Elm Street. The destination computed to be only fifteen minutes north of her position. What were the chances the brothers, her brothers, were still there? Not, likely, she thought. No need to call out the Cavalry, but she had to check it out. What would Jason do? She missed him, especially right now. Cassie glanced at her watch. Five minutes before five. Plenty of time to investigate the situation on Elm Street, come back and test the accuracy of the radiation monitors, and still get back to the airport to meet Russo at six-thirty. Easy. Not nearly as difficult as being double-teamed and shooting a jumper from the corner with one second left on the clock. Different stakes. Higher consequences.

Cassie didn't exactly want to depart the reservation. She couldn't talk to Jason, but she felt she had to talk to someone, just to cover herself. She hit the speed dial on her cell phone, knowing she would have to leave a message.

"Hi Boss, it's Reilly. I wanted you to know about an anonymous tip..." She told Russo she was going to check out Elm Street, without divulging information which might compromise Tony.

Rubber burned from the loaner cruiser. Cassie departed the expressway at Exit 56, took a left on Wagon Wheel Drive and sped north on South Boulder Highway and then right onto North Major Avenue. She noticed a Pizza Hut and a large shopping plaza with a grocery store off to the right. Traffic was spotty on the divided highway allowing Cassie to pressure the accelerator.

In less than a minute Cassie saw several school-age kids crossing the street ahead. She reduced her speed and looked left across the street where there was a sign that read, "Henderson City Park." Her eyes were drawn to a basketball court where several teenage boys and two girls were shooting hoops. Cassie smiled. As she shifted her gaze to the road ahead, a vehicle traveling in the opposite direction caught her attention. She did a double take.

Was that a silver Toyota? Cassie turned to get a direct look at the car rapidly disappearing behind her. There was only one person, a man, in the car. But, it was definitely a silver Toyota Camry. She looked down the road at several vehicles a few hundred yards ahead approaching in the oncoming lane.

Without a second thought, Cassie jack-knifed the Crown Vic in a cloud of dust across the median of desert dirt and small rocks in pursuit of the silver Toyota. She glanced in her rear-view mirror to see the oncoming vehicles were still a comfortable distance back. Now Cassie was concerned she might be on a wild goose chase. She had left the office with the simple chore of checking a couple of monitors, and now a few distractions later it was getting complicated. She knew she had to solve this riddle and get back on task. Cassie kicked in the passing gear to catch the Toyota and identify the driver.

Before she could catch the car, she saw it turn left into the shopping center ahead. Keeping a safe distance, she turned left and followed. Was it one of the brothers? She couldn't tell.

The Toyota turned down a row of cars in the parking lot of the grocery store and drove towards the rear of the lot. Cassie followed. The Toyota turned into an open space on the right. Cassie slowly passed behind it and looked closely at the man. It was Ali al Din.

She passed two cars and turned to the right into an empty space. Cassie stepped out of her car with her Glock in hand car to see that Ali, wearing green coveralls, was already out of the Toyota. He reached back into the car and was getting a piece of luggage from the rear seat. He closed the door, locked the car, picked up the metal suitcase and turned around to see he was facing Special Agent Cassandra Reilly.

"Hello, Ali. How are you?" Cassie speaking in perfect Arabic stood partially shielded by the rear fender of the car parked in the adjoining space, her weapon down by her side.

Ali stood mute.

"Ali, keep your hands where I can see them and slowly set the luggage on the ground."

Ali said nothing. Slowly, he lowered the Halliburton towards the ground with his left hand. But Cassie was watching his right hand that was slowly coming up towards the pocket of his jacket. Ali released the Halliburton on the pavement and as he straightened up, jerked the pistol from his pocket. The 9mm from Cassie's Glock entered on the bridge of his nose between his eyebrows.

Cassie watched in shock as Ali al Din dropped like a corpse cut from a hanging tree.

She felt the burning sting in her back before the loud bang registered in Cassie's brain. Her world shifted to slow motion. She tried to turn around, but her knees buckled and she fell flat of her back on the black asphalt. Now, she heard no sounds and felt no pain. She could not expand her chest to take a breath. Her blurred vision was growing dimmer with every passing second. She could barely perceive Abdul standing over her extolling some insult. He spat on her. And that's the last thing Cassandra Reilly would see.

Chapter 49

Monday, January 28 (Moon in Cancer to Leo 3:29 a.m.) Glee and gloom often occupy the same room. Benevolence is a virtue. The beasts of yesterday reappear.

"Well, Vince, it's finally come down to the final four in the World Series of Poker Main Event here at the Rio. Annabelle Duquemin has about twenty million chips, a commanding chip lead over her three opponents. Can she hold on to take the bracelet and the five million dollars and be the first woman to be crowned world champion?

"She has to be considered the odds on favorite at this point, Mike, but you can't count out these other three guys. 'The Pounder' and 'Birmingham Bernie' each have about four million chips, but the surprise of the tournament, a satellite qualifier and former FBI agent Jason Lancer, whom they've named 'Mr. Invincible,' is in second place with ten million chips, and cannot be taken lightly.

"You're right, Vince, this former G-man has made some remarkable reads so far in this event. If they try to bluff him, he calls and takes their money, and when they have the goods, he folds to stay out of harm's way.

"Let's get back to the table, Mike. The action is on our G-man, Mr. Invincible who, look at this, Mike, he's holding pocket kings!"

"Raise," Jason said. "One million."

Jason recalled the last time he had had pocket kings was in the early round of the satellite tournament. Even though that was only last week, it seemed far removed from the crowds and the glare of the television lights under which he had now found himself. He had placed a raise three times big blind only to be called by one of the donkeys. The flop had no kings, but had three diamonds and the donkey went all in. In keeping with what Belle had told him about not risking all his chips early, he folded. Of course, the donkey immediately flipped his cards to show he had flopped a flush. Had Jason called, he would have most likely been eliminated. Instead he played on, concentrating on what was happening in the moment at the table and was amazed at how accurate he had become at reading players and evaluating hands.

One other strategy difference in his new style of play had served Jason well through the qualifier and on to the final table in the main event: he had looked at neither a horoscope nor a tarot card.

"Call," The Pounder said, He pushed in a stack of chips.

"Look at this, Vince, The Pounder is setting a trap. Right now he has the best hand, the weapons of mass destruction, pocket aces."

"Call," echoed Birmingham Bernie. He squeezed a pair of queens.

"Look at the cagey one, Mike. Birmingham Bernie must think his pair of ladies is good, so he throws in a smooth call."

Belle folded her cards and slid them towards the muck while casting a knowing look at Jason. She had returned early from

Aruba after not cashing in the tournament when her aces full were busted by a straight flush on the river. "That's poker," she had said when she returned, telling Jason she was happy to be back early so she could be with him.

The flop was king, king, and queen.

"Vince, how can Mr. Invincible appear so cool? He has flopped the grand tsunami, the perfect storm; he has four kings against aces over and queens full. You know all the money's going in the pot right here. Let's see how he plays it."

Jason contemplated for a moment then tapped the table, indicating a check.

"All in!" said The Pounder.

"All in!" repeated Birmingham Bernie.

"Call," Jason said. He turned over his two pocket kings to the dismay of Bernie and The Pounder.

When the turn card was not an ace, the hand was over with Jason accumulating a total of almost eighteen million chips. It suddenly hit Jason that he was heads up with his idol in the poker world, his mentor. And, yes, his new love.

The ceremonious money presentation was very impressive. Shotgun-toting guards watched a horde of beauties pile large stacks of cash on the table. Eight million dollars. Five million for the champion and three million for the runner-up.

"So now we're heads up here at the Rio to crown a new world champion and to bestow life changing money on both of these talented players. Will the winner be the darling of the poker world, Annabelle Duquemin, or the newcomer 'Mr. Invincible,' Jason Lancer, the former FBI agent? Let's get to the action with

Annabelle looking at a pair, the ten of clubs and the ten of hearts."

"Raise, one million," Belle said.

"Call," Jason said.

"Vince, Mr. Invincible just smooth called one million chips. He must think he has Annabelle beaten, but we don't know what he has because he hasn't exposed his cards to the pocket-cam."

The flop was the queen, five, and two, all spades.

"Two million," Belle said.

"Call."

"Annabelle could not have liked the G-man's call, Mike. She has to be worried about those three spades on the board."

"Maybe the queen paired him, Vince. Why doesn't he show us his cards?"

The turn card was the three of diamonds, no visible help to the board, or anyone else.

"Two million," Belle said.

Jason again smooth called, slowly pushing his chips forward.

"He did it again, Vince. Is Mr. Invincible letting his inexperience show here?"

"The only thing I can figure, Mike, is he has a read on Annabelle, and he's planning to make a move to pick up this monster pot on the river. Let's see what happens."

The river card revealed the seven of clubs, still no help. Belle hesitated for a moment, and looked at the chips in front of her.

"All in," she said, pushing her chips forward and staring down at the table.

"This could be it, Vince! If Jason Lancer calls, his tournament life is on the line because we know Annabelle has him covered. This is really a poor semi-bluff Annabelle is trying to pull, representing she has a flush. If Mr. Invincible calls, he can probably beat a pair of tens and could severely cripple Annabelle. This decision is for all the marbles, right here. What does he have in the hole, and is he going to call?"

Jason, still shielding his hand from everyone, including the pocket-cam, peeked down at his hole cards. He returned his gaze to Belle, regarding her with careful contemplation.

"I call," he said.

Belle was shocked. She clearly was not expecting Jason to call.

"Good call, Jay," Belle said. She gave a conciliatory nod and turned over her two tens.

"Nice hand," Jason said. He caught Belle completely by surprise as he quickly mucked his cards without exposing them. "Congratulations. I thought you were totally bluffing."

Belle appeared to feel happy, then sad. Jason walked around the table and she melted into his arms, not seeming to care that the cameras were still rolling.

She held him close for the longest moment. Under her breath she said, "You had me, didn't you? Why did you muck your cards? How did you know?"

Jason whispered softly in her ear. "I'm happy for you, Belle, so very happy."

Jason's eyes were drawn to the table and the stack of money, not yet comprehending what three million dollars would mean to him. Looking beyond the table, he saw Clayton Spaulding hurrying towards him with a man he hadn't seen in a while. It was Alfredo Russo.

Chapter 50

Monday, January 28 (Moon in Cancer to Leo 3:29 a.m.) There are dragons to be slain, but the speedy stallion may not be a steadfast steed. Consider all information and trust your instincts.

"Enjoy the moment, sweetheart, you've earned it," Jason said. He left Belle to receive her accolades and slipped away into the crowd toward Clayton and Russo. He knew from the look on Clayton's face and the very presence of Russo that something was wrong.

"Jay! Did you win?" Clayton asked.

I didn't win the bracelet, but I won a bunch of money," Jay said. He glanced back at Belle posing for pictures with the champion's bracelet and the pile of cash.

"Hello, Jay," Russo said. He offered his hand to Jason. They shook hands.

"What's wrong?" Jason asked. "What's happened?"

"Jay," Russo said. "I know this is bad timing, but the Bureau needs your help."

"You've got to be kidding."

"Listen to what he has to say, Jay," Clayton said. He led the three of them toward a less crowded corner of the room.

"I went through all of this with Cassie a couple of weeks ago," Jason said. He looked around. "Where is she? Where is Cassie?"

The quick glance between Clayton and Russo told Jason the news was not good.

"Jay, Cassie's been shot," Russo said.

"What? How? Is she … "

"We don't know," Russo said. "Cassie was following a lead when she must have spotted Ali driving the silver Toyota Camry. She followed him to a grocery store parking lot and tried to arrest him. He made the mistake of getting into a shootout with Cassie and you know exactly what happened there. Ali took one between the eyes."

"Then, how did Cassie get shot?"

"Witnesses reported another man, we know it had to be Abdul, pulled up in a white van and shot Cassie in the back. After saying a few words in a foreign language over his dead brother and spitting on Cassie, he grabbed a piece of silver luggage from the scene and sped away in the van."

Clayton's cell phone vibrated.

"Spaulding. What? When? Where? Oh! Dear God."

"What is it?" Russo asked.

"That was my company dispatch. The investigators from the shooting in the parking lot called and said they found an employee of the Hoover Dam power plant dead in the trunk of the silver Toyota. He was identified by his driver's license and his green coveralls, but he was missing his government ID. And his right thumb."

"What does that mean?" Russo asked.

"It means Abdul is headed for the dam with a suitcase nuke, that's what," Jason said.

"We gotta run, Jay! What do you think?" Russo asked. He was almost pleading now.

"I think I haven't been to the restroom in hours. Excuse me a moment," Jason said.

Jason's mind was churning. He hurried into the men's room in a physical and mental state that was somewhere between disoriented and queasy. The ghastliest of all nightmares had become a reality; a terrorist with a nuke was in the country and detonation was imminent. Did the public know? Were they evacuating the area? Was Cassie alive? What could he do? So many questions. No answers. He was no longer with the Bureau, so how could he help? Or, more to the point, how could he not help? He needed guidance. He needed direction.

When Jason left the urinal, he spotted a newspaper on the empty shoeshine stand nearby. Regardless of his promise to Belle, he needed reassurance and confidence to face this extreme situation. He grabbed the newspaper and tore it open to read his horoscope.

Libra. September 24–October 23. Leave nothing to chance today. Keep both feet on the ground in mind, body, and spirit.

"Dear God in Heaven!" Jason exclaimed to no one in particular. "This can't be!"

Before another second passed, Jason reached in his back pocket and pulled out the miniature deck of Rider-Wait tarots he always kept with him. He shuffled them three times, cut them once, and flipped the top card.

DEATH!!!

Jason dropped to his knees, feeling faint, his mind flooded with images of his mother, and of his last day with the Bureau. His mother had chosen to do her duty, even though the stars forecast sure death, and he had chosen the opposite. He was awestruck by the fact he had just won three million dollars and suddenly it seemed insignificant.

Jason looked up and gazed at the mirror. He was staring at a beaten man. Behind him in the mirror he saw an image of Belle. She said *"Put away the tarot deck and forget about your horoscope for a while. React to what you perceive happening at the moment, not what some soothsayer has written or the chance flop of some medieval mystic on a card. What do you think?"*

Replacing her image, an image Russo appeared. *"We gotta run! Jay. What do you think?"*

Belle reappeared: *"What do you think?"*

Russo reappeared: *"What do you think?"*

An image of Cassie appeared: *"What do you think?"*

Jason's mother appeared: *"What do you think? What do you think? What do you think?"*

The images disappeared when Jason placed both hands under the automatically dispensing faucet and splashed water on his face. He was seeing clearer now and was looking at a determined reflection of himself. He dried his face and raced outside where Clayton and Russo were waiting.

"Let's go!" Jason said.

Chapter 51

Monday, January 28 (Moon in Cancer to Leo 3:29 a.m.) In the gale, be calm. In the moment, be omnipotent. You could have a chance to excel today.

"Ladies and Gentlemen," the voice on the casino public address system announced, *"this is the Director of Security speaking. The Mayor and the Governor, under direction of the President and the FBI, are directing an orderly but immediate evacuation of the city of Las Vegas. It is believed an attack is imminent. Take evacuation routes to the north, west, and south of the city only. Do not, I repeat do not evacuate in the vicinity of Lake Mead or Hoover Dam. I repeat..."*

Jason followed Clayton and Russo toward the lobby but instead of exiting through the front door they dashed into an elevator.

"Where are we going?" Jason asked.

"The streets will be gridlocked; we're taking a chopper from the roof," Clayton said.

"A chopper?" Jason asked.

Leave nothing to chance today. Keep both feet on the ground in mind, body, and spirit.

Jason thought again of the last day of his mother's life and swallowed hard. He took several deep breaths and followed them into the helicopter. They were airborne as soon as the door slammed closed and Jason was transported into a moment so surreal it was like the opening scene from a thriller movie. The only sound was the hypnotic drone of the chopper blades. Below, the salient lights of the Las Vegas strip masked the certain anguish of a city trying desperately to evacuate. Above, foreshadowing the heavens filled with stars, was a full moon.

The chopper landed in the employee parking lot of Hoover Dam. A white Bureau of Reclamation van was parked near the entry door. When they approached the cheese grater, they all saw it at the same time: blood on the thumb scanner of the PrintScan entry device.

"We're too late," Clayton said. He used his master key to disable the device and allow them entry. "He's already here!"

Two Crown Vics screeched into the parking lot and eight more FBI agents followed them through the cheese grater and into the large elevator. When they began the five-hundred foot journey downward, Jason's eyes were drawn to something on the floor in the back of the elevator. It was a bloody human thumb in a plastic bag.

The elevator doors opened and the agents entered the area leading to the tunnel with their guns drawn. There was no sign of Abdul. They started down the long tunnel with Jason, close behind Russo and Clayton, feeling naked without a weapon of his own. When they emerged from the tunnel into the gigantic room, the vibrating hum of the generators smothered the sound of their footsteps and all normal conversation.

Russo directed the agents to spread out for the search while he, Clayton, and Jason made their way to the center of the facility. They scurried past the ninth generator and found what they were looking for.

"There he is!" Jason said.

Abdul was leaning on a counter at the Nevada-Arizona dividing line intensely studying the control panel and the flashing lights of the suitcase nuke. He inserted a card key into the device and began pushing buttons. He glanced up and saw them!

"Stop!" Abdul shouted, "or you will be standing in hell!"

They all froze in their tracks.

"If you shoot me, this thing blows!" Abdul said. His readied his finger that was pressed against a button on the panel. His face was covered with sweat.

Jason took a step in front of the group, showing his hands so Abdul could see he was unarmed.

"Mr. Lane, we meet again," Abdul said. He sneered. "FAA, FBI, what's the difference?"

"Abdul, it's time to give it up."

"Stay where you are or I'll blow it!"

"Abdul, your brother's dead. Your sister's dead. This has gone far enough."

"I don't have a sister, and my brother's with the virgins."

"Abdul, you shot your sister in the back, and your brother will be buried in a pig farm." Jason said.

Behind Jason, Russo whispered to Clayton, "What the hell is he talking about?"

"I have no idea," Clayton said.

Jason was completely focused on Abdul. The words of Belle echoed in his mind: *"You must be totally in the moment. If you are harboring preconceived biases, you are inviting disaster. What it really comes to, my sweet, in poker and in life, is the ability to read people. Then you must act on your intuition, which in reality is only a subconscious assessment of tells."*

"No! You must not dishonor my brother!" Abdul shouted.

"Tell me how we can avoid that happening?" Jason asked.

Abdul appeared frustrated for a few moments and made a demand. "Have a fully fueled 757 at Las Vegas airport in one hour with the body of my brother on board. Give me safe passage to the airport. I will leave the country.

"What's he thinking?" Russo whispered. "How can we do that?"

Jason took a step closer. Abdul crouched closer to the panel of buttons on the bomb.

"Stop! Or I'll end it here!" Abdul's voice was like an angry growl.

Strong means weak. Weak means strong.

Abdul cocked his head slightly and Jason noticed Abdul's inability to maintain eye contact. He took another step forward.

"Jason! What are you doing?" Russo yelled. "Step back! I'm ordering you to step back!"

"I'm exploding it! I'm exploding it!"

Jason began walking towards Abdul.

"Stop, Jason stop!!! I'm ordering you to stop! Okay Abdul, you win," Russo shouted. "We'll get you the airplane!"

Jason kept walking.

"Here it goes!!!" Abdul screamed.

Jason kept walking. In a calm voice he said, "You're all in, Abdul. And you're drawing dead."

When it became obvious Jason was not going to stop, Abdul took his hand off the bomb and attempted to pull the revolver from his pocket. Jason grabbed the gun with his left hand and connected with a right hook to the jaw which knocked Abdul to the floor.

"You low-life scum bag!" Jason spat. When Abdul attempted to get up, Jason pummeled him in the mouth and several of his teeth hit the floor before he did.

"That's for Cassie," Jason said. He straddled Abdul, who was barely moving, lying face up on the floor. "And this is for Sandra Thompson!" Jason raised his right boot and stomped Abdul violently in the crotch! A primal scream could be heard throughout the plant, even over the noise of the loud generators. Abdul collapsed into unconsciousness.

While checking Abdul for more weapons, Jason found an item, and slipped it into his pocket. He reached over to the control panel of the bomb and flipped a red-guarded switch which turned off the flashing lights.

Jason stared down at Abdul as he reached into his pocket and removed the miniature tarot deck. He shuffled them three times, cut them, and flipped the top card onto Abdul's chest. It was the card of Justice.

The hint of a smile came to Jason's face. He tossed the entire tarot deck at Abdul and walked away.

Epilogue

Monday, March 18 (Moon in Taurus) There are scores to be settled. And there are roses to be smelled. Celebrations await. Scorpio very much involved.

The ceremony was scheduled for the Rose Garden, but inclement weather forced the affair inside to the East Room of the White House. Jason received the Medal of Freedom Award from the President, the highest honor bestowed upon a civilian by our country. Jason thought of his mother throughout the event and how she would have been proud of him for his actions 'above and beyond the call of duty.'

Belle clung to Jason's arm while they watched the snow falling gently outside the south entrance of the White House while they were waiting with the other invitees for their transportation. A tall brunette with her arm in a sling approached them.

"Congratulations, Jay," she said. They embraced warmly. "I'm so proud of you."

"Thank you. I'm glad you were here," Jason said. He hugged her again, but not too tight. "Oh! I don't think you two have met. Belle, I'd like you to meet Cassandra Reilly. Cassie, this is Annabelle Duquemin."

"It's nice to meet you, Annabelle. And I can tell you right up front, I never want to get in a poker game with you."

"And I never want to get in a shootout with you," Belle said. "It's a pleasure meeting you." Cassie walked slowly away.

"Oh! Wait!" Jason called. "I have something for you."

Cassie stopped and turned.

"I didn't think Abdul would need this anymore," Jason said. He handed her a wallet-sized photograph.

Cassie looked at the picture and her eyes filled with tears. It was the first time she had ever seen a picture of her birth mother.

"Oh! Thank you, Jay. Thank you," she said. She kissed him on the cheek and walked away.

"Good luck in rehab. Call me."

"You don't have a phone!"

"Oh! Yea, I forgot," Jason said. He laughed out loud.

Jason spotted Russo approaching in a hurry, as usual. "Thank you again, Jay, and congratulations. Remember, if you ever want to come back … "

"I know, thank you. That's very nice of you," Jason said. It was obvious he did not want to revisit the subject.

"Abdul told us everything," Russo said. "By the way, how did you know he didn't have the code to detonate the bomb?"

"In the words of a famous poker player, I read him like a book." He glanced at Belle with a smile. "He had the key, why didn't he have the code?"

"It went to the fishes in the Gulf, along with Scar Face," Russo said. He turned and scurried away.

"Ouch!" Jason winced, waving goodbye. "See you soon. Well, maybe not."

"Agent Lancer!" An attractive blond in a simple black wool dress called to Jason. "I don't quite know how to say this, but I wanted to thank you for saving my life."

"That's very nice of you. By the way, I have something for you." Jason reached into his coat pocket and handed her a large envelope labeled *scholarship*. She opened it and huge tears started running down her cheeks.

"How can you do this? How can you do this?" She asked. She hugged him tightly.

"I just can."

"Thank you! Thank you so very much!"

"You're welcome. Take good care of Tiffany," Jason said. He watched her walk away. She looked back and waved.

"Wow! Who was that, and what was that all about?" Belle asked.

"That was Sandra Thompson. She's always wanted to go to law school, and now she can."

Their driver arrived and they were ushered into the back seat of the warm government car. When the car pulled away, they looked out the back window at their tracks in the snow.

"Well, Miss Annabelle Duquemin, where would you like to go?" Jason asked. There was no way she could get the answer to that question wrong, as long as they were together.

"I would like to go where the sun is shining, the weather is warm, and we can drink fruity drinks, and play some poker."

"You mean, like Texas Hold 'em?"

"No telling."

Ω

Where to Find this Book

Autographed copies and info about live appearances:
http://www.bennettshelfer.com

General trade paperback, $17.99:
http://www.unlimitedpublishing.com/shelfer

Order by mail, $17.99:
Unlimited Publishing LLC, Box 99, Nashville, IN 47448
For faster service, send payment by Paypal to
operations@unlimitedpublishing.com and include your postal
address.
Includes free shipping to U.S. addresses.

100 page e-Book Preview in Portable Document Format, $4.99:
Unlimited Publishing LLC, Box 99, Nashville, IN 47448
For faster service, send payment by Paypal to
operations@unlimitedpublishing.com and include your e-mail
address.
Includes 10% discount code for paperback orders.

Paperback + PDF e-Book Preview, $19.99:
Unlimited Publishing LLC, Box 99, Nashville, IN 47448
For faster service, send payment by Paypal to
operations@unlimitedpublishing.com and include your postal
and e-mail addresses.
Includes free shipping to U.S. addresses.

Coming Soon:
e-Book editions for Kindle, Kindle-for-iPad/iPhone, Mac, PC and
smartphones.
Visit Amazon.com for details.

About the Book

"Might there have been even *more* teams ready to hijack
aircraft on 9-11? Bennett Shelfer dares to say 'yes' with
Drawing Dead, his surprising, thrilling, no-punches-pulled debut
that will keep you pinned to the couch. Don't miss it!"
— Carl Ellsworth, Screenwriter, *Red Eye, Red Dawn* (2012)

FBI Special Agent Jason Lancer is obsessed with horoscopes and
tarot cards after losing his mother in a plane crash. She had
ignored the warnings of the stars and the cards. Lancer is
pursuing terrorist hijackers and is ordered to take a plane to St.
Louis but faces the same warnings that spelled doom for his
mother. He resigns and moves to Las Vegas. A sexy poker
professional persuades him to ignore the stars and the cards
and teaches him to read people. Lancer confronts his obsessions
and the terrorists at Hoover Dam using his newly acquired skills.

About the Author

BENNETT SHELFER is a former instructor pilot for the U.S. Air
Force, National, Pan Am, and Delta Airlines. He piloted the
White House Press Corps, accompanying two Presidents
overseas and to every state in the union. He is the only known
living pilot to have been hijacked twice.

Before penning DRAWING DEAD, Mr. Shelfer co-authored two
musicals and "Struttin'," an award winning screenplay. Mr.
Shelfer, teaming with one of his daughters, has captured five
national tennis championships. He and his wife divide their time
between Florida and Georgia, while Mr. Shelfer is working on
his next book, a memoir.

Made in the USA
Charleston, SC
21 May 2012